THE BARON'S SONS

BY DR MAURUS JÓKAI

THE BARON'S SONS

A Romance of the Hungarian
Revolution of 1848

BY

DR MAURUS JÓKAI

AUTHOR OF

"MIDST THE WILD CARPATHIANS," "BLACK DIAMONDS,"
"DEBTS OF HONOUR," "THE HUNGARIAN NABOB," ETC.

Translated from the Hungarian by
PERCY FAVOR BICKNELL

Fredonia Books
Amsterdam, The Netherlands

The Baron's Sons:
A Romance of the Hungarian Revolution of 1848

by
Maurus Jókai

ISBN: 1-4101-0467-2

Copyright © 2004 by Fredonia Books

Reprinted from the 1901 edition

Fredonia Books
Amsterdam, The Netherlands
http://www.fredoniabooks.com

CONTENTS.

TRANSLATOR'S PREFACE.

No page of history is more crowded with thrilling interest than that which records the uprising of the Hungarians, in 1848–49, in a gallant attempt to recover their
constitutional rights. The events of that stirring period,
even when related by the sober pen of the annalist, read
more like romance than reality; and thus they cannot
fail to lend themselves admirably to the purposes of
historical fiction. More than one of that brilliant series
of novels with which the genius of Hungary's greatest
story-writer has enriched the literature, not of his own
country merely, but of the world, takes its theme from
those memorable scenes in which the author himself
played no unimportant part. Into none of these fascinat-
ing romances has the writer succeeded in crowding so
much of the life and colour, of the heroism and self-sacri-
fice, the triumph and the despair, of that national con-
vulsion, as into the pages of "The Baron's Sons" ("*A
Köszivü Ember Fiai*," literally, "The Sons of the Stonyhearted Man"). Especially effective is his description
of the historic flight over the Carpathians of the two
hundred and twenty hussars who, at the outbreak of the

Revolution, deserted the Austrian army and hastened to their country's aid. No chapter in all the author's writings exceeds this one in breathless interest and in the skilful handling of detail.

The necessity of abridging the author's text, while regretted by no one more than by the translator, has, it is believed, tended to contribute to the story an element of unity and compactness which, owing to the undue elaboration of certain minor details, seems somewhat lacking in the original. It is with extreme hesitation and diffidence, however, that I venture, even in self-defence, to impute the slightest blemish to a style in which so many of the author's admirers can see no fault. The curtailment has necessitated, in some chapters, a certain amount of adaptation, and a slight departure from strict literalness of rendering; but it is hoped that the spirit of the original has nowhere been sacrificed.

P. F. B.

Malden, Mass., April, 1900.

THE BARON'S SONS.

CHAPTER I.

SIXTY MINUTES.

THE post-prandial orator was in the midst of his toast, the champagne-foam ran over the edge of his glass and trickled down his fat fingers, his lungs were expanded and his vocal chords strained to the utmost in the delivery of the well-rounded period upon which he was launched, and the blood was rushing to his head in the generous enthusiasm of the moment. In that brilliant circle of guests every man held his hand in readiness on the slender stem of his glass and waited, all attention, for the toast to come to an end in a final dazzling display of oratorical pyrotechnics. The attendants hastened to fill the half-empty glasses, and the leader of the gypsy orchestra, which was stationed at the farther end of the hall, held his violin-bow in the air, ready to fall in at the right moment with a burst of melody that should drown the clinking of glasses at the close of the toast.

At this point the family physician entered noise-lessly and whispered a few words in the ear of the hostess, who was presiding at the banquet, and who immediately rose and, with a mute gesture of apology to those of the guests who sat near her, withdrew from the room.   Meanwhile the orator continued :

"May that honoured man who, like a second Atlas, bears the burden of our country on his shoulders, whom all future ages will reverence as the type of true patriotism, who is the leader of our party's forces in their march to victory, and whom we all regard as our light-giving pharos, a tower of strength to our side and the bulwark of our cause, though at present he is un-fortunately unable to be with us in person,— may he, I say, live to enjoy renewed health and strength and to bear forward the banner of his party for many, many years to come ! "

The final words of this peroration were drowned in a storm of cheers, an outburst of music, and the con-fused din caused by the pushing back of chairs and the dashing of wine-glasses against the wall, while the guests fell into one another's arms in an ecstasy of enthusiasm.

"Long life to him ! " they cried ; "may he live a thousand years ! "

He to whom the assembled company wished so long a life was the renowned and honoured Baron Casimir Baradlay, lord lieutenant of his county, the owner of large estates, and the leader of a powerful party. The high dignitaries assembled about his hospitable board had gathered from far and near to determine upon a programme which should ensure their country's welfare for the coming years. As a fitting close to this important conference, Baron Baradlay was treating his partisans to a banquet in the great hall of his castle, and in the unavoidable absence of the host himself his wife was presiding at the festive board. The administrator, however, Benedict Rideghváry, had taken the absentee's place at the conference.

At the close of the toast, when those near the head of the table turned to touch glasses with the hostess, her absence was noticed, and the butler who stood behind her empty chair explained that the physician had just entered and whispered something in the lady's ear, whereupon she had left the room. Probably, said he, her husband had sent for her. Upon this information a number of the guests made anxious inquiry whether their honoured host was seriously ill ; and the administrator hastened to reassure all present, as far as his voice could reach down the long table, by telling them that it was merely a return of the baron's chronic ailment. Some of the better-informed supplemented this announcement by explaining to their neighbours that the gentleman had, for perhaps ten years, been subject to frequent attacks of heart-failure, but could nevertheless, by observing very regular habits, be expected to live for another ten years or more.

Therefore, as it was only one of his habitual attacks, all joined in wishing their honoured host many, many years of life and happiness. The family physician, however, had whispered in the wife's ear these four words : " Only sixty minutes more ! "

" I have been waiting for you," said the husband, as his wife entered the sick-room, and the words sounded like a reproach.

" I came as soon as I could," returned the other, as if in apology.

" You stopped to weep, and yet you knew my time was short. Let us have no weakness, Marie. It is the course of nature ; in an hour I shall be a senseless form ; so the doctor told me. Are our guests enjoying themselves ? "

A silent nod was the reply.

" Let them continue to do so ; do not disturb them, or hasten their departure. Having assembled for a conference, let them remain for the funeral banquet. I have long since determined upon all the details of the burial ceremony. The funeral anthem will be sung by the Debreczen College chorus — no opera music, only the old psalm tunes. The customary addresses will be delivered by the superintendent, in the church, and by the sub-dean, in the house, while the local pastor will repeat the Lord's Prayer over the grave, and nothing more. Have you followed me carefully?"

The wife was gazing abstractedly into vacancy.

"I beg you, Marie," urged the speaker, "to bear in mind that what I am now saying I shall be unable to repeat. Have the goodness, then, to be seated at this little table by my bed, and write down the directions I have just given, and also those that I am about to add. You will find writing materials on the table."

The baroness did her husband's bidding, seating herself at the little table and writing down what had just been told her. When she had finished the patient continued as follows:

"You have been a true and faithful wife to me, Marie, ever since our marriage, and have obeyed all my commands. For an hour longer I shall continue to be your lord and master, and the orders that I give you during this hour will furnish you occupation for the rest of your life. Nor shall I cease after my death to be your lord and master. Oh, my breath is failing me! Give me a drop of that medicine."

The wife administered a few drops in a little gold teaspoon, and the patient breathed more freely.

"Write down my words," he continued. "No one but you must hear them or see them. I have performed a great work which must not perish with me. The earth is to pause in its course and stand still; or, if the earth as a whole will not stop, yet our small portion of it must do so. Many there are who understand me, but few that know how to follow out my designs, and still fewer that have the requisite courage. I have three sons who will take my place when I am dead. Write down, Marie, what my sons are to do after my death. They are all too young to assume their duties at once. They must first be trained in the school of life, and, meanwhile, you will be unable to see them. But don't sigh over that; they are big boys now, and are not to be fondled and petted any longer.

"My eldest son, Ödön,[1] is to remain at the court of St. Petersburg; it is a good school for him. Nature and disposition have too long fostered in him an ardent enthusiasm which can bring no good to our stock, and of which he will there be cured. The Russian court is a good training school, and will teach him to distinguish between men born with certain inherited rights, and those born with no rights whatever. It

[1] The vowel *ö* is sounded much like *oe* in *Goethe*. *J*, as in *Jenö*, is pronounced like *y*. In pronouncing other Hungarian proper names in the book, let it be noted that *a* is sounded nearly like *o* in *not; á* like *a* in *far; e* like *e* in *met; é* like *a* in *fate; o* like *o* in *whole*, but somewhat shorter; *ó* like *o* in *hole; cz* like *ts; s* like *sh; sz* like *s* in *soft; g* is hard; *gy* is sounded like *dy* in *would you.* The stress of voice is on the first syllable in every case, though less pronounced than in English. For typographical reasons the diæresis has been substituted for the double acute accent; the latter gives the same sound to the vowel over which it is placed as the former, only lengthened.

will teach him to stand on the heights without feeling dizzy, to recognise the true rights of a wife in the eyes of her husband, to cast aside all foolish youthful enthusiasm, and, upon his return hither as a man, to grasp the rudder from which my hand has fallen. You are to supply him with money enough to play his part worthily among the young nobles of the Russian court. Let him drain the cup of pleasure to the dregs. Leave him to his extravagances. To gain the serene heights of indifference, a young man must first sow his wild oats."

The speaker paused to look at the clock, which admonished him to hasten, as time was short and there was still much to say.

"That young girl," he continued, "on whose account he was sent away from home, you must try to marry to some one. Spare no expense. There are men enough suitable for her, and we will provide the dowry. Should the girl prove obstinate in her resolution, you must endeavour to bring about her father's removal to Transylvania, where we have many connections. Ödön is to remain abroad until the family has moved away or he himself has married. The matter need not, I think, cause you any anxiety. My second son, Richard, will remain a month longer in the royal body-guard; but it offers no opening for a career, and he will leave it for the cavalry, where he is to serve a year, after which he must seek an appointment on the general staff. Skill, valour, and fidelity are three excellent aids to a man in making his way upward, and all three are developed by service. There are victories yonder waiting to be won, and my son is to take the lead. There will be war in Europe when once the earthquake begins, and a Richard Baradlay will find work enough ready to his hand. His fame shall cast its glory over us all. He must never marry : a wife would only be in his way. Let his part be to promote the fortunes of his brothers. What an excellent claim for their advancement would be the heroic death of their brother on the battle-field ! But you are not writing, Marie. Surely, you are not weeping ? I beg you to overcome such weakness, as there are only forty minutes left, and I have yet much to say."

The wife mastered her feelings and wrote on.

" My third and youngest son, Jenö, is my favourite ; I don't deny that I love him best of the three ; but he will never know it. I have always treated him harshly, and you too must continue so to treat him. Let him remain at Vienna in the civil service and make his way upward step by step. The struggle will give him address, shrewdness, and fruitfulness of resource. Let him learn to supplant others by dint of superior intelligence and amiability, and to take all possible pains to please those whom he is afterward to use as ladders for his own upward progress. Do not spoil him with tender treatment at home, but let him learn to adapt himself to strangers and judge of their worth. His ambition must be fostered, and an acquaintance cultivated with powerful and influential men that shall lead to valuable family connections."

A momentary distortion of the patient's features bore witness to his acute suffering. It lasted but a second, however, when the noble will overcame the weakness of the flesh and enabled the speaker to continue his dying instructions.

"Three such strong supports — a diplomat, a soldier, and a high government official — will uphold and preserve the work of my hands. Alas! why could I not have continued my task a little longer, until they were farther advanced in their careers? Marie, my wife, I beg and most solemnly adjure you to obey my behests. Every muscle in my body is wrestling with death, but my thoughts are not now upon that final dissolution which must so soon overtake me. This cold sweat on my brow is not caused by the death-agony, but by the fear lest all my past striving shall have been for naught, lest the work of a quarter of a century shall be buried with me. Ah, Marie, if you but knew how my heart pains me! No, no more medicine; that cannot help me. Show me my sons' pictures; they will bring relief."

The baroness brought three miniature likenesses

and held them before her husband's eyes. The man with the heart of stone looked at them, one after the other, and his sufferings abated. He forgot his death pangs, and pointing with his wasted forefinger at the portrait of the eldest, he whispered : "He will be most like me, I believe." Then, waving aside the three miniatures, he continued, coldly : "But no sentimentality now ! The time is short and I shall soon be gathered to my fathers and leave to my sons what my ancestors left to me. But my house will remain as the fortress and defence of true principles. Nemesdomb will live in history as the centre and focus of our national policy. And you, too, will remain after I am gone."

The writer looked up inquiringly.

"You look at me as if to ask what a woman, a widow, can effect in a task under which a man broke down. I will tell you. Six weeks after my death you are to marry again."

The pen fell from the woman's hand.

"That is my command !" continued the stonyhearted man sternly ; "and I have chosen a husband for you in advance. You will give your hand to Benedict Rideghváry."

At this the wife could no longer contain herself. She left the writing-table, sank down upon her knees by the bedside, seized her husband's hand and wet it with her tears. The patient closed his eyes and sought counsel in the darkness. He found it.

"Marie," said he, "do not give way in that manner; it is now no time for tears. My orders must be obeyed. You are young yet, — not forty years old. You are beautiful and will not lose your beauty. Twenty-four years ago, when I married you, you were not a whit fairer than you are to-day. You had raven-black hair and bright eyes, and you have them yet. You were gentle and modest, and you have not lost those virtues. I have always loved you warmly, as you well know. In the first year of our married life my eldest son, Ödön, was born; in the next year my second son, Richard; and in the third my youngest, Jenö. Then God visited me with a severe illness, and I have ever since been an invalid. The doctors said I was doomed, and that a single kiss from your beautiful lips would kill me. And so I have been wasting away for the last twenty years at your side like a condemned criminal. Before your eyes the bloom of my life has withered away, and during all this time you have been merely a dying man's nurse. I have dragged out my existence from day to day, possessed by a great purpose which alone enabled me to retain the breath of life in my body amid the most grievous tortures. Oh, what a life it has been, — a life bereft of every pleasure! Yet I endured it, denying myself everything for which other men live. I lived simply for the sake of the future, a future which I wish to be, for our country, the perpetuation of the past. For that future I have reared my sons, for it I have spent my strength, and in it my name will live. On that name now rests the curse of the present, but it will be glorified by the radiance of the future. It is for that name, Marie, that I have suffered so much. But you must live to enjoy yet many years of happiness."

The wife sobbed in mute protest against his commands.

"It is my will," cried the man, and he snatched his hand from her grasp. "Go back to the table and write. 'This is my dying command: six weeks after my death my wife is to marry Benedict Rideghváry, who is the man most worthy to follow in my footsteps. Only thus shall I rest easily in my grave and enjoy peace in heaven.' Have you written that, Marie?"

The pen slipped from the writer's fingers; she buried her face in her hands and remained silent.

"The hour is fast going," stammered the dying man, struggling against the approaching dissolution; "but *non omnis moriar*. The work that I have begun will survive me. Marie, lay your hand on mine and leave it there until mine begins to stiffen. No foolish sentimentalism, no tears! I will not let you weep now. We shall not take leave of each other: my spirit will remain with you and never leave you. Every morning and evening it will demand of you an account how you have discharged the duties I have laid upon you in this my dying hour. I shall be near you constantly."

The woman trembled from head to foot, but the dying man folded his hands calmly and murmured in broken accents: "The hour is nearly gone. The doctor was right: I no longer feel any pain; everything grows dark around me, only my son's pictures are still visible. Who is that coming toward me out of the darkness? Halt! Advance no farther; I have yet more that I must say."

But the grim spectre's approach was not to be stayed; it laid its invisible hand over the dying patient's face, and the powerful man with the heart of stone succumbed to a force mightier than himself. He voluntarily closed his eyes and pressed his lips together, not calling upon any one to help him die, as do ordinary weak mortals; but proudly and unshrinkingly, as becomes a nobleman, he surrendered his great, indomitable soul to the master jailer, Death.

When the baroness saw that her husband was dead, she fell upon her knees by the table and, folding her hands upon the written page before her, stammered forth: "Hear me, Lord God, and be merciful to his forsaken soul, as I now vow to be merciful and to execute the very opposite of all the wicked commands he has with his last breath enjoined upon me. This is my fixed resolve, O God, and I pray Thee in Thine infinite power to help me."

A cry, unearthly and terrible, rang out on the sepulchral stillness of the room. The startled woman threw a look of horror at the dead form stretched out upon the bed. And see! his closed lips had parted, his eyes had opened, and his right hand, which had been folded in his left upon his breast, was raised toward his head.

Perhaps the departing soul had been overtaken in its flight by the kneeling woman's vow, and had turned back to reënter its mortal tenement and protest with that one fearful cry against the violation of its commands.

CHAPTER II.

THE baron's funeral took place a week later. The funeral sermon was very long, and the baroness wept through it all with a grief as unaffected as that of any peasant widow in the land.

"The poor lady is having a good cry once for all," remarked one of the distinguished attendants at the funeral to his neighbour. "They say she was not allowed to shed a tear during her husband's lifetime."

"The baron was indeed a stern man," answered the other, "and would not suffer his wife to give way to grief or pain, however severe."

Meanwhile the lady thus referred to removed her tear-moistened handkerchief from her eyes occasionally, and sought to compose her features.

"She is really a beautiful woman still," whispered one of the gentlemen to the other.

"For twenty years she has been virtually a widow," was the reply.

"I doubt whether she remains one another twelve months," observed the first speaker.

The funeral anthem followed at this point. The village church could boast of an organ, the generous gift of the deceased. The choir sang, in excellent time and tune, one of the most beautiful of funeral melodies, — from the opera "Nebuchadnezzar," with words, of course, adapted to the occasion. Did the lamented Casimir Baradlay hear this opera selection sung over his remains? Administrator Rideghváry gave utterance to this query as he turned to the gentleman at his side.

"Didn't he like opera music?" asked the latter.

"On the contrary, he was always highly incensed when any such music was introduced into the church service. Indeed, he went so far as to give express directions in his will that no operatic airs should be sung at his funeral."

"Are you, then, so familiar with his last will and testament?" inquired the other.

But the administrator merely lowered his eyelids and twirled his mustache, implying thereby that he knew more than he cared to admit.

The funeral anthem did not close the service. Side by side on the bench near the pulpit sat three priests, who were evidently there for a purpose. When the singing ceased one of them mounted the pulpit.

"Are they all three going to preach to us?" asked the administrator's companion, already becoming restless.

"No," was the reply; "one of them is the local pastor, who is to offer a prayer at the grave."

"Ah, is he the one whose"— but here the two gentlemen fell to whispering so softly to each other that the concluding words of the sentence could not be overheard.

"And is the daughter here?" asked one. "Ah, yes, there she is in that corner, dressed in brown, her handkerchief in her hand. A lovely girl, truly!"

"Poor child!" whispered another. And, indeed, she was to be pitied, for she seemed little likely ever to see again the one for whom she was weeping.

At length the service came to an end, twelve haiduks, splendidly attired, raised the magnificent coffin upon their shoulders, the administrator offered his arm to the widow, and the funeral procession issued from the church and took its way toward the family vault, where yet one last ceremony was to be observed.

Upon depositing the remains in their final resting-place, it is customary for the local pastor to offer a prayer for the repose of the departed soul. Many were curious to see and hear the eccentric priest, Bartholomew Lánghy by name, whose duty it was to perform this office. The old preacher was wont to speak in the pulpit like an Abraham-à-Sancta-Clara, and in the county assembly like Lawrence the Club-bearer. After the third hymn a space was cleared

B

for the preacher before the entrance to the vault, where he took his stand with bared head, surrounded by the mourners. On each side of his forehead, which was high and bald, hung a few thin locks of hair; his face was smoothly shaven, as was then the custom in the Church, and the heavy eyebrows over the keen, dark eyes gave his countenance a look of resolute determination.

Folding his hands, he prayed as follows: "O Thou Judge of the living and of the dead, almighty Father of us all, incline Thine ear to our petition. Lo! with much earthly pomp and splendour the ashes of one of Thy servants are borne to the marble sepulchre prepared for their reception, while in the same hour his soul, naked and trembling, cowers at heaven's portals and sues for admission to paradise. What are we poor mortals that we should take our departure from this life amid such vain display and idle pomp, — we whose brothers are the worms and whose mother is the dust beneath our feet? The memory of a single good deed lights our path better than the flare of a thousand torches, and the unspoken benison of our neighbours is a fairer ornament for our coffin than all the escutcheons and orders in the world. O Lord, be merciful to those who in their lives have shown no mercy. Inquire not too sternly of the trembling soul before Thee, 'Who art thou, who led thee hither, and what say they of thee down yonder?' For to what but thine infinite mercy can he appeal who, though great and powerful in this life, yet stands before Thee stripped of his earthly glory? Called upon to answer Thy dread questions, 'Hast thou given help to the needy, raised up the fallen, protected the persecuted, lent thine ear to those that appealed to thee in despair, wiped away the tears of the sorrowing, shown compassion to the oppressed, and repaid love with love?'— he must answer, 'No.' And when Thou askest him, 'What use hast thou made of the power which I entrusted to thee? Hast thou given happiness to those under thy charge? Hast thou built for posterity? Hast thou honestly served thy country, or didst thou render homage to strange idols?' — what answer can he make, to whom turn for help, with what escutcheon or orders shield his breast, whom call upon as intercessor?"

The priest's face glowed, he seemed to increase in stature, and his hearers could not repress a feeling of awe and dread as they listened to him.

"O Lord," he continued, "let justice be tempered with mercy, avert Thy scrutiny from this man's past, and remember only that he walked in darkness here below and saw not Thy face. Weigh not his errors and his failings, but ascribe to him good intentions even where he erred. Forgive Thou him in heaven even as those against whom he sinned forgive him here on earth. Blot out the remembrance of his works, that none may thereby be reminded of him. But if the sinner must atone for his sins, if Thou art inexorable toward him and wilt not dismiss him unpunished from before Thy throne, then let his atonement be the return of his soul, which now sees all things in the clear light of Thy truth, and not as through a glass, darkly,— let his soul, we pray thee, return to the earth and take up its abode in his three sons, in order that the sins of the father may be transformed into virtues in the sons, and that the soil of his fatherland, which was his tomb as long as he lived, may now, when his bones rest therein in death, become the cradle in which he shall at last wake to life everlasting.   Hear, O Lord, Thy servant's prayer, Amen."

The closing of the iron portals of the vault terminated the ceremony, and the procession wound its way to the castle, where tables were spread in different rooms for the nobility, the students and the domestics.

The old priest, however, lingered behind and, while all the rest turned their faces toward the castle, took his daughter by the hand and went another way.   In vain had a cover been laid for him in the great hall of the castle.

CHAPTER III.

In a splendid hall formed entirely of malachite—its slender columns hewn each from a single block and resembling tropical tree-trunks, its niches filled with rare exotic plants, its centre occupied by a mammoth aquarium, and its arched doorways each affording a glimpse into a seemingly endless series of other magnificent apartments — was gathered a brilliant company. Among the gold-trimmed and order-bedecked costumes of the men was occasionally seen the plain black attire of an attaché to some embassy, and not infrequently these soberly clad young men received quite as much attention from the ladies as did the cavaliers in gaudier array.

One such black-clothed figure seemed to be the object of unusual interest. His handsome face showed at once youth, high birth, and an air of modesty and refinement. A woman might well have envied him his large blue eyes, shaded by their long lashes ; but his noble profile, finely cut lips, and tall and slender,

although muscular and elastic, form betokened the
early maturity of vigorous manhood.

A gentleman in a dazzling military uniform, with a
diamond order on his breast and a silk sash extending
over his shoulder and down to his hip, addressed the
young man and linked his arm in his.   He had known
the youthful attaché's father, whom he esteemed as
an able and highly gifted man, and he prophesied a
yet more brilliant career for the son.   As he drew
him forth in his promenade, he told him to prepare to
be presented to the grand-duchess.

It was a formidable ordeal for a young and unknown
man, who had not even a uniform to brace his courage, to be summoned before one of the greatest ladies
of the vast empire, in the presence of so many august
dignitaries, and to be called upon to frame, on the instant, suitable replies to her questions, and perhaps to
repay her gracious words with an improvised compliment or two.

But he stood the test, and many more beside.
Dancing began, and on his arm floated one charming
partner after another, each a type of beauty and grace.
The lovely Princess Alexandra, only daughter of a
Russian noble, a blonde beauty whose golden locks
seemed to have been spun out of sunbeams, had
whirled around the room twice on his arm when, as
they again reached her seat, she gave him a stealthy
pressure of the hand, as much as to say, "Once

more ! "— and so they danced around the hall a third time. It was a piece of boldness on her part that is seldom committed except out of wantonness or — love.

The youth bowed, and left his partner, feeling neither weariness nor any undue quickening of the pulse. There was a charm about him which lay in his calm, passionless bearing, and his unfailing self-control where other young men would have shown excitement. Royal pomp and splendour did not appeal to him, nor did beautiful eyes, sweet words, or the secret pressure of a fair hand rob him of his self-possession.

When midnight had struck and the orchestras in the various rooms were all playing national airs, as a signal that the grand-duchess was about to retire to her private apartments, the black-clothed young man hurried into the malachite hall, and reached for a glass of sherbet from the tray which a servant was bearing around the room. Suddenly, however, some one pulled his hand away, and said : " Don't drink that ! "

The young man turned, and for the first time that evening a smile of genuine pleasure lighted up his face.

" Ah, is it you, Leonin ? " he exclaimed.

Leonin was a young officer of the guard in tightly fitting uniform, a muscular young fellow with full face, carefully kept blond mustache and side-whiskers, and thick blond eyebrows which went well with his keen and animated gray eyes.

"I thought I had lost you in the dancing-hall," said he, with friendly reproach in his tone.

"I was dancing with your betrothed. Didn't you see me? She is a charming girl."

"Charming indeed; but how does that help matters for me? I can't marry her till I am of age and wear rosettes on my epaulets; and that won't be for two years yet. A man can't live all that time on a pair of beautiful eyes. Come with me."

The other hesitated. "I am not sure whether we ought to run away so early," said he.

"But don't you hear the bands playing the national hymns?" asked his companion. "Besides, we can slip out through the rear door; a sleigh is waiting for me there with my furs. Surely you haven't any more engagements with the wax dolls here?"

"Yes, I have," was the reply; "I am down for a quadrille with the Princess N——, to whom I was just now presented."

"Oh, I beg you, have nothing to do with her," urged the young officer. "She will only make sport of you, as she does of all the others. Come with me."

"Whither do you wish to take me?"

"To the infernal regions. Are you afraid to follow?"

" Not at all."

" Will you come with me to paradise, too, if I ask you ? "

" With all my heart."

" And if I invite you to a stuffy little inn on Kamennoi Island, where the sailors are having a dance, will you come ? "

" Yes, anywhere you please ; it's all one to me."

" Good ! That's what I like." And Leonin embraced his friend, after which he led him forth from the marble palace by passages known to himself. Once in the open air, they ran in their light ball-room costumes to the bank of the Neva, where a sleigh awaited their coming, wrapped themselves in warm furs, and in a moment were speeding across the ice behind two fleet horses, to the silvery music of tinkling bells.

These two young men were the Russian noble, Leonin Ramiroff, and Ödön, eldest son of the house of Baradlay.

As the sleigh glided along the moonlit row of palaces, Ödön remarked to his companion that they were not going in the direction of Kamennoi Island.

" Nor do we wish to," returned Leonin.

" Why, then, did you say we were going thither ? "

" So that no one should by any possibility overhear our real destination."

" And what, pray, may that be ? "

"You can see for yourself : we are on the Petrofski Prospect, headed straight for Petrofski Island."

"But there's nothing there except hemp factories and sugar refineries."

"You are right; and we are going to call on a sugar-boiler."

"I have no objection," returned Ödön, wrapping his mantle more closely about him, and leaning back in his seat. Possibly he even went to sleep.

Half an hour later the sleigh crossed the Neva again, and drew up before a red building at the end of a long park. Leonin aroused his companion.

"Here we are," said he.

All the windows of the long factory were lighted up, and as the two young men entered, they were greeted by that unsavoury odour peculiar to sugar refineries, and suggestive of anything but sugar. A smooth-faced man of sleek appearance advanced to meet them, and asked them in French what they wished.

"To see the sugar works," answered Leonin.

"Only the factory, or the refinery as well?" asked the Frenchman.

"Only the refinery," whispered the other, pressing a bank-note into the hand of his questioner.

"*Bien,*" replied the latter, and pocketed the money. It was a hundred-ruble note. "Is this gentleman going with you?" he asked, indicating Ödön.

"To be sure," answered Leonin. "Give him a hundred rubles, Ödön: that is the entrance fee. You won't regret it."

Ödön complied, and the Frenchman then conducted them through various passages and past doors from which issued hot blasts of air, stifling odours, and a fierce hissing of steam. Coming at last to a low iron portal which their guide opened to them by pressing a hidden spring, they passed into a dimly lighted passage and were directed to go on, as they could now find their way unaided.

Leonin, as one well acquainted with the place, took his friend's arm and led him forward. They descended a winding stairway, and as they went downward the clanking of machinery and hissing of steam gave place to the sound of distant music. At the foot of the stairs there sat at a little table an old woman dressed in the latest mode. Leonin threw down a gold coin.

"Is my box open?" he asked.

She bowed and smiled, whereupon he advanced to one of a row of tapestry portières and held it aside for Ödön to enter. They passed through another door and found themselves in a sort of opera-box whose front was screened by a light grating. The music was now distinctly audible.

"Is this a theatre or a circus?" asked Ödön, adding, as he peeped through the grating, "or is it a steam bath?"

Leonin laughed. "Anything you will," said he, throwing himself down on a divan and taking up a printed sheet that lay on the railing. It proved to be a programme, prepared in due form. He read it while the other looked over his shoulder.

"'*Don Juan au Sérail.*' That is a fine piece ; too bad we missed it. '*Tableaux Vivants*'— awfully tiresome. '*Les Bayadères du Khan Almollah*'— exceedingly amusing ; I have seen it once before. '*La Lutte des Amazones.*' '*La Rêve d'Ariane*'— charming, only I don't know whether Persida is at her best to-night."

The door of the box opened and a servant looked in.

"Waiter, serve us some refreshments," ordered Leonin.

"For how many ? "

"Three."

"Who is the third ? " asked Ödön.

"You will soon see, " replied Leonin.

The waiter spread the table and brought a roast, side dishes, and champagne in a cooler ; then he left the gentlemen to themselves. Leonin bolted the door after him.

"This is a queer kind of a sugar refinery, " remarked Ödön, glancing through the grating.

The other laughed. "You thought we only knew how to sing psalms, I suppose," said he.

"But such a resort here in a government building ! " exclaimed Ödön.

Leonin smiled and put his finger on his lips.

"Aren't you afraid of being discovered?" asked the other.

"If we were we should all take a trip to Siberia."

"Don't you fear the musicians may betray you?"

"They can't see. Every member of the orchestra is blind. But don't listen to the music. That is well enough for old gentlemen: something better is in store for us."

Leonin knocked twice on the partition wall separating them from the next box, the signal was repeated above, and in a few minutes a door opened in the partition and a woman's form appeared.

A more beautiful creature could not have stepped out of the pages of the "Arabian Nights." She wore a long Persian caftan that reached to her ankles and defined rather than veiled her shapely figure. Her slim waist was encircled by a golden girdle, while around her neck and on her bosom hung strings of pearls. The long, flowing sleeves of her caftan were slit up in front and gathered only at the shoulder, thus exposing to view the most perfect pair of arms ever dreamt of by sculptor. The face was of a noble Caucasian type, with finely shaped nose, full lips, arched eyebrows, and bright eyes of the deepest black. The sole ornament of her head was furnished by two magnificent braids of hair that fairly touched the wearer's heels.

She paused in surprise on the threshold. "You are not alone," said she.

"Come in, Jéza," returned Leonin. "This young gentleman is one half of my soul, of which you are the other half." So saying, with a quick movement he embraced the two and pressed them to his breast, after which he seated them side by side on another divan opposite his own.

"There, Ödön," he exclaimed, "isn't she different from those cold beauties of the upper world? Don't you find it more interesting here in the lower regions?"

Jéza met Ödön's unmoved inspection of her charms with a sort of timid wonder.

"Did you ever see such eyes as those?" asked Leonin, "or a mouth like that, which can smile, pout, tease, laugh, beg, and scold, so that you don't know which best becomes it?"

"Do you wish to sell me?" asked the Circassian girl.

"The purchaser would have to give me a new world in exchange," was the answer. "But if you should fall in love with one who is my friend and brother, he should receive you as a present."

Jéza sank back in a corner of the divan, lowered her eyelids and let her hands fall into her lap.

"Ödön, you really ought to have been an animal-tamer," said Leonin, as he took in both his hands

one of the Circassian girl's dainty little red-slippered
feet. "This young creature is naturally wild, impul-
sive, talkative, and full of whims; but as soon as she
meets the severe glance of your *mal occhio*, she sub-
sides and sits there like one of the novices in the
Smolna nunnery. Jéza, you are lost. All of those
beautiful wild beasts known as women become mute
and helpless the moment this lion-tamer looks at
them."

The Circassian girl tossed her head and turned a
defiant look upon Ödön; but no sooner did she meet
his eye than she blushed in spite of herself — perhaps for the first time since the slave-dealer at
Yekaterinograd had severed her girdle.

"Come, let us drink, my children," cried Leonin,
striking off the head of one of the champagne bottles.
Filling three glasses, he handed one to Ödön and one
to Jéza; and when they had half emptied them he
exchanged and refilled them.

"Drink to the bottom this time," he said. "That
is right. Now you have drunk love to each other."

The wine loosed the girl's tongue and she began
to chatter in the liveliest fashion. From the hall the
notes of the orchestra reached them, and she sang an
accompaniment. Ödön sat with his back against the
grating and did not once turn around to see any of
the pieces that were being presented. Leonin, on
the other hand, looked through the grating at every

new number and indulged in various random comments.

"Well, Jéza," he asked at length, "haven't you
any number to-night?"

"No, I am having a holiday," she replied.

"But couldn't you oblige my friend by giving one
of your productions?"

Jéza sat upright and stole a look at Ödön. "If he
wishes it," she answered.

"What shall I ask for?" asked Ödön, turning to
Leonin.

"Oh, I forgot," replied the latter; "you didn't
know that Jéza was an *artiste*, and above all things
unexcelled as a rider. Her number is always given
the place of honour, — at the end of the programme.
Choose any of her rôles."

"But I am not acquainted with the young lady's
repertoire," returned the other.

"Barbarian! not to know Jéza's masterpieces after
living for half a year in a civilised country. Well,
I'll name the best ones to you. '*La Reine Amala-
sunthe;*' '*La Diablesse;*' '*Étoile qui File;*' '*La
Bayadère;*' '*La Nymphe Triomphante;*' '*Diane
qui Chasse Actæon;*' '*Mazeppa*' —"

"No, that is not among them!" cried the girl,
interrupting the speaker.

"Ödön, don't let her fool you," said Leonin;
"choose Ma—"

But he was stopped by Jéza, who had sprung from her seat and was holding her hand over his mouth. He struggled to free himself, but meanwhile Ödön ended the contest by making his choice.

"Mazeppa!" he called, and Jéza turned her back to them both in a pet and leaned against the wall. Leonin, however, gained his point.

"You have always refused me that," said he; "but I told you the time would come when you would have to yield."

The girl threw a look at Ödön. "Very well, then; it shall be done." And therewith she disappeared.

Ödön now turned his attention for the first time to the arena, a vaulted space of sixty yards in diameter, half enclosed by a semicircle of grated boxes. No spectators were to be seen, but the cigar-smoke that made its way through the gratings betrayed their presence. The side of the arena unenclosed by boxes was draped with hangings on which were depicted various mythological scenes, while an occasional door broke up the wall-space and relieved the monotony.

For a few minutes after Jéza's exit from Leonin's box the arena was quite empty, save that two Moorish girls in Turkish costume were busy smoothing the sand,—a sign that an equestrian act was to follow.

A knock was heard at the door of Leonin's box.

c

and he went to open it. A servant stood without, bearing a letter on a silver tray.

"What have you there?" asked Leonin.

"A letter for the other gentleman, sir."

"How did it come?"

"A courier brought it, sir, with instructions to find the gentleman without delay, wherever he might be."

"Fee the courier and send him away."

Leonin took the letter and fingered it a moment. Its seal was black and its address was in a woman's hand.

"Here is a billet-doux for you," said he, as he handed the letter to Ödön. "The Princess N—— sends you word that she has taken arsenic because you failed to claim her hand for the quadrille." With that he turned to the grating and drew out his opera-glass, as if resolved not to lose a moment of Jéza's impersonation of Mazeppa; but he added, over his shoulder, to Ödön: "You see, in spite of my precautions, we failed to cover our tracks. Oh, these women have a thousand-eyed police in their service, I verily believe. They have us watched at every turn."

The overture began. At the ringing of a bell the blind musicians struck up the Mazeppa galop. Behind the scenes could be heard the barking of the dogs which, as a substitute for wolves, were to pursue Mazeppa as he was borne away, fast bound upon a wild horse's back; and the cracking of whips also

sounded, arousing the horse to a livelier display of his
mettle. Finally the beating of the animal's hoofs
was heard, a loud outcry was raised, and Mazeppa's
wild ride began amid cheers and hand-clapping from
behind the gratings.

"Oh, beautiful! Infernally beautiful!" exclaimed
Leonin. "Look, Ödön, look! See there!" But
what did he behold as he turned his head for an instant toward his friend?

Ödön's hand was over his eyes and he was weeping.

"What is the matter?" cried the other in amazement. Ödön handed him the letter without a
word, and he read its brief contents, which were in
French.

"Your father is dead. Come at once.

"Your affectionate MOTHER."

Leonin's first impulse was one of resentment. "I'd
like to get hold of that blockhead of a courier who
brought you this letter. Couldn't he have waited
till morning?"

But Ödön arose without a word and left the box.
Leonin followed him.

"Poor fellow!" he exclaimed, seizing his friend's
hand. "This letter came very *mal à propos.*"

"Excuse me," returned the other; "I must go
home."

"I 'll go with you," was the hearty response. "Let those stay and see Mazeppa who care to. We promised that we would go with each other to hell, to heaven — and home. So I shall go with you."

"But I am going home to Hungary," said Ödön.

Leonin started. "Oh, to Hungary!"

"My mother calls me," explained the other, with the simple brevity of one overcome with grief.

"When do you start?"

"Immediately."

Leonin shook his head incredulously. "That is simply madness," he declared. "Do you wish to freeze to death? Here in the city it is twenty degrees below zero, and out in the open country it is at least twenty-five. Between Smolensk and Moscow the roads are impassable, so much snow has fallen. In Russia no one travels in winter except mail-carriers and tradesmen."

"Nevertheless I shall start at once," was the calm rejoinder.

"Surely your mother wouldn't have you attempt the impossible. Where you live they have no conception what it means to travel in midwinter from St. Petersburg to the Carpathians. Wait at least till the roads are open."

"No, Leonin," returned Ödön, sadly; "every hour that I waited would be a reproach to my conscience. You don't understand how I feel."

"Well, then," replied the other, "let us go to your rooms."

Reaching his quarters, Ödön first awakened his valet and bade him pack his master's trunk and pay whatever accounts were owing. Then, so great was the young man's haste, he proceeded to build a fire with his own hands rather than wait for his servant to do it. Meanwhile Leonin had thrown himself into an easy chair and was watching his friend's movements.

"Are you really in earnest about starting this very day?" he asked.

"You see I am," was the reply.

"And won't you delay your departure to please me, or even at the Czar's request?"

"I love you and respect the Czar, but my mother's wishes take precedence of all else."

"Very well; so that appeal will not serve. But I have a secret to tell you. My betrothed, Princess Alexandra, is desperately in love with you. She is the only daughter of a magnate who is ten times as rich as you. She is beautiful, and she is good, but she does not care for me, because she loves you. She has confessed as much to me. Were it any one else that stood in my way, I would challenge him; but I love you more than my own brother. Marry her and remain here with us."

Ödön shook his head sadly. " I am going home to my mother."

"Then, Heaven help me! I am going with you," declared the young Russian. " I shall not let you set out on such a journey alone."

The two embraced each other warmly, and Leonin hastened away to make preparations for the journey. He despatched couriers to order relays of horses, together with drivers, at all the stations; he loaded his travelling-sledge with all kinds of provisions, — smoked meat, smoked fish, biscuits, caviare, and brandy; a tea-kettle and a spirit-lamp were provided; two good polar-bear skins, foot-bags, and fur caps for himself and his friend were procured; and he also included in their equipment two good rifles, as well as a brace of pistols and a Greek dagger for each of them, — since all these things were likely to prove useful on the way. He even had the forethought to pack two pairs of skates, that they might, when they came to a stream, race with each other over the ice and thus warm their benumbed feet. The space under the front seat he filled with cigars enough to last them throughout their twenty days' journey. When at length, as twilight was falling, he drove up with a merry jingle of bells before Ödön's lodging, he felt himself thoroughly equipped for the journey. But first he had to dress his friend from top to toe, knowing well from experience how one should be attired for a winter journey in Russia.

The Russian sledge stood ready at the door, its runners well shod, its body covered with buffalo-hide, the front sheltered by a leather hood, and the rear protected by a curtain of yet thicker leather. Three horses were harnessed abreast, the middle one standing between the thills, which were hung with bells. The driver stood with his short-handled, long-lashed whip before the horses.

The young Russian stopped his friend a moment before they took their places in the sledge. "Here, take this amulet," said he; "my mother gave it to me on her death-bed, assuring me it would shield the wearer from every danger."

The trinket was a small round cameo cut out of mother-of-pearl and set in gold; it represented St. George and the dragon. Ödön felt unwilling to accept the gift.

"Thank you," said he, "but I have no faith in charms. I only trust to my stars, and they are — loving woman's eyes."

Leonin grasped his friend's hands. "Answer me one question: do you see two eyes or four among your stars?"

Ödön paused a moment, then pressed his comrade's hand and answered. "Four."

"Good!" exclaimed Leonin, and he helped his companion into the sledge.

The driver pulled each of his horses by the fore-lock, kissed all three on the cheek, crossed himself, and then took his place on the front seat. In a moment more the sledge was flying through the snow-covered streets on its way southward.

CHAPTER IV.

THE TWO OTHERS.

"THE King of Hungary" was, at the time of our narrative, one of the finest hotels in Vienna, and much frequented by aristocratic Hungarian travellers and by Hungarian army officers.

A young hussar officer was ascending the stairs to the second story. He was a handsome, well-built, broad-shouldered youth, and his uniform fitted his athletic figure well. His cheeks were ruddy, his face full, and on his upper lip he wore a mustache, the ends of which pointed upward with a sprightly air. His cap was tilted well forward over his eyes, and he carried his head as proudly as if he had been the only captain of horse in the whole wide world.

On reaching the landing his attention was arrested by a strange scene in the passageway leading to one of the guest-chambers. An old gentleman with a smooth face, and wearing a peasant's cloak, was vociferating wrathfully before three waiters and a chambermaid. Both the waiters and the chambermaid were exerting themselves with every demonstration

41

of respect to gratify his slightest wish, which only increased the old gentleman's anger, and caused him
to renew his scolding, now in Hungarian, and now in
Latin. Catching sight of the hussar, who had been
brought to a standstill by the clamour, he called to
him in Hungarian — feeling sure that no hussar could
be of any other nationality — and begged his assistance.

"My dear Captain," he cried, "do have the goodness to come here, and explain matters to these
hyperboreans, who seem to understand no language
that I can speak."

The officer approached, and perceived that his interlocutor was, to all appearances, a minister of the
gospel.

"Well, reverend father, what is the trouble?" he
asked.

"Why, you see," explained the other, "my passport describes me rightly enough, in Latin, as *verbi
divini minister*, that is, a preacher of God's word.
Well, now, when it came my turn to show my papers
to the custom-house officer, they all began to salute
me, as if I had been a minister of state, calling me
'your Excellency,' and paying me every sort of compliment, right and left, — porters, cab-drivers, waiters,
and all. I thought they would kiss the ground I
stood on before I was at last shown up to this splendid apartment. Now this style is more than I can

afford. I am only a poor pastor, and I have come to Vienna not for pleasure, but forced by necessity. Pray explain matters for me to these people. I can't speak German, it is never used at home among our people, and no one here seems to understand any other language."

The hussar officer smiled.

"Good father," he asked, "what languages do you speak?"

"Well," was the reply, "I can speak Latin, Greek, Hebrew, and, in case of need, some Arabic."

"They will hardly be of any service here," rejoined the other, laughing. Then, turning to the head waiter, he asked him a question in a low tone, to which the servant replied by winking mysteriously and pointing upward.

"Well, reverend father," said the hussar to the poor priest, "you go into your room now, and in a quarter of an hour, I will return and arrange everything for you. Just now I am in haste, as some one is waiting for me."

"But, I beg to assure you, my business is even more pressing than yours," was the other's reply, as he seized the young officer's sword-tassel to prevent his escape. "If I so much as set foot in this state apartment, it will cost me five florins at least."

"But, sir," explained the other, apologetically, "my affair is far more important. Five comrades of mine are expecting me in the room above, and one of them is to fight with me. I really cannot wait."

The priest was so startled by this announcement that he dropped the sword-tassel.

"What!" he exclaimed, "you are on your way to a duel? Pray tell me the reason of such a piece of folly."

But the young man only pressed his hand with a smile. "You wait here quietly till I come back," said he. "I shall not be gone long."

"Supposing you are slain?" the old gentleman called after him, in great anxiety.

"I'll look out for that," replied the hussar, as he sprang blithely up the stairs, clinking his spurs as he went.

The old priest was forced to take possession of the splendid apartment, while the whole retinue of servants still persisted in honouring him with the title, "your Excellency."

"This is fine, to be sure," said the good man to himself, as he surveyed his surroundings. "Silk bed-curtains, porcelain stove — why, I shall have to pay five florins a day, if not six. And then all the good-for-nothing servants! One brings my valise, another a pitcher of water, a third the bootjack, and each one counts on receiving a good big fee from 'his Excellency.' I shall be expected to pay for the extra polish on the floor, too."

Thus grumbling and scolding, and estimating how

much all this splendour would probably cost him in
the end, the priest suddenly heard a stamping of feet,
and a clashing of swords in the room above. The
duellists were surely at it over his very head. Now
here, now there, he heard the heavy footsteps, accompanied by the ringing of steel against steel. For five
or six minutes the sounds continued, the poor parson
meanwhile in great perplexity as to what course he
ought to pursue. He felt half inclined to open the
window and call for help, but immediately bethought
himself that he might be arrested by the police for
disturbing the peace. Then it occurred to him to run
up-stairs, throw himself between the combatants, and
deliver them a sermon on the text (Matt. 26 : 52) :
" Put up again thy sword into his place : for all they
that take the sword shall perish with the sword."
But while he was still debating the matter the tumult over his head subsided, and in a few minutes he
heard steps approaching his door, which opened and
admitted, to his great relief, the young hussar officer,
safe and sound.

The priest ran to him and felt of his arms and
breast, to make sure that he had actually received no
injury. " Aren't you hurt, then, in the least ? " he
inquired.

" Of course not, good father," replied the other.

" But did you slay your opponent ? "

" Oh. I scratched him a little on the cheek."

"And is he not in great pain?" asked the kind-hearted pastor, with much concern.

"Not at all; he is as pleased over his wound as a boy with a new jacket."

But the minister of the gospel found the matter no subject for light treatment. "How, pray, can you gentlemen indulge in such unchristian practices?" he asked, earnestly. "What motive can you possibly have?"

"My dear sir," returned the other, "have you ever heard the story of the two officers who fought a duel because one of them maintained that he had picked sardines from a tree in Italy, and the other refused to believe him? So they fought it out, and it was only after the first had received a slash across the face that he remembered, — 'Ah, yes, quite right; they were not sardines, after all, but capers.' So here you may imagine some such cause as that."

"And you fought for such a trifle!" exclaimed the pastor.

"Yes, something of the sort, if I remember rightly. You see, I have just joined the regiment after serving in the life-guard, and I have been promoted captain; so I must fight with a dozen comrades in succession, until they either cut me to pieces or learn to endure my presence among them. That is the custom. But let us discuss your affairs now. You said you were here on urgent business ; pray tell me its nature."

" Certainly," responded the other ; " if you will have the kindness to hear me, I shall be most grateful. I am an entire stranger in the city and have no one to render me any assistance. I have been summoned hither *ad audiendum verbum*, having had some differences with the landlord of the village where I am settled as pastor. You must first understand that the squire was a great oligarch, while I am nothing but a poor country parson. There was discord between our families, arising from the squire's having a young cavalier as his eldest son and my having a pretty daughter. I refused to listen to certain proposals on the part of the squire, and the upshot was that the son was sent away to Russia. That, however, did not greatly concern me. But not long afterward the squire departed this life and was buried with all the pomp of the Church. I made the prayer at the grave, and it is true, I said some hard things ; but what I said was for God's ear, not for man's. And now, because of that prayer of mine to Heaven, I am called to account by the mighty ones of this earth. Already I have appeared before the consistory and before the county court, accused of impiety and sedition. I am expelled from my pastorate, and yet they are not content ; they summon me hither, I know not before whom, to answer the charge of *lèse-majesté.* But see here and judge for yourself; I have the text of the prayer in my pocket. Read it and see whether it contains a single word by which I have made myself guilty of any such offence."

The old man's lips trembled as he spoke, and his eyes filled with tears. The hussar took the writing from his hand and read it through, the other watching meanwhile every line of the young man's face, to see what impression the perusal would make on him.

"Well, sir, what do you say to it?" he asked when the young officer had finished reading. "Would you condemn me for anything in that prayer?"

The other folded the paper and returned it to the old man. "I should not condemn you," he replied gently. He appeared to be much moved.

"Now may God bless you for those words!" exclaimed the priest. "Would that you were my judge!"

And, indeed, he was his judge at that moment; for he was no other than Richard Baradlay, the son of him over whose body the prayer had been offered.

"But let me give your Reverence a piece of advice," added the young man. "First, stay here quietly in your room until you are summoned. Visit no one and make your complaint to no one. You cannot be found guilty of the offence charged against you. But if you should undertake to defend yourself,

I could not answer for the consequences. Just stay here in your room, and if you are sent for, answer the summons. Go whither you are called, and hear in silence what is said to you. When that is over, bow yourself out and hasten back to your hotel without saying a word to any one on the way or answering a single question."

"But I shall be taken for a blockhead," objected the other.

"No, believe me, silence is a passport that will carry a man half-way around the world."

"Very well, I will do as you direct ; only I hope the process will be brief. The Vienna air is costly to breathe."

"Don't worry in the least about that, reverend father. If some one has compelled you to make the journey against your will, you may be sure he will pay your score."

The old man wondered not a little at these words, and would gladly have inquired who the unknown "some one" was.

"But now my engagements call me away," concluded the young officer, and he took his leave before the other could question him further.

Soon after he had gone a waiter appeared with coffee, which, in spite of the old priest's protestations that he never took any breakfast and was in general a very light eater, the German domestic insisted on

D

leaving upon the table. At length, as the coffee was there on his hands, the reverend gentleman proceeded to drink it in God's name; for it would have to be paid for in any case. The warm breakfast did him good. The servant now appeared, to carry away the breakfast service. The old gentleman had learned one German word on his journey, and he hastened to make use of it.

"Pay?" he said inquiringly, producing from the depths of his pocket a long knit purse, a birthday present from his daughter, in which his scanty savings were carefully hoarded. He wished to settle at once for his breakfast, both because it troubled him to be in debt for even an hour, and also that he might gain some idea from this first payment how much his total daily expenses would probably be.

Great was his surprise, however, when the waiter, smiling politely and waving aside the offered purse, assured him that the breakfast was already paid for.

"So that young man was right, after all," said the good priest to himself. "Why didn't I ask him his name? But who can it be that is paying my bills?"

The unknown benefactor was, of course, none other than Richard Baradlay, who, on leaving the hotel, had handed the head waiter two ducats and bidden him provide for all the old gentleman's wants, adding that he, Baradlay, would pay the bill. After that the young officer repaired to the military riding

school and exercised for an hour in vaulting, fencing
on horseback, breaking a lance or two, and mastering
a vicious horse. Then he went to walk for an hour
around the fortifications, looked at all the pretty faces
he met, and at length, toward noon, returned to his
quarters. He kept bachelor's hall on the fourth floor,
occupying a sitting-room and a bedroom, while across
the passageway was a little room for his servant, and
a diminutive kitchen.

His domestic was an old hussar who answered to
the name of Paul, and who was rather more inclined
to command his master than to receive orders from
him. He was sixty years old and more, and still a
private and a bachelor. He was serving out his
fourth enlistment and wore on his breast the cross
given to the veterans of the Napoleonic wars.

"Well, Paul, what is there to eat to-day?" asked
the captain, unbuckling his sword and hanging it
up in his closet, which showed a collection of ancient
swords and daggers.

The reader must here be informed that Paul was
at once body-servant and cook to his young master.

"What is there to eat? A Greek rose-garland,"
answered the old servant, with humourous phlegm.

"Ah, that must be delicious," returned Richard;
"but what is it made of?"

"Angels' slippers," was the reply.

"Excellent! And is it ready?"

Paul surveyed his master from top to toe. "Do we eat at home again to-day?" he asked.

"Yes, if we can get anything to eat."

"Very well; I will serve dinner at once," answered Paul, and he proceeded to spread the table — which was accomplished by turning its red cloth, ornamented with blue flowers, so that it became a blue cloth adorned with red flowers. Then he laid a plate of faience ware and a horn-handled knife and fork, together with an old-fashioned silver spoon, first wiping each article on a corner of the table-cloth. He completed these preparations by adding an old champagne-bottle filled, as the reader will have guessed, with cold water.

The cavalry captain pulled up a chair and seated himself comfortably, stretching his legs out under the table. Meanwhile Paul, his hands on his hips, thus addressed his master:

"So we are stranded again, are we, — not a kreutzer in our pockets?"

"Not a solitary one, as sure as you live," answered Richard, as he took up his knife and fork and began to beat a tattoo on his plate.

"But this morning I found two ducats in your vest pocket," remarked the old servant.

Captain Richard laughed and asked, in expressive pantomime: "Where are they now?"

"Good!" muttered the other, as he took up the

decanter that stood before his master's plate and went out. Having brought it back filled with wine, which he had procured in some way, he set it down again and resumed his discourse.

"No doubt they went to buy a bouquet for a pretty girl," said he. "Or have the boys drunk them up in champagne?" With that he took up a plate with a sadly nicked edge from the sideboard and added, with philosophic resignation, as he went out: "Well, I was just that way when I was young." Soon he returned, bearing his master's dinner.

The "Greek rose-garland" proved to be a dish of beans, while the "angels' slippers," cooked with them, were nothing but pigs' feet. The old hussar had prepared the meal for himself, but there was enough for two, and Richard attacked the camp fare with as keen a relish as if he had never known anything better in his life. While he ate, his old servant stood behind his chair, although his services were not needed, as there were no plates to change, the first course being also the last.

"Has any one called?" asked Richard as he ate.

"Any one called? Why, yes, we have had some callers."

"Who were they?"

"First the maid-servant of the actress — not the blonde one, but the other, the pug-nosed one. She brought a bouquet and a letter. I stuck the flowers into a pitcher in the kitchen, gave the maid a pinch on the cheek, and kindled the fire with the letter."

"The deuce take you!" exclaimed Richard; "what made you burn up the letter?"

"It asked for money from the captain," was the reply.

"But how did you know that, Paul? I thought you couldn't read."

"I smelt it."

Richard laughed aloud. "Well, who else has been here?" he asked.

"The young gentleman." This title was always used by Paul to designate one particular person.

"My brother? What did he wish?"

As if in answer to this inquiry, the young gentleman suddenly appeared in person.

The youngest Baradlay was a slender youth of frail physique. On his smooth, boyish face sat a somewhat affected expression of amiability, and if he carried his head rather high, it was not from pride, but on account of the eye-glasses which he wore on his nose. As he shook hands with his older brother, the latter was somehow reminded of the regulation that requires certain government officials, as a part of their duties, to show the utmost courtesy to every one — *ex officio*.

"Your servant, Jenö. What's up now?"

"I came to tell you," replied the other, "that I have received a letter from mother."

"I received one, too," said Richard.

"She informs me," continued Jenö, "that she is going to double my monthly allowance, and, in order to enable me to fit up my rooms as becomes one of my rank, she sends me a thousand florins."

"And she writes to me," said the older brother, "that if I continue to spend money as I have in the past, I shall soon run through my share of the property; and unless I am more economical she will send me no more funds."

"But my difficulty," rejoined the other, "is that if I begin now to spend a good deal of money, those over me will notice it. You can't imagine how one is made to suffer for it when once his superiors in the government service begin to suspect him of playing the independent gentleman. Really, I don't know what I shall do. Look here, Richard; do you know what I came for this morning? I came to share with you the money that mother sent me."

The other continued to chew his toothpick. "What interest?" he asked.

"Don't insult me with such a question!" protested Jenö.

"Then you offer to divide with me simply because you don't know how to spend the money yourself and

want my help in getting rid of it? Good! I am at
your service."

"I thought you could make a better use of it than
I," said the youth, handing over the half of his thousand florins, and pressing his brother's hand as he did
so. "I have something else to give you also," he
added, with assumed indifference, — "an invitation
to the Plankenhorsts' reception to-morrow evening."

Richard rested his elbows on the table and regarded
his brother with a satirical smile. "How long have
you been acting as advertising agent of the Plankenhorst receptions?" he asked.

"They begged me most cordially to invite you in
their name," returned the other, moving uneasily in
his chair.

Richard laughed aloud. "So that is the usury I
am to pay?" said he.

"What do you mean by that?" asked Jenö, with
vexation, rising from his seat.

"I mean that you would like to pay your court to
Miss Alfonsine if her mother, who considers you a
very raw youth as yet, were not in the way. Madame
Antoinette herself claims to be not devoid of personal
charms, and, if her *friseur* is to be believed, she is
still a beautiful woman. When I was in the guard
I used to dance with her often at the masked balls,
and I recognised her under her domino more than
once when she mistook me for an acquaintance and

fell to chatting with me. You know all that very well, and you say to yourself: 'I'll take my brother along as elephant.' All right, brother; never fear, I am not going to hand back the five hundred florins. Your charges are high, but I'll be your elephant. Climb up on my back, and while you beguile the daughter I will keep the mother amused. But first I must impose one condition. If you really want my company at the reception, do me the favour to intercede with your chief on behalf of a poor priest who has been summoned to Vienna. Have him sent home in peace. I don't need to tell you he is our pastor at Nemesdomb, and he has been set upon because of the funeral prayer he saw fit to make."

"How did you learn all that?" asked Jenö, in surprise.

"Oh, I picked it up," replied the other; "and I tell you he is an honest man. Let him go."

Jenö assumed his official expression of countenance. "But really," said he, "I have reason to know that the chancellor is greatly incensed against him."

"Come, come!" cried the elder brother, impatiently; "don't try to impose on me with your great men. I have seen any number of them, in all sorts of undress, and I know that they are built just like other mortals, —eat and drink, yawn and snore exactly like the rest of mankind. Your great magistrate wrinkles his brow. talks in a harsh tone to the innocent vic

tim before him, and when he has let him go, the
mighty man laughs aloud at the terrible fright he
gave the poor wretch. This priest is an honest fellow, but his tongue sometimes runs away with him.
Yet he is a servant of God, and he must be allowed
to depart in peace. May he long minister to his little
flock!"

"Well, I will speak to his Excellency," returned
Jenö.

"Thank you. Now sit down and drink with me,
to seal our compact. Paul!"

The old hussar appeared.

"There is a ten-florin note. Go and get two
bottles of champagne,—one for us and one for
yourself."

Old Paul shook his head as he withdrew, and
muttered, "I was just such another myself when
I was a youngster."

CHAPTER V.

THE Plankenhorst family in Vienna was an entirely respectable one, although its name lacked the prefix which denotes nobility. Nevertheless the widow was honoured with the title of baroness, as she was of noble birth, and her daughter, too, was similarly addressed by her admirers. They lived in a house of their own in the inner city; and that signifies a great deal in Vienna. But the house was an old-fashioned one, built in the style of Maria Theresa, and the ground floor was given up to shops. They were admitted to court circles and were often seen there; yet it was the men rather than the women that sought their society. Barons and princes not seldom offered an arm to the amiable Madame Antoinette to escort her to the supper-room, or begged of the charming Miss Alfonsine the pleasure of a dance. But no baron or prince was ever known to seek an intimate acquaintance with either of them.

Their receptions were well attended, and it was there that many political and love intrigues were hatched. To be sure, the Sedlniczkys, the Insaghis, and the Apponys never graced these functions, but their secretaries were to be seen there. No one ever thought of seeking the Princes Windischgrätz and Colloredo in that house; yet military celebrities with decorated breasts and gold-laced collars were to be found there in plenty, as well as jovial officers and guardsmen of good family. The ladies, too, in attendance, both matrons and misses, belonged to families distinguished either for high official station or for birth.

The tone of these assemblies was thoroughly respectable, while they offered peculiar facilities for enjoying oneself without irksome restraint, — an advantage not found everywhere.

For all that, however, when at nine o'clock of the appointed evening Jenö betook himself in full evening dress to his brother's quarters, he found the young cavalry officer not yet attired for the reception, and, apparently, utterly indifferent to the great pleasure awaiting him. He was lying on his lounge, reading a novel.

"Well, aren't you going to the party?" asked the younger brother.

"What party?"

"At the Plankenhorsts'."

"There now, I had forgotten all about it," exclaimed Richard, springing up and summoning his servant.

"Do tell me, Richard, why you have such an aversion to these people? They are so friendly and cordial, and one is always sure to pass a pleasant evening at their house."

"What's wanted now?" inquired Paul, appearing at the door.

"Come in, Paul, and shave me," returned his master.

The old hussar was barber as well as cook.

"Why don't you answer my question?" persisted Jenö, while old Paul beat up the lather. "What have you against the Plankenhorsts?"

"The deuce take me if I can tell," answered Richard; "but they are such tuft-hunters!"

"Better not talk now, or I shall be cutting your face," interposed the old servant. "Let the young gentleman go on ahead, and you can follow him as soon as I have made you presentable. You won't need any rope ladder or skeleton key to get into the Plankenhorst house."

Jenö adopted this suggestion, and half an hour later his brother joined him in the Plankenhorst parlours. Jenö hastened to present the newcomer to the hostess and her daughter, both of whom remembered that they had already had the pleasure of meeting him. The mother declared herself delighted to welcome him under her own roof, to which Richard replied with an appropriate compliment, and then made room for other arrivals.

"Shall I introduce you to some of the people here?" asked Jenö.

"No, don't trouble yourself; I know them better than you do. That marshal over there, with the military figure and a voice as loud as if he were commanding a brigade, is an officer in the commissary department. He spends his time in weighing out provender, and has never smelt gunpowder except on the emperor's birthday. The young prince yonder, with the condescending smile and his eye-glasses stuck high up on his nose, is secretary to the chief of police, and a very influential man. The duenna in the coffee-coloured dress and with paint on her cheeks, is the wife of Blumenbach, the banker, who lends money to the spendthrift young aristocrats, and, consequently, knows all that is going on in high society. And the young lady near us, talking and smiling so confidentially with a young man about your age, is the most accomplished detective that ever ferreted out a secret; but aside from that she is a very nice little innocent creature."

Jenö felt not entirely at his ease as he listened to his brother, whom he suspected of entertaining no very high opinion of the whole company.

"The little maid that I met on the stairs," resumed Richard, "pleases me more than all this company put together. I don't know whether she belongs in the house, but I came here to-night wholly on her account. I pinched her cheek as she was running away from me, and she gave me a slap on the hand that I can feel now."

The last words received but scant attention from Jenö, as a certain illustrious ornament of society had caught sight of the two brothers and was hastening toward them. He was a tall, angular man, with a sharp nose and a little pointed beard. Greeting Jenö on the way, he made straight for the elder brother, and placed his bony hand familiarly on the young man's shoulder.

"Your humble servant, my dear Richard!" he exclaimed in Hungarian.

The other returned the greeting with much coolness and indifference.

The angular gentleman pulled at his beard as if not wholly pleased with his reception, and Jenö bit his lip in vexation at his brother's conduct.

"Well, how are you?" asked the tall gentleman, with gracious condescension.

"Well enough," replied Richard nonchalantly; "and I see you are in good trim, too."

The other seemed not exactly to relish this answer. "I am going to leave for home to-morrow," said he; "what word shall I carry to your mother from you?"

"Ah, you live in our neighbourhood, do you?" blandly inquired the young hussar officer.

At this the polygonal gentleman nearly lost command of himself, while Jenö tried to look as if his attention were elsewhere engaged.

"What message, then, do you wish to send?" resumed Richard's interlocutor.

"I kiss her hand," answered the young man briefly.

"Ah, that commission I will execute with the greatest pleasure, in person," exclaimed the other, with effusive friendliness.

"Oh, you needn't feel obliged to convey my respects in such a literal sense as that," returned Richard. "I was speaking figuratively."

Jenö meanwhile had opened a conversation with the innocent-looking young lady near him; but he kept one eye on his brother, and as soon as he saw that the angular gentleman had departed, he took leave of the young lady and returned to Richard.

"Well, now, you've put your foot in it this time!" he exclaimed.

"How so?" asked the other, with much composure.

"Didn't you know that man? It was Rideghváry."

"Well, he might have been Meleghváry, for all I care."

"But he is an intimate friend of the family, and you have often seen him at our house."

"As if I could remember all the faces I saw in our house when I was a little boy, before I was sent away to the military academy. I didn't keep an album of them, — the Rideghvárys and all the other várys."

Jenö tried to draw his brother aside where they would not be overheard. "You must know," said he, "that Rideghváry is a very influential man."

"What is that to me?" asked the other, indifferently.

"He is the administrator of our county."

"Well, that is the county's affair, not mine."

"And, still more, he is likely to be our stepfather."

"That is our mother's affair." So saying, Richard turned his back on his brother, who wished to detain him, but the other shook him off. "Don't bother me with your Rideghváry. We didn't come here to see him. Go and court Alfonsine; there's no one with her now but the little secretary with the squeaky voice."

The hussar officer danced for awhile and otherwise sought to amuse himself. Cards were never played at the Plankenhorst parties. Young ladies were there in plenty, and Richard enjoyed the reputation of a veritable Don Juan; but the very ease of his conquests destroyed their value in his eyes. A little maid-servant, however, who slapped him and ran away because he pinched her cheek, was something new. No man had ever defeated him in a duel, nor woman triumphed over him in a love affair.

Entering the supper-room later with his brother, he saw the little maid-servant presiding over the lemonade, and he pointed her out to Jenö.

E

"You bungler!" exclaimed the latter, under his breath; "you only fall from one blunder into another. She isn't a servant, but Miss Edith Liedenwall, a relative of the family."

"What! She one of the family? And do they leave her alone on the stairs in the evening, and let her serve lemonade to the guests?"

Jenö shrugged his shoulders. "Well, you see, she is the daughter of some poor relations, and her aunt here has taken pity on her. Then, too, she is little more than a child, — only about fifteen years old, — and no one heeds her."

Richard looked at his brother coldly. "Was your Baroness Plankenhorst never of that age herself?" he asked.

"But what would you have them do with an adopted waif like that?" returned the other. "They can't rear her as if she were to be a great lady."

"Then they ought not to have adopted her," objected Richard. "No gentleman will pay court to her as long as she fills a menial's place, and no poor man will venture to do so on account of her high birth."

"Quite true, but what can we do about it?" said Jenö.

Richard left his brother and advanced to the side-board, where the girl was serving lemonade. She presented an exceedingly attractive appearance, her abundant dark hair coiled high on her head, her black eyes full of life, and a ready smile on her coral lips. She seemed to enjoy the part allotted to her, and met the guests' friendly advances in an unconstrained but modest manner. Upon Richard's approach she did not turn away from him, as he might have expected from their earlier meeting, but met his look with a roguish smile in her bright eyes, and said to him, as he came nearer:

"Aha! now you are afraid of me, aren't you?" And she had hit the truth, for the young officer really felt abashed in her presence.

"Miss Edith," said he, "I beg you to pardon me; but why do they let you wander about alone in the evening, where you are sure to meet so many people?"

"Oh, they all know me," she answered, "and I had an errand to do. You took me for a maid-servant, didn't you?"

"That is, indeed, my only excuse," he replied.

"Well, don't you think maid-servants have any rights that others are bound to respect?" asked the girl.

The question was a hard one for Richard to answer; he could find nothing to say.

"Now tell me what to give you," said Edith, "and then go back to the dancing-hall, where they are waiting for you."

The young man refused all the offered refreshments, but asked the girl to reach him the tip of her little finger in sign of forgiveness for his offence.

"No, no!" she cried, "I won't shake hands with you. Your hand has been wicked."

"If you call my hand wicked," he returned, "I will go to-morrow and fight a duel and have it cut off. Do you really want my poor hand to be chopped off for offending you? If you do, just as surely as I stand here you shall see me day after to-morrow with only one hand."

"Oh, don't talk like that!" exclaimed Edith. "I won't be angry any longer." So saying, she gave him her hand — not merely her little finger, but the whole of her soft, warm little hand — and let him press it in his own. No one was near them at the moment.

"And now, not to offend you even with a look," said he, "I promise on my honour not to raise my eyes higher than your hand."

He kept his word, dropping his eyes as he released her hand and took his leave with a low bow.

As the two young men returned home together after midnight, Jenö noticed that his elder brother no longer teased him.

CHAPTER VI.

THE *BACKFISCH*.

ONE evening, after the habitual frequenters of the Plankenhorst house had taken their departure, as Alfonsine was undressing with the help of her maid, she turned to the latter and asked :

" What is the *backfisch* doing nowadays, Betty ? "

Backfisch, be it observed, means literally *a fish for frying*, but, as commonly used in German, it denotes a girl who is no longer a child, but not yet a young lady ; one who is still innocent and harmless, and who feels strange emotions stirring in her breast, but fails to understand them ; who takes jest for earnest and earnest for jest, and who believes the first pretty speech poured into her ear to be so much refined gold.   That is the *backfisch.*

" The *backfisch* is learning to swim," replied Mademoiselle Bettine.

" Still holding on to the guard-ropes ?   Not yet able to strike out alone ? "

" She will be able before long," was Betty's reply, as she took down her mistress's hair and coiled it up anew for the night. "A day or two ago, as I was doing her hair, she asked me: 'Whose hair is the longer, mine or Alfonsine's?'"

"Ha, ha! The *backfisch!*"

"And I told her that her hair was the more beautiful."

At this both laughed.

"She knows already, without any one's telling her, that she is a pretty girl," said Alfonsine. "Does she ever talk about any of the gentlemen that visit us?"

"Oh, yes, we gossip about all the men that come to the house, and she tells me her opinion of each; but there is one she never names at all, and if I happen to mention him she blushes up to her eyes."

"And do you think he is after her?" asked Alfonsine.

"He is very cautious," answered the maid, "and whenever he meets her alone he can hardly find two words to say to her. But I know what that means."

"Poor little *backfisch!*" murmured the other. "We'll give her a pleasant surprise, Betty. To-morrow she shall have a new gown. The dressmaker spoiled one of mine, and it will do nicely for her."

Mademoiselle Bettine laughed. "The pink tarla-tan?" she inquired. "That is a ball-dress."

"Never mind. She shall have it and be happy. You make her believe that we have been rather slighting her hitherto because she was only a child, but that now she is to be regarded as a young lady. We will have her taught dancing, playing, and singing."

"Really?"

"Oh, well, let her think so, and that she is to be introduced to society and treated like one of the family."

"If I tell her that now, I sha'n't get a wink of sleep all night long; she will chatter about it till morning. She is fairly crazy to take singing lessons."

"Poor little *backfisch!* We'll gratify her for once."

Oh, the heartless Jezebel!

A few days later Richard received an invitation to take tea and play whist at the Plankenhorsts'— quite *en famille.* Alfonsine was to sing also.

The young hussar officer refused no invitation from the Plankenhorst ladies, nor was he ever tardy on such occasions, but was wont to set his watch ahead so as to have an excuse to offer if he was the first guest to arrive. Thus it occurred in this instance that he saw no signs of a previous arrival when he handed his cloak and sword to the footman in the anteroom.

"Am I the first one here?" he asked.

The footman smiled and replied in the affirmative as he opened the drawing-room door for the guest.

Entering, he came upon Betty, who seemed busy with something about the room.

"Am I too early, Miss Betty?" he asked.

The maid courtesied and smiled. "The baroness has not come in yet, but she will soon be at home. The young lady is in the music-room."

At this moment, indeed, he heard some one singing in the next room, but the voice sounded fuller and richer than Alfonsine's. He concluded, however, that it was with her as with so many others, who sing their best when alone.

He passed into the music-room, but halted suddenly in surprise. At the piano sat, not Alfonsine, but another young lady whom at first he failed to recognise. It was Edith, in a new gown and with her hair arranged as he had never seen it before. She wore a low-necked pink dress which exposed to view her beautiful neck and shoulders, and she was singing a ballad, in an untrained voice, but with expression and feeling, picking out the air on the piano with one hand like a person unskilled in playing. She was quite alone in the room.

Richard feasted his eyes on the little white hand dancing over the keyboard, until Edith, glancing up from her music, caught sight of him. Her first impulse was to cover her bare neck with both hands, so new and strange did her costume still seem to her. But recognising that this was exactly the wrong thing to do, she let her hands fall and advanced to meet the young officer. Her face flushed a rosy red and her heart beat violently as, in a voice that nearly failed her, she announced that the baroness was not at home.

Richard pitied her embarrassment. "And Miss Alfonsine?" he asked.

"They both went out together," she replied. "They were called to court and will not return until late."

"Has my brother been here?"

"Yes, but he went away again some time ago."

"And did not the baroness say that she expected company?"

"She said she had ordered the footman to go around to the houses of the invited guests and tell them that the whist party was postponed until to-morrow."

"Strange that he didn't say anything about it to me when he let me in. Pardon me, Miss Edith, for disturbing you. Please present my compliments to the baroness."

So saying, he bowed with much formality and withdrew, purposing to call the footman to account for his negligence. But he failed to find him in the anteroom, and the front door, by which he had entered, proved to be locked and the key removed. He was forced to go back through the drawing-room and seek an exit by the servants' door; but this also was locked. One other door was known to him, leading into the kitchen, and he tried it. It would not open, however. In the dining-room was a bell-cord communicating with the servants' quarters; he pulled it sharply three times in succession, but no one answered his summons. Returning once more to the anteroom, he found it still empty. Evidently he and Edith were the only ones in the house. His heart beat tumultuously. He felt himself the victim of a curious plot whose outcome he could not foresee. Once more he returned to the music-room. At the sound of his step Edith came toward him. Her face was no longer flushed; she was very pale. But she met the young man's eyes calmly, with no sign of trembling or embarrassment.

"Pardon me, Miss Edith," he began, "I have tried all the doors and found them locked, nor is there any one in the house to let me out."

A life-size portrait of Alfonsine hung on the wall. To Richard, at that moment, the fair face seemed to smile down upon the scene with a malicious triumph.

Edith, however, lost none of her composure. "The servants must have gone down into the courtyard," said she; "but I know where there is another key to the front door, and I will let you out."

Against the wall hung a wicker-work device for holding keys, and in order to reach it Edith was forced to pass by Richard. When she was very near him he suddenly stepped in front of her.

"One word, Edith," said he. "Do you know what is in my mind at this moment?"

In his fancy the fair lady on the wall seemed to be carrying on a diabolical dialogue with his loudly beating heart. The world was on fire around him. Yet the young girl whom he was confronting stood there calmly and answered him with great presence of mind:

"Yes; you are thinking: 'I once promised this girl never to offend her even with a look, and not to raise my eyes, when I stand before her, higher than her hands.'" Therewith she folded her hands and dropped them in front of her.

"That is it," nodded Richard, feeling as if a hundred-pound weight had been removed from his breast. "And one thing more I must ask of you, Miss Edith," he added. "I have an urgent message to write to the baroness. Can you furnish me with writing-materials?"

Edith opened her aunt's desk and, with a motion of her hand, invited him to be seated.

Richard sat down and wrote. His letter was brief and soon written. He enclosed it in an envelope and sealed it, Edith meanwhile standing quietly on the other side of the desk with her hands still folded and resting upon her lap. Then he rose and advanced with the sealed note to where she stood. Nobility spoke in his face and pride in his bearing. The girl's very soul was in her eyes as she met his gaze.

"Can you also tell me, Miss Edith," he asked, "what I have written in this letter which I hold sealed before you?"

The young girl slowly raised her hands and pressed them to her forehead, unmindful that in so doing she invited him to raise his eyes and look into hers, where he could not but read the mingled expression of pain and delight, of despair and rapture.

"In this letter," he continued, "I have written the following: 'My dear Baroness: I beg herewith to prefer my petition for Miss Edith Liedenwall's hand in marriage. I shall be of age in a year's time, and will then come and claim her. Until then pray let her be regarded as my affianced bride.'" Therewith he handed the letter to Edith, who pressed its seal to her lips in a long kiss, after which she returned it to him. His lips also touched the seal, while it was still warm with the kiss of his beloved. That was their betrothal kiss.

"Will you deliver this letter to the baroness?" asked Richard.

Edith inclined her head without speaking, and stuck the note into her bodice.

"And now we shall not have another such interview for a year. Good-bye." He withdrew and let himself out by aid of the key which Edith had given him.

When he had gone Edith sank down and pressed a kiss on the spot still marked by her lover's footprints in the soft carpet.

It was late when the baroness and her daughter returned, and Edith had already gone to her room, — that is, the room which she shared with the maid.

"Send the *backfisch* to us," commanded Alfonsine, addressing Betty.

"Not gone to bed yet, Edith?" asked the baroness, as her niece entered the room.

"No, aunt."

Antoinette looked into the girl's eyes with searching scrutiny, but failed to find there what she sought. She saw, on the contrary, a proud self-consciousness that was new to the girl.

"Have any callers come while we were out?" inquired the baroness.

"Yes; Captain Baradlay."

The two ladies' eyes directed a cross-fire upon Edith, but with no effect. She no longer blushed at the mention of that name. It was now enshrined in her heart and would not again drive the tell-tale blood to her cheeks.

"Did the captain wait for us?" asked Antoinette.

"Only long enough to write this letter," was the girl's calm reply, as she delivered Richard's note to her aunt.

Now it was the latter's turn to feel the hot blood mounting to her face as she read the missive.

"Do you know what is in this letter?" she asked, giving the girl a penetrating look.

"Yes," answered Edith, with modest dignity.

"You may return to your room and go to bed," said the baroness.

Edith withdrew.   Antoinette tossed the letter wrathfully to her daughter.

"There!" she exclaimed, "that's what comes of your fine scheme."

Alfonsine turned pale and trembled with passion as she read the letter.   Her voice failed her.   Her mother's face was distorted with anger.

"You evidently thought," said the baroness, biting her words off one by one, "that every man was an Otto Palvicz!   Your stupid game is lost, and now we will try my plan."

CHAPTER VII.

THE OLD CURIOSITY SHOP.

As Richard made his way homeward, he seemed to himself to be riding on a winged steed. He was entirely satisfied with the issue of that day's adventure. Reviewing in imagination the temptation to which he had been exposed, he exulted in the victory he had won over himself. Consequently, when he reëntered his bachelor quarters, he could not but feel an unwelcome sensation as his eye fell on certain objects that he would gladly have banished from sight. They were sundry souvenirs of certain love affairs, and no longer possessed the value in his eyes that they had once had.

Summoning Paul, he bade him make a fire.

"But the wood is so confoundedly wet that it won't burn," returned the old hussar.

At this Richard rummaged in the drawer of his writing-desk and produced a bundle of letters, whose delicate tint and perfume betrayed their probable nature. "There," said he, "take these; they will start the fire."

This order gave old Paul much pleasure, and soon the billets-doux were blazing merrily on the hearth.

"Paul," began Richard after a pause, "to-morrow we break up and go away for the annual manœuvres."

The old soldier showed his satisfaction at this announcement.

"But we can't take all this trumpery with us," added the young officer. "You'll have to sell the furniture, but the souvenirs, pictures, and embroideries may be thrown into the fire."

Paul bowed dutifully.

Opposite the young man's bed hung a large oil painting in a great gilt frame; it was the portrait of a famous beauty who had caused herself to be painted as Danaë, and had presented the picture to Richard. The latter now bade his servant get rid of it with the rest of the rubbish. After thoroughly ransacking his drawers for old love-letters, faded flowers, bits of ribbon, and other miscellaneous articles, he left the entire collection for old Paul to destroy, while he himself went out with a lightened conscience to his supper.

The next morning, when Paul brought his master's boots, Richard made some remark on the thoroughness with which his faithful servant had executed his orders. "But surely," he added, "you can't have burnt up the frame of the large painting. What has become of it?"

"Do you suppose I burnt up the picture, either?" asked Paul in his turn. "I am not so crazy as to throw a fine work of art like that into the fire."

"What then have you done with it?" demanded the other, kicking off his bedclothes. "You haven't pawned it, I hope?"

Paul shrugged his shoulders. "Captain Baradlay said I was to get rid of it," he replied.

"Yes, and that meant that it was to be burnt up," declared Richard.

"Well," returned the servant, "I understood you to mean that it was to be carried to old Solomon and sold for what it would bring."

"And is that what you did with it?"

"There's where it is now."

Richard was very near being downright angry with his old servant. "Go at once and bring the painting back!" he commanded, as sternly as he could.

But old Paul was not one to be easily disconcerted. Laying his master's stockings within their owner's reach, he replied, with unruffled composure: "Solomon will not give it back to me."

"Not if I demand it?"

"He sends his compliments to Captain Baradlay, and begs him to have the goodness to go and speak with him in person about the picture," returned the old hussar, handing Richard his trousers.

F

The young officer fairly lost his temper. " Paul, you are a donkey !" he exclaimed.

Quickly, and with no little vexation, the hussar officer completed his toilet and hastened to old Solomon's shop in Porcelain Street, before the Jew should hang the picture where it could be seen and, perhaps, recognised.

Solomon's establishment was a little basement shop, lying lower than the sidewalk and lighted only from the door, which was consequently always kept open. On both sides of the entrance old furniture was placed on exhibition, while within was gathered such a heterogeneous collection of all sorts of second-hand wares as fairly baffles description. But the most ancient and curious object in the whole shop was its owner, who sat in a big leather armchair, wrapped in a long caftan, fur shoes on his feet and a fur cap tilted over his eyes. There he was wont to sit all day long, rising only to wait on a customer. The leather covering of his chair-cushion was worn through with long service and had been replaced by a sheet of blotting-paper.

Solomon was in the habit of opening his shop early and taking his seat in the doorway ; for no one could tell when good luck might bring him a customer. It was hardly eight o'clock when Richard strode down the narrow street and paused at the old Jew's door.

"Is this Solomon's shop ?" he asked.

The old man in the caftan drew his feet from under his chair, rose from his seat, and, pushing back his fur cap so that his caller might have a good view of his smiling face, made answer:

"Your humble servant, sir. This is the place, and I shall be most happy to serve Captain Baradlay."

"Oh, do you know me?" asked the young officer, in surprise.

"Why should I not know Captain Baradlay?" returned the old man, with an ingratiating smile. "I know him very well, and he is a man I am proud to know."

Richard could not imagine how this acquaintance had risen. It was hardly probable that he had ever met Solomon at a military review or a court ball, and he was sure he had never borrowed any money of the old Jew.

"Then you doubtless know also," said he, "that I have come to see you concerning a picture that my servant left here yesterday by mistake. I did not intend to offer it for sale."

"Yes, yes," rejoined the Jew, "I know that very well, and for that reason I made bold to request the favour of a visit from you to my poor establishment, in order that we might talk about the picture."

"There is nothing more to be said about it," interposed Richard, with vexation. "I will not sell it; I am going to destroy it."

"But, my dear sir," protested the other, smiling blandly, "why lose our temper over the matter? That is bad for the health. I certainly have no intention of retaining the picture by force. I merely desired the honour of a call from you, and you are perfectly free to do as you choose in the matter. We like to cultivate new acquaintances. Who knows but they may be useful some day? Do me the honour, Captain, to enter my house. The painting is up-stairs. Pray walk up."

Richard complied and ascended to the next floor, while the Jew locked his shop-door before following him. Reaching the head of the stairs, the young man was astonished at what met his eyes. He almost thought himself in a royal museum. Three communicating apartments were filled with the costliest articles of luxury, — carved furniture, Japanese and Etruscan vases, rare old china, jewelry of the finest workmanship, ancient armour and weapons, and many masterpieces of painting and sculpture.

"Well, how do you like the looks of things up here?" asked Solomon, when he had rejoined his guest. "It is worth while coming up to look around a little, isn't it?"

Richard could not sate himself with examining all that met his view. Meanwhile the Jew continued his confidential chat.

"The gentlemen and ladies," said he, "even those

in the very highest circles, honour me with their patronage and confidence, knowing that I can be as mum as an oyster. I know who sent in each one of these articles, — one from Count So-and-so, another from Prince Blank, a third from Baron X——, and so on ; but no secret of that kind ever passes my lips. Solomon knows the history of all these things, and why they were sold, but he never breathes a word to any mortal soul."

"Very commendable on his part, I am sure," assented Richard ; "but where is my picture ?"

"Why in such a hurry ?" asked the other. "Am I likely to run off with it ? Have the kindness to look around a bit, and meantime perhaps we can drive a little bargain."

" No, not so far as the painting is concerned," declared the hussar officer. "It is a portrait ; and, even though I may be at odds with the original, yet I cannot insult her by selling her likeness."

The old shopkeeper drew his guest with him into the adjoining room, whose walls were covered with portraits of all sorts and sizes, in oil, water-colours, and pastel, mostly representing young men and women, while a pile of unframed pictures stood in one corner.

"How did you ever get hold of so many portraits ?" asked the astonished visitor.

"Oh, that is simple enough," replied the Jew ; "you see, young people have a way of falling in love and then falling out again. They hang a portrait over their bed, and presently their taste changes and another takes its place. Then when a young gentleman wishes to marry, he finds it inadvisable to keep a lot of strange portraits in his house."

"And so he sells them?" asked Richard.

Solomon made a significant gesture with his open hands. "Judge for yourself," said he.

"Well," rejoined the other, "I am not much surprised at people's selling some of these faces; but how in the world do you find purchasers for them. Who would ever want one of this collection?"

Solomon smiled knowingly, and tilted forward and backward on his toes and heels.

"I know the original of your picture," said he. "She visits me occasionally. What if she should see her likeness among the others? That kind of costume-portrait always fetches a magnificent price."

"Such an injury, however," declared the cavalry officer, "I will not do her. Though we may not be on the best of terms, I will not give her cause to despise me."

"A most praiseworthy determination!" exclaimed the dealer, warmly. "But may I ask whether you are thinking of marrying, and so wish to put another portrait in the old one's place? In that case, at what price would you part with this Miss Danaë?"

Richard made an impatient movement. "I have already told you that I will not sell the picture," said he. "I demand it back."

"Well, well, no offence," returned the other, soothingly. "I didn't presume to offer you any ten or twenty florins for it; that would be an insult to a Richard Baradlay. But, how about an exchange for some other beautiful picture, — some mythological study? I have a large collection to choose from."

Richard laughed in spite of himself. "No, friend Solomon," said he, "we can't make a trade to-day. I will not give the Danaë in exchange for any picture, however beautiful or mythological. I won't exchange it for all the world."

"Well, well, why so positive? Supposing we should find something, after all. Let's look around a bit; it won't cost us anything."

So saying, the old dealer drew his guest toward the pile of unframed portraits leaning against the wall in a corner, and began to turn them over, one by one. Suddenly the young man at his side uttered a passionate interjection.

"Aha!" cried the Jew, in triumph; "have we found something at last worth hunting for?" And he drew out the picture that had caused the other's hasty exclamation, dusted it with his sleeve, and held it up to the light, where Richard could see it.

"That is my portrait!" cried the young man.

"Yes, to be sure, it is," replied the other. "It has been here six months or so. Miss Danaë, as you see, was less scrupulous than you, and she sold it to me half a year ago. Five silver florins was the price I paid for it."

"And what will you take for the picture now?"

"This picture? Your own picture? As I have already said, I'll give it in exchange."

"Done!" cried Richard.

"Ah, Captain, you are too hasty in closing a bargain," said the old man. "Be more cautious. Any one but old Solomon would be likely to take advantage of you. You might have made me pay you something to boot."

"Send home my picture, and I shall be glad enough to wash my hands of the whole affair," returned Richard. "After that you may squeeze Miss Danaë for a million, as far as I am concerned."

"Oh, Captain," protested the Jew, in an injured tone, "Solomon never does that sort of thing; he always does what is right and just. Every man knows his worth, and Solomon is content with whatever price is named. He is no extortioner. Look here, just to show you how fair I am, I want to call your attention to the frame. We agreed to exchange the pictures, but how about the frame?"

"What frame?"

"Why, the frame to the Danaë. She sent me

your portrait without any frame. Probably she used it for another picture. So you see the frame to your Danaë isn't included in the bargain."

The old man's anxiety to be fair began to vex Richard. "Oh, don't worry about the frame!" he cried, impatiently. "Surely you don't want me to insist on your paying five florins for it?"

"Well, well, why waste so much noble wrath?" rejoined the old dealer. "A paltry five florins, indeed! I made you no such pitiful offer, but I have all sorts of curiosities here that might please Captain Baradlay. Suppose we arrange another little trade. Let us look about for a few moments; it won't cost us anything. I have some splendid weapons here, — all sorts of swords and daggers."

"Thank you, but I am already supplied. I have a whole arsenal of them at home."

"But what if we should find something here that you lack?" persisted the Jew. "It won't cost you a penny to look around. Perhaps we can make another trade, after all. Well, well, I won't mention the frame; I'll merely reckon it in and charge you so much the less for anything here that may take your fancy. You shall pay me something in cash, so that a florin, at least, may pass between us. You see, we have a superstition that, unless the first sale of the day leaves us with a little money in our hand, even though it be but the merest trifle, the whole day will be unlucky. For that reason the first customer in the morning is likely to make a good bargain on his purchase; for we won't let him go without selling him something, even if we are forced to sell below cost, just so that we see the colour of his money."

Richard yielded perforce to the old man's importunity and followed him into a third room, which was filled with a large assortment of armour and weapons of all nations.

"A regular arsenal, isn't it?" exclaimed Solomon, rubbing his hands complacently.

The young officer felt in his element as, with the eye of a connoisseur, he surveyed the splendid collection. Suddenly his attention was arrested by a brown blade with a simple hilt and without a scabbard. He took it up and examined it more closely.

"Aha!" cried the dealer, much pleased, "you've hit it the first time. I was sure it wouldn't escape the eye of an expert. That is a genuine Crivelli blade, and I have been offered ten ducats for it; but I won't part with it for less than fifteen. It is positively genuine, no imitation."

Richard held the sword up to the light. "That is not a Crivelli," he declared.

The dealer was deeply injured. "Sir," he protested, "Solomon never deceives. When I say it is a genuine Crivelli, you may trust my word for it."

Therewith he bent the blade in his trembling hands and caused it to encircle his visitor's waist like a belt. "See there!" he cried triumphantly; "the point kisses the hilt."

"Good!" exclaimed the other, taking the sword from him again; "and now I'll show you a little trick, if you have an old musket that is of no use."

"Take any you choose," returned Solomon, pointing to a pyramid of rusty firearms.

Richard selected one of the heaviest and leaned it obliquely against the pile, barrel upward. "Now stand aside a little, please," said he.

The old Jew drew back and watched the young man curiously. The latter gave the sword a quick swing through the air and brought it down sharply on the musket-barrel, which fell in two pieces to the floor, cleanly severed. Old Solomon was lost in amazement. First he examined the sword-blade, next the divided musket-barrel, and then he felt of Richard's arm.

"Heavens and earth, that was a stroke!" he exclaimed. "When I cut an orange in two I have to try three times before I succeed. You are a man I am proud to know, Captain Baradlay, — a man of giant strength! Such a thick musket-barrel, and cut in two with one stroke as if it were of paper!"

"This sword is not a Crivelli," repeated Richard, as he returned the weapon; "it is a genuine Al-

Bohacen Damascus blade, and worth, between you and me, one hundred ducats."

"Heaven forbid!" exclaimed the Jew, with a deprecatory gesture of both hands. "I have named the price as fifteen ducats, no more and no less. That is my figure; but if Captain Baradlay will give the Danaë and frame, with one ducat into the bargain, he may have the sword. I won't sleep another night under the same roof with such a weapon."

Richard smiled. "But the Danaë I have already exchanged for my own portrait," said he.

"Oh, your portrait doesn't go out of my house now for any money," declared the Jew. "This is the first time in my life that a gentleman has said to me: 'Solomon, what you offer me for fifteen ducats is worth not fifteen, but a hundred; it is not a Crivelli, but an Al-Bohacen.' Such another portrait is not to be found in all the world. It is a rarity, it is unique. No, no, that portrait doesn't leave my house; it stays here. Take the sword and pay me a ducat to boot; then we shall be quits."

The young man hesitated. Solomon guessed his thoughts. "Have no fear, sir," he hastened to add reassuringly; "no one shall see your portrait in my house. I will hang it up in my bedroom, of which, since my wife's decease, I am the sole occupant, and which no stranger will ever enter. What do you say? Do you agree to the terms?"

Richard gave his hand to the dealer in sign of assent.

"Very well, then. Now pay me a ducat into the bargain." The old Jew touched the coin with his lips and then dropped it into his long purse. "Let me wrap up the sword for you," he added. "My servant shall deliver it at your door. I am truly delighted to have had the honour; and perhaps it won't be the last time, either. If Captain Baradlay is about to marry, I am always at his service. I deal in all the rare and beautiful things that ever charmed a pair of pretty eyes."

"Thank you," returned Richard; "but she whom I am to marry does not expect to live in a palace."

"So she is a poor girl, is she?" asked the old man. "Tell me, have I guessed aright?"

But the young officer would not tarry longer; he moved toward the door and prepared to take his leave.

"Very well, then," said the dealer; "I won't trouble the captain with any more questions. But old Solomon knows a good many things of which other folks never dream. Captain Baradlay, you are a man of gold — no, I mean of steel, Damascene steel. You know, of course, how that is made: gold and steel are wrought into one. Only remain as you are now, — of gold and steel. I will not pry into your affairs, but let me ask you to remember the old shopkeeper at Number 3 Porcelain Street. I tell you, an honest man is not met with every day. Remember my words. Some day you will fall in with old Solomon again, and then you will understand what I mean."

CHAPTER VIII.

A WOMAN'S REVENGE.

"ARANKA, my dear girl, if you are looking for your father, you will look in vain; he won't come back. My husband has just received a letter from Pest. He says your dear father's affair is going badly. The consistory forbids his appearing in the pulpit, and he has been summoned to Vienna. He will be sentenced to ten years, at least, and sent to Kufstein. Yes, my dear, there's no help for it. But you mustn't weep so. There is a good Father in heaven, and he will care for the forsaken. God be with you, my dear!"

With this cheerful morning greeting the wife of Michael Szalmás, the notary, saluted the pastor's daughter, as the latter came to the door of the little parsonage for the hundreth time and looked up the street along which she had seen her father drive away two weeks before.

The young girl went back into the house, sat down at her work-table, and resumed her sewing. She had hardly done so, however, when a carriage drove up and stopped in front of the parsonage. She sprang to her feet and hastened joyfully to the door. Was it really her father come back to her? Upon opening the door she started back in surprise. Not her father, but the widowed Baroness Baradlay, dressed in deep mourning, which accentuated her pallor, stood before Aranka.

The girl bowed and kissed with deep respect the offered hand of the high-born lady.

"Good morning, my child," said the visitor. "I have come to have a talk with you on certain matters that must be settled between us."

Aranka offered the lady a seat on the sofa. The widow motioned to the girl to be seated opposite her.

"First," she began, "I must inform you, to my great regret, that your father has got into trouble on account of his prayer at my husband's funeral. I am sorry, but it can't be helped. He will probably lose his pastorate, and that is not the worst of it."

"Then the rumours that we hear are true," sighed the girl.

"Even his personal liberty is in danger," continued the lady. "He may be imprisoned, and if so, you will not see him for a long time."

Aranka bowed in silence.

"What will you do when you are left alone and thrown upon your own resources?"

"I am prepared for the worst," was the calm reply.

"Pray look upon me as your well-wisher and would-be benefactress," said the widow. "My bereavement is the indirect cause of your misfortune, which I should like to make as light for you as possible. Speak to me unreservedly, my child. Whither will you go, and what do you intend to do? I will help you all I can."

"I shall stay here, madam," returned the other, straightening herself with dignity and calmly meeting her visitor's look.

"But you cannot remain here, my dear, for the parsonage will be handed over to another."

"My father owns a small house in the village; I will move into it."

"And how will you support yourself?"

"I will work and earn money."

"But your work will command only a mere pittance."

"I shall be content with little."

"And when your father is held in confinement in a strange city, shall you not wish to be near him? You may count on my aid; I will provide for your support."

"I thank you, madam, but if I must be alone I can endure my loneliness better here than in a strange place; and if I am to be separated from my father,

G

it is all one whether a wall three feet thick parts us, or a distance of thirty miles."

"But I wish to make amends, as far as possible, for the misfortune which my bereavement has indirectly brought upon you. I will make such provision for you as to render you independent. Being a fellow-sufferer in my loss, you shall also share a portion of my wealth. Put your trust in me."

The girl only shook her head, without speaking.

"But pray remember," pursued the baroness, "that good friends forsake us in misfortune, and all are but too prone to censure the unfortunate, if only as an excuse for withholding their aid. You are young and beautiful now, but sorrow ages a person very rapidly. In a new environment you would meet with new people, while here every word and look is sure to injure and distress you. Accept my proffered assistance, and you shall at all times find a friend and protectress in me."

At this the girl rose to her feet. "I thank you, madam," said she, "for your kindness; but I shall remain here, even if I have to go into service in some peasant's family in order to earn my bread. You know the history of this ring," — showing the ring which she wore on the little finger of her left hand. "This ring holds me here, immovable. He who placed it on my finger said to me, as he did so: 'I am going out now into the world as a wandering pilgrim; I am driven forth; but whithersoever fate may lead me, I shall circle around this spot as a planet about its sun. Do you, however, stay here. I shall come back to you some day.' Therefore, madam, you will understand that I cannot go away; that no promises, no threats can move me. I will suffer want, if I must, but I will remain here."

Baroness Baradlay now rose from her seat also, and took in her own the girl's hand on which was the ring. "Do you, then, love my son?" she asked; "and don't you believe that I love him too? One of us must give him up. Which shall it be?"

Aranka, in despair, sought to free her hand; but the other held it fast. "Oh, dear madam," she cried, "why do you ask me that question? Whichever one of us dies first will give him up. Do you wish to make me take my own life?"

The widow released Aranka's hand and stood looking into her eyes with a kindly smile. "No," she replied, "I wish him to belong to both of us. He shall be yours, and you shall be mine. You shall be my daughter. Come home with me and keep me company until my son returns; then you shall love each other, while I will content myself with what crumbs of love you may have to spare."

The young girl could not believe her ears; she thought she must be dreaming. "Oh, madam," she cried, "what you say is too beautiful to be true. I cannot understand it."

The baroness sighed. "Is my face then so cold," she asked, "and my voice so chill, that you cannot think me capable of wishing your happiness? But I will convince you." So saying, she drew the girl to her side on the sofa and took a letter from her bosom. "Look here," said she, "I have just received a letter from Russia, from my son, whom I have called home from St. Petersburg. I restrained my desire to open this letter, and brought it to you, that you might open it and read it to me. Are you aware what that means in a mother?"

Aranka bowed her head and touched the other's hand with her lips.

"There, take the letter," said the baroness, "and read it aloud. You know the writing?"

Aranka received the letter, but had no sooner looked at the address than the glad smile vanished from her face. She shook her head and turned her large eyes with surprised inquiry upon the baroness.

"What is the matter?" asked the latter.

"That is not his writing," stammered the girl.

"What do you say?" demanded the other. "Let me look again; I ought to know my son's handwriting. That is his *B*; that strong downward stroke, the manly firmness in every letter —"

"Are very cleverly imitated," interrupted Aranka, completing the sentence.

"But look again," urged the baroness; "the very words of the address — *à ma très-adorable mère* — can only have been written by my son. Open the letter and you will be convinced."

A look of joy lighted up the young girl's face when the beginning of the letter met her eyes. "That is really his writing, — 'My dear mother.'"

"There, didn't I tell you so!" declared the other in triumph.

But, as when a cloud suddenly passes over the sun, Aranka's bright face lost its radiance the next moment.

"What is it this time?" asked the baroness.

"Only those first three words are in his hand; the rest is written by some one else, and in French."

"By some one else? Oh, read quickly!"

The letter trembled in the girl's hands. "'Dear madam,'" she read; "'forgive the well-meant deception committed by me on the cover of this letter. To spare you unnecessary alarm, I have imitated my friend's handwriting — for which I must go to the galleys if you betray me. Ödön wished to write himself, but after the first three words the pen fell from his hand. He is still very weak. Don't be alarmed, however. He was in great danger, but is now happily on the road to recovery. In two weeks more he will be able to resume his journey.'"

"He was in great danger!" exclaimed the anxious mother. "Oh, read on, read on!" Despite her own agitation, she did not fail to note how deeply the girl was affected. Aranka was forced to use the utmost self-command in order to go on with the letter.

"'I will write you everything without reserve, just as it occurred. When Ödön received your letter calling him home, he dropped everything and hastened to set out. I resolved to accompany him as far as the border, but would that I had not! Then he would have stopped over at Smolensk, and would not have been overtaken by a snow-storm; we should not have been chased by wolves and compelled to save our lives by skating for two hours down the Dnieper.

"'Your son Ödön, my dear madam, is a son to be proud of. When one of my skates came off in the course of our headlong flight, and I was left helpless by the accident, he turned, single-handed, against our pursuers, and, with dagger and pistols, warded them off while I buckled on my skate again. He killed four of the pack, and I owe it to him that I am now alive.'"

This praise of her son brought a flush of pride to the mother's cheek; but she saw that the maiden's colour left her face entirely as she read on, and that her agitation nearly made her drop the letter. The girl's love was not that of the Spartan mother, and the heroic deed of daring dismayed her while it delighted the other.

" ' Then we resumed our flight, and it was a race for life, with a pack of two hundred wolves at our heels.' "

" Heavens ! " exclaimed the mother, herself now greatly alarmed. Aranka read on with halting accents.

" ' We were nearing a place of refuge, — a military guard-house, — when we came to a dangerous spot, where some fishermen had cut a hole in the ice. Not noticing the place, as it was frozen over with a thin sheet of ice, we broke through and sank.' "

" Merciful God ! " cried the baroness, losing her self-control. Aranka sank back in a faint and was with difficulty restored to consciousness by the ministrations of her companion. At length the two, holding the letter before them both, read on in silence.

" My amulet saved my life. It was a parting gift from my mother, and I had tried to induce my friend to wear it, but he would not. ' My stars are my protection,' said he, and confessed that his stars were loving women's eyes. When we had been rescued from our cold bath by the fishermen, I remained constantly by Ödön's side until he was able to answer my question, ' Do your stars still shine upon you ? ' ' All four of them,' said he."

At this each of the readers felt the electric thrill that ran through the other.

"Ödön was taken with a fever as a result of this mishap, but he is now happily over the worst of it. I am at his side night and day. This morning he was determined to write a letter, but it was too much for him, as you see. I was obliged to take the pen and write for him. He is entirely out of danger, and in two weeks we shall resume our journey. Until then I beg Ödön's stars not to weep on his account; for under Russian skies star-tears turn to snow, and of snow we have already more than enough.

"Leonin Ramiroff."

The two pairs of stars looked at each other and beamed with heavenly joy. Baroness Baradlay drew Aranka to her and kissed her on the forehead, whispering tenderly: "My daughter!"

CHAPTER IX.

THE UNDERSCORED LINES.

SOME one was expected at the castle: a letter had been received from Ödön — this time written by his own hand and mailed at Lemberg — announcing in advance his early arrival. In the afternoon the baroness ordered her carriage and drove to meet her son. Halting at Szunyogos, she there awaited his coming. Ödön arrived promptly at the appointed time. The meeting of mother and son was tenderly affectionate.

"How you frightened me with your accident!" exclaimed the baroness, half in reproach.

"That is now happily over," rejoined Ödön, kissing his mother. "We have each other once more."

Entering his mother's carriage, the young man proceeded without delay, in her company, to Nemesdomb. After he had exchanged his travel-stained clothes for fresh garments, his mother led him into his father's apartments.

"These rooms," said she, "will now be for your use. You must receive the people that come to visit us. Henceforth you are master here and will exercise that supervision over the estate which it so sadly needs. Our house enjoys great repute in the county, and you must decide what position you will take, what circle of acquaintances you will gather around you, and what part you will play as leader. Have you taken thought that as eldest son you will be called upon to assume the lord-lieutenancy of the county, which has so long been in our family?"

"An administrator, as I am told, now sits in the lord lieutenant's chair," observed the son.

"Yes," replied the mother, "because the actual lord lieutenant was an invalid and unable to preside in person over the county assemblies. But you are well and strong, and it rests with you to see that no one usurps your rights."

Ödön looked into his mother's eyes. "Mother," said he, "it was not for this reason that you called me home."

"You are right. I had another motive. I must tell you that your father left directions in his will that, six weeks after his death, I should give my hand in marriage to the administrator. A betrothal ceremony, accordingly, is the immediate occasion of the coming together of our acquaintances. Your father wished our house to gain a new support, able to bear the burden that will be imposed upon it."

"If it was my father's will and is yours also —" began the son.

"Is my will, then, of supreme authority with you?" asked the mother.

"You know that it is my highest law," was the reply.

"Very well. Now I will tell you what my will really is. The house of Baradlay needs a master and a mistress, — a master to command and guide, a mistress with power to win hearts. A master it will find in — you."

Ödön started in surprise.

"You will be the master, and your wife the mistress, of this house."

The young man sighed heavily. "Mother, you know this cannot be," said he.

"Will you not marry?"

"Never!"

"Make no such rash vow. You are but twenty-four years old. You were not born to be a Carthusian monk. The world is full of pretty faces and loving hearts, and even you are sure to find one for yourself."

"You know there is none among them for me," returned the young man.

"But what if I have already found one?"

"Your quest has been in vain, mother."

"Say not so," rejoined the other, tenderly drawing her son to her side. "Can you pass judgment without first seeing? She whom I have chosen is good and beautiful, and loves you fondly."

" She may be as beautiful as a fairy and as good as an angel, with a heart more full of love than even your own ; yet I care not to see her."

" Oh, do not speak so rashly ; you might repent it. I am sure you will retract your words when you see her face. Come, I will show it to you in the next room."

" It will have no effect on me," declared Ödön.

The mother led her son to the door and let him open it and enter first. There stood Aranka, trembling with expectant happiness.

Hastening to her own room, the baroness drew from her portfolio the memorable document dictated to her by her dying husband, and underscored with a red pencil the lines referring to the event which that day had witnessed.

" Thus far it is accomplished," she said to herself.

CHAPTER X.

THE BETROTHAL.

It was no longer a secret, but was in everybody's mouth, that six weeks after the funeral there was to be a betrothal ceremony in the Baradlay house, and the latter was, they said, to receive a new name. Friends and neighbours from the country around had been invited in the baroness's name to a family festival.

There was a great bustle of expectation when it was announced that the hero of the day, Benedict Rideghváry, was coming, seated in a brand-new coach which was drawn by five splendid horses. On the box was perched a magnificent hussar, who sprang down to open the carriage door and to help the great man alight with all the dignity demanded by his lofty rank and the importance of the occasion.

"My dear sir," one of the administrator's friends hastened to announce to him, with considerable concern in his tone, "I notice a good many strange faces in there."

"Very likely, Zebulon," answered the administrator, briefly.

"That is, I know the faces well enough," explained the other, "but the people are strangers to me."

"I don't understand," returned Rideghváry, with a laugh.

"Don't understand?" repeated Zebulon Tallérossy impatiently; "but you will understand as soon as you are pleased to look around. The hall is full of people belonging to the opposition; we know them, but we are not on terms of acquaintance with them."

The great man now found the matter worthy of his attention, but did not allow it to cause him undue concern. The principal men of the county, he said to himself, had come to pay their compliments to the son and heir, without regard to party. It was merely a conventional form, and was, he felt sure, entirely without political significance. Nevertheless, he would have preferred not to meet in that house his inveterate opponent at the Green Table, Tormándy; but the Baradlay mansion was on that day open to all comers, of whatever party.

Among the early arrivals was the much-persecuted priest, the Reverend Bartholomew Lánghy, Aranka's father, whose appearance was a surprise to many of the guests. His bearing was that of one whose part in the festivities of the day was to be of no small importance. Indeed, the preparations for a grand function were so manifest on every side that Rideghváry's good friend, Zebulon Tallérossy, soon came to him for further information.

"So there is to be a grand ceremony, is there?" he asked.

"Certainly," was the reply; "the bridegroom's spokesman goes to the bride's representative and makes formal petition for her hand in marriage. Receiving a favourable reply, he returns to the bridegroom, the double doors are thrown open, and the retinue of ladies enters with the bride at its head. Then comes the rest of the ceremony."

"Ah, that will be a fine spectacle."

The two gentlemen then went in quest of Count Paul Gálfalvy, whom the administrator had chosen to act for him in this important matter. After shaking hands, they began to exchange witticisms over the great number of their political opponents who had assembled there to witness their enemy's triumph. Thus talking and laughing, they failed to note that Tormándy was at that moment engaged in earnest consultation with the Reverend Bartholomew Lánghy. They were therefore unpleasantly surprised when Tormándy's stentorian voice fell on their ears, imposing a sudden hush on all present.

"Silence in the hall, gentlemen!" he cried. "We all know to what a glad festival we are this day invited. A new sun has risen over the house of

Baradlay in the person of its new head, to whom, both for his own sake and for that of our fatherland, we heartily wish long life and prosperity. The bridegroom, whom Providence has called to be the head of this house in the vigour of his youth, —"

"He puts it rather strongly," commented Rideghváry to himself.

"— has commissioned me as his spokesman — "

"What's that?" exclaimed Rideghváry and his friends, looking at one another in amazement.

"— to ask the representative of the bride whether he gives his consent to the desired union."

By this time the administrator and those at his side were fairly dumb with astonishment. If Tormándy was spokesman for the bridegroom, what part was Paul Gálfalvy supposed to play? And who was to reply for the bride? The superintendent was expected to discharge that function, but he was nowhere to be seen. The confusion became still worse confounded when the Reverend Bartholomew Lánghy stepped forward in response to Tormándy's address, and in clear tones thus made answer:

"Those ordained of heaven for each other let naught but death put asunder. Let them who are already one in love be joined together in holy matrimony."

"The parson is crazy!" exclaimed Zebulon in utter bewilderment.

But the solution of the enigma was not long delayed. The double doors at the farther end of the hall were thrown open and the procession of ladies entered, led by the widow Baradlay, who presented Aranka Lánghy to the assembled company as the bride. It was a beautiful sight, — the elder lady in a trailing black gown, a garnet diadem in her hair, and a long-unwonted smile lighting up her face and giving her the aspect of a beautiful queen; and the fair young bride at her side, in robe of white with white hyacinths for her ornaments and a modest blush adding its charm to her sweet maidenly dignity. Each type of beauty, so entirely opposite in character, was perfect in its kind.

There was a murmur of surprise and admiration among the guests, and all pressed forward in eager expectancy. A marble table with a gold plate on it stood near the folding doors. Over the plate was spread a lace napkin. The bridal party took their places at this table, and the priest, Aranka's father, removed the napkin from the plate, revealing two simple gold rings. One of these he then put on Ödön's finger, and the other on Aranka's. Finally he placed the bride's hand in the groom's. No word was spoken, there was nothing but this simple ceremony; but it was impressive in the extreme. The whole company broke into cheers, and even Zebulon Tallérossy caught himself shouting to the full capacity

H

of his lungs ; he only recognised his mistake upon meeting the glance of the administrator, who looked at him
with severe disapproval, whereupon the other endeav-
oured to atone for his misplaced enthusiasm by acting
on a brilliant suggestion that suddenly occurred to him.

"So there is to be a double betrothal," he
remarked, blandly, to the would-be bridegroom ;
but the latter only turned his back upon him with
a muttered imprecation.

Administrator Rideghváry was the first to take his
departure ; but before he went he had a final interview with the woman whom he had hoped to claim
as his bride that day.

"Madam," said he, as he bade her farewell, "this
is the last time I shall have the happiness to be the
guest of the Baradlay family. I should not have
believed the greatest prophet, had he foretold to me
this morning what was about to occur. And yet I
myself am not without the spirit of prophecy. You,
madam, and your son have deviated from the course
laid down for you in his dying hour by that great
man, your husband and my sincere friend. That
course he communicated to me before broaching the
matter to you. You have chosen the very opposite
path to that which he opened for you, and I beg
you to remember in future what I now say : the way
you have chosen leads upward, but the height to
which it leads is — the scaffold !"

CHAPTER XI.

THE FIRST STEP.

THREE days after the betrothal a county assembly was held under the presidency of Administrator Rideghváry.

At an early hour the white feathers and the black — the badges of the Progressive and the Conservative parties respectively — began to appear. But not only were white and black feathers conspicuous; loaded canes, also, and stout cudgels were seen peeping out from overhanging mantles, to be brought forth in case some convincing and irrefutable argument should be needed in the heat of debate.

Punctually at nine o'clock Rideghváry called the meeting to order. The Progressives had planned an energetic protest against an alleged unconstitutionality in the administration, and their best speakers were primed for the occasion, hoping to bring the matter to a vote. The Conservatives, on their part, had summoned to their aid all the most tiresome and long-winded speakers to be found in the neighbouring counties, to kill the motion.

Nevertheless, the white feathers held their ground, being determined to sit the meeting out if it lasted all night, and well knowing that, the moment the chairman should note any preponderance of blacks in the hall, he would put the question to vote and it would be lost. Therefore they kept their places patiently until it came the turn of their chief orator, Tormándy, to speak.

When he rose to address the assembly, the black feathers seemed to unite in an effort to silence him, disputing his every statement and making constant interruptions. But Tormándy was not to be disconcerted. If a hundred voices shouted in opposition, his stentorian tones still made themselves heard above the uproar. In the heat of debate it could not but occur that an occasional word escaped the speaker's lips that would have been called unparliamentary in any other deliberative body, and a repetition of the offence would have necessitated the speaker's taking his seat. Not so here, however. As soon as Tormándy's ardour had betrayed him into the utterance of an unusually insulting expression, Tallérossy and his comrades immediately set upon him, like a pack of hounds after the game, and called out in concert: "*Actio, Actio!*" Thereupon the assembly, *stante sessione*, passed judgment on the case and imposed a fine.

Tormándy, however, was not so easily put down.

Coolly drawing out his pocketbook, he threw down two hundred florins, — the usual fine, — and continued his philippic. Upon a second interruption of the same kind, he merely threw down another two hundred, without pausing in his speech. And so he continued his oration, interspersed with occasional invectives, until he had emptied his pocketbook and surrendered his seal ring and his insignia of nobility in pledge of payments still lacking. His speech, however, was finished; he had succeeded in saying what he had to say, to the very last word. But his concluding sentences were drowned in an uproar. Deafening huzzas on one side, and shouts of "Down with him!" on the other, turned the meeting into a veritable pandemonium, each party trying in vain to drown its opponents' cries.

Meanwhile the presiding administrator sat unmoved, listening to the uproar as an orchestra conductor might listen to the performance of his musicians.

The customary tactics of the Conservatives had failed. In the first place, there were more white feathers than black in the hall. Secondly, the former were not to be routed from their position either by the high temperature of the room, — it would have almost hatched ostrich eggs, — or by the pangs of hunger, or by the long-winded harangues of their opponents. Thirdly, they refused to be silenced by any fines; they paid and spoke on. Fourthly, both parties seemed disinclined to begin a fight, — a diversion which hitherto had commonly resulted in the white feathers abandoning the field and taking flight through doors and windows. A fifth expedient still remained, — the adjournment of the meeting.

Rideghváry rang his bell, and was beginning to explain, in a low tone, that the excessive noise and confusion made further debate impossible, when suddenly he found himself speaking amid a hush so profound that one could have heard a pin drop.

"To what noise and confusion does the chairman refer?" asked Tormándy, with a smile.

Rideghváry perceived that the meeting was under other control than his own. The white feathers had received orders to hush every sound the moment they heard the chairman's bell; their opponents, observing that their leader was trying to make himself heard, would voluntarily become silent. Thus it was that the chairman found himself completely outwitted.

"I admit, there is no noise now," said he, "but as soon as the debate is resumed, the uproar will begin again, and therefore I claim the right, as presiding officer, to adjourn the meeting."

But not even then did the result follow which he had expected. The storm did not break out again; the emergency had been foreseen, and all his stratagems were too well known to catch his enemies napping.

Tormándy first broke the silence. "Mr. President," said he, rising and calmly addressing the chair, "I beg to propose that, if the chairman declines to preside longer over this meeting, we proceed to elect a substitute, after which we will continue our debate."

A hundred voices were raised in approval of this suggestion, and as many against it. The cries increased until confusion and uproar were again supreme. Assuming a stern expression and leaning forward over his table, Rideghváry tried to make himself heard.

"This is an open affront," he declared, "a violation of the law. But it lies in my power to put an end to such unbridled license. If the members oppose the adjournment of the meeting I shall call for their expulsion by force of arms."

"We will stand our ground," shouted back Tormándy, crossing his arms and facing the administrator defiantly.

But the latter had resources still in reserve. Summoning the sheriff, he bade him clear the hall, whereupon that officer threw open the folding doors behind the president's chair and revealed a body of men standing there with drawn swords, ready to do his bidding. Both the sheriff and his posse were creatures of the administrator.

In the first moment of surprise every one thought this must be a joke of some sort, so many years had

passed since swords had been drawn in a county
assembly. But when one and another zealous patriot
was seen to fall wounded beside the green table, and
bloody blades were brandished before their eyes, all
took fright in earnest. The next moment, however,
the scene changed. Some of the young Progressives
drew their swords and ranged themselves against the
sheriff's posse. Such a clashing of steel and din of
battle then ensued as had never before been heard in a
meeting of that kind, — and all under the eye of the
presiding officer, and, apparently, with his approval.

But what speedily followed was not so much to
his liking. The valiant young wearers of the white
feather soon succeeded in driving the sheriff and his
force into a corner, where they struck the swords out
of their hands, and sent the men themselves flying
through the windows. At that moment a newcomer
opened the door and entered the hall.

It was Ödön Baradlay. In his rich mourning
attire, and with stern displeasure on his brow, he
looked like an angry god. Without uncovering, —
whether from forgetfulness or design, — he advanced
to the president's chair, his face flushed with wrath
and his eyes flashing resentment. Rideghváry eyed
him askance, like the jackal that suddenly encounters
a tiger in the forests of India.

"I hold you responsible for this shameful occurrence, which will stand as a disgrace to our country

before the world," declared Ödön, sternly confronting the occupant of the chair.

"Me responsible?" cried Rideghváry, his voice betraying a mixture of anger, haughtiness, alarm, and astonishment.

"Yes, you!" repeated the other, and, laying his hand on the back of the president's chair, he shook it in the excess of his wrath. "And now leave this seat," he continued. "This is the chair that my ancestors have occupied, and only during my father's illness were you authorised to take his place. The lord lieutenant is well again."

At these words there was an outburst of cheers in every part of the hall, — yes, in every part. Those familiar with Hungarian political assemblies will recall many a similar instance where one fearless stroke has gained the admiration and support of all parties. Likes and dislikes, political prejudices and private interests, are all forgotten, and the whole assembly is swept off its feet as one man — whither, no one asks.

Such a miracle was wrought on the present occasion. Rideghváry read only too plainly in the faces of his partisans and hirelings that his rule was at an end. Here was no place for him now. Pale with shame and fury, he rose from his chair. With one look of wrath and hatred at the assembly, he turned to Ödön and, with lust for revenge in his tones, muttered between his teeth:

"This is the first step to that height of which I have warned you."

Ödön measured him with a look of scorn. He knew well enough from his mother what height was meant, but he deigned no reply.

The door closed upon the administrator, and the young lord lieutenant took the president's chair amid the huzzas of all present. Then at length he removed his fur cap. His action had been, it must be admitted, unconstitutional, since he had not yet been installed as lord lieutenant, and so was unqualified to assume the duties of the office. But the enthusiasm which greeted his appearance was warm and genuine, and he accepted it as a sanction of his course. His had been a bold stroke, and one pregnant with results for himself, for his county, for his native land, — yes, for his generation. But it succeeded. His action formed a turning-point in his country's history. Whither the course he had adopted would lead, he knew not, and no little courage was called for in facing its possible issue.

What else occurred in that assembly is simply a matter of history, but the glory of that day belongs to Ödön Baradlay.

CHAPTER XII.

It was the 13th of March, 1848, the day of the popular uprising in Vienna.

The Plankenhorst parlours were even on that day filled with their usual frequenters; but instead of piano-playing and gossip, entertainment was furnished by the distant report of musketry and the hoarse cries of the mob. Every face was pale and anxious, and all present were eager to learn the latest news from any newcomer.

At length, toward evening, the secretary of the police department entered. His mere outward appearance indicated but too well that things were going badly for the government. Instead of his official uniform, he wore a common workman's blouse, and his face was pale and careworn. As soon as he was recognised in his disguise, all pressed around him for the latest tidings.

"Well, are you sweeping the streets?" asked the high official of the commissary department, in anxious haste.

"There is no making head against the rascals," answered the secretary in a trembling voice. "I have just left the office and only escaped by means of this disguise. The mob has broken into the building, thrown down the statue of Justice, and wrecked the censor's office."

"But, for heaven's sake, can't more soldiery be sent out against them?"

"We have soldiers enough, but the emperor will not permit any more bloodshed. He is displeased that any lives at all should have been sacrificed."

"But why ask his permission? He is too tender-hearted by far. Let the war department manage that."

"Well, you go and tell them how to do it," returned the secretary petulantly. "What is to be done when the soldiers fire in such a way that a whole platoon volley fails to hit a single man? In St. Michael Square I saw with my own eyes the cannoneers stick their slow-matches into the mud, and heard them declare they wouldn't fire on the people."

"Heavens! what will become of us?"

"I came to give you warning. For my part, I believe the people have fixed upon certain houses as objects of their fury, and I would not pass the night in one of them for all the Rothschild millions."

"Do you think my house is one of the number?"

asked Baroness Plankenhorst. The only reply she got
was a significant shrug of the shoulders.

"And now I must hasten away," concluded the
secretary. "I have to order post-horses and relays
for the chancellor."

"What! has it come to that already?"

"So it seems."

"And do you go with him?"

"I shall take good care not to remain long behind.
And you too, madam, I should advise at the earliest
opportunity — "

"I will consider the matter," returned Antoinette
composedly, and she let him hurry away.

Jenö Baradlay never left his room all that day.
The brave who laugh at danger little know the agony
of fear that the timid and nervous must overcome before resolving to face peril and rush, if need be, into
the jaws of death. Finally, at nine o'clock in the
evening, his anxiety for Alfonsine's safety impelled
him to seek her. With no means of self-defence, he
went out on the street and exposed himself to its unknown perils. What he there encountered was by
no means what he had, in the solitude of his own
room, nerved himself to face. Instead of meeting
with a violent and raging mob, he found himself surrounded by an exultant throng, drunk with joy and
shouting itself hoarse in the cause of "liberty."

Jenö's progress toward his destination was slow, but at last he managed to push his way into the street where the Plankenhorst house was situated. His heart beat with fear lest he should find the building a mass of ruins. Many a fine residence had that day fallen a sacrifice to the fury of the mob.

Greatly to the young man's surprise, however, upon turning a corner he beheld the house brilliantly illuminated from basement to attic, two white silk banners displayed from the balcony, and a popular orator standing between them and delivering a spirited address to the crowd below.

Jenö quite lost his head at this spectacle, and became thenceforth the mere creature of impulse. Reaching the steps of the house, he encountered nothing but white cockades and faces flushed with triumph, while cheers were being given for the patronesses of the cause of liberty by the throng before the house. Pushing his way into the drawing-room, he saw two ladies standing at a table and beaming with happy smiles upon their visitors. With difficulty he assured himself that they were the baroness and her daughter. The former was making cockades out of white silk ribbon, with which the latter decorated the heroes of the people, fastening bands of the same material around their arms. And meanwhile the faces of the two ladies were wreathed in smiles.

The young man suffered himself to be swept along

by the crowd until Alfonsine, catching sight of him, gave a cry of joy, rushed forward, threw her arms about his neck, kissed him, and sank on his breast, exclaiming :

"Oh, my friend, what a joyful occasion!" and she kissed him again, before all the people and before her mother. The latter smiled her approval, while the people applauded and cheered. They found it all entirely natural. Their shouts jarred on Jenö's nerves, but the kisses thrilled him with new life.

In the days that followed, Jenö Baradlay found it quite a matter of course that he should be at the Plankenhorsts' at all hours, uninvited and unannounced, amid a throng of students, democrats, popular orators, all wearing muddy boots, long swords, and pendent feathers in their caps. He also found nothing strange in the fact that Alfonsine frequently received him in her morning wrapper and with her hair uncurled, that she embraced him warmly on each occasion, and that she took no pains to conceal her endearments either from strangers or from friends. It was a time when everything was permitted.

As the two turned aside one evening in their walk, to join a throng of eager listeners who were being addressed by one impassioned speaker after another, Jenö was startled at seeing his brother Ödön mount the platform as one of the orators of the occasion.

He, too, it appeared, was on the side of the people; he was one of the parliamentary speakers who were making their voices heard in favour of popular rights and legislative reform. His speech swept all before it; no one could listen to his words without feeling his heart stirred and his pulse quickened. Alfonsine waved her handkerchief in her enthusiasm, but her companion was suddenly seized with a mysterious fear and dread. What premonition was it that seemed to whisper in his ear the true significance of that elevated platform on which his brother stood?

When the two had returned from their stroll, weary with walking the streets, and Jenö had been dismissed with a good-night kiss, Alfonsine, at last alone with her mother, threw her hat with its tricol-oured ribbons into a corner and sank exhausted upon a sofa.

"Oh," she cried, "how tired I am of this horrid world!"

CHAPTER XIII.

THE REVERSE OF THE MEDAL.

AFTER a troubled night's rest Jenö rose and, telling his servant that he should not return until late in the evening, betook himself to the Plankenhorst residence, thinking thus to avoid all possibility of meeting his brother Ödön, who, he feared, might try to persuade him to return home to their mother.

"Welcome, comrade!" cried Fritz Goldner, chairman of the standing committee, as Jenö entered the drawing-room; "we were just speaking of you. Do you know that our cause is in great danger?"

Jenö had known that from the beginning.

"We must step into the breach," continued the chairman. "The reactionary party is bent on compromising us and bringing disgrace on our patriotism by stirring up the dregs of the people to the most outrageous excesses. The false friends of liberty are inciting the mob to acts of violence and riot against the manufacturing and property-holding classes. Last night the custom-house was burnt and property destroyed in the outlying villages. To-day the rioters are expected to attack the factories and the religious houses within the city limits, and our duty will be to confront them and turn their misguided zeal into proper channels.   We have not a moment to lose, but must hasten to meet this movement and rescue our flag from the dishonour with which our false friends are striving to stain it.   Let us oppose our breasts to the flood and dam its course with our bodies."

Poor Jenö!   To offer his own person as a check to the fury of the mob, and to stand as a target between two fires — that of the rioters on one side, and of the soldiery on the other — was hardly to his liking.   But he made haste to assure his friend Fritz of his hearty acquiescence in the plan proposed, and bade him go on ahead; he himself would run home and get his sword and pistols and then follow in a cab.   Before Alfonsine he could not betray how little stomach he had for the undertaking.

Gaining the street, he hailed the first empty cab he saw, and hired it for the day, directing the coachman to drive around whithersoever he chose, without halting, except at noon at some outlying inn, and late in the evening at his lodging.

His friends and co-workers in the cause of freedom did not wait for him, but marshalled their forces and pushed forward to check the fury of mob violence that was now gaining fearful headway.

The Granichstadt distillery was a mass of smoking

ruins. The machinery had been wrecked, the brandy casks rolled into the street and their heads knocked in, whereupon their contents had rushed out over the pavement in a stream that soon caught fire. This blazing Phlegethon, pouring through the streets, had been the salvation of the St. Bridget Convent; for as long as the fiery stream barred the way in that direction, the mob could not offer the nunnery any violence. Yet the rioters were taking measures to overcome this obstacle, and were bringing sand, mud, ashes, — anything that would serve to make a road through the burning flood. At the entrance to the convent, however, a squadron of hussars had been posted early in the morning; its commander was Captain Richard Baradlay.

It was nearly a year since he had changed his quarters and moved out of the city into the barracks in the suburbs. His purpose in making the change had been to devote himself entirely to the duties of his calling. He was no longer seen idling in the town, he attended no balls, paid court to no ladies, but lived wholly with his men, contenting himself with their society, and became one of the most industrious of officers. He had learned from Jenö that Edith was at a boarding-school, to which her aunt had sent her the day after he had asked her hand in marriage; and with this information he was content. The young girl was doubtless well cared for, and at the proper time he would go and take her away. So why disturb her meanwhile?

In the last few days Captain Baradlay had received six successive and mutually contradictory orders, all relating to the maintenance of order, and each signed by a different hand and valid only until its writer's deposition from office. Finally, the young commander found himself left entirely to his own discretion. He was all night in the saddle, leading his troop hither and thither, but utterly unable to subdue a mob that broke out in one quarter after another and always melted away at his approach, to muster again immediately afterward in another part of the town.

At length the light of the burning distillery had led him in that direction. After drawing up his men across the street and before the entrance to the convent, he was calmly watching the mob's advance, when suddenly a strangely clad figure approached him. A black coat faced with red, black, and gilt, a sash of the same colours, a straight sword with an iron hilt, a broad-brimmed hat adorned with a black ostrich feather, — these were the accoutrements of the stranger, who wore a thin beard and mustache, and was of a bold and spirited bearing, though evidently not of military training. Hastening up to Richard, the newcomer greeted him heartily.

"Good day, comrade!" he cried. "Hurrah for the constitution and public order!"

Richard offered no objection to this sentiment, and the young gallant next extended his hand, which the hussar officer did not refuse.

"I am Fritz Goldner," he explained, without further ceremony, "an officer in the second battalion of the Aula."

"What news do you bring?"

"I heard that a mob was collected here and was likely to bring dishonour on our cause, and so I came to quiet the storm."

The other surveyed him doubtfully. "What, you alone?" he asked. "Heavens and earth, man! I have been doing my best for three days, at the head of my squadron, to put down the mob, and it is growing stronger every minute."

The young hero of the Aula threw up his head proudly. "Yes, I alone will quell the disturbance," he declared.

"I leave you a free hand, comrade," returned Richard; "but I cannot abandon my position, as it would be no easy matter recovering it again."

"Very well, then," assented the other; "you stay here as a passive onlooker. But first may I ask your name?"

"Richard Baradlay."

"Ah, glad to meet you. Your brother and I are good friends."

"My brother Jenö?"

"Yes, he is attached to our headquarters at the Plankenhorsts'."

"Headquarters at the Plankenhorsts'?" repeated Richard, in surprise.

"Yes, indeed. Didn't you know about it? Both of the ladies are most zealous friends of the cause, and they give us the happiest advice and suggestions."

By this time Richard had dismounted and thrown his horse's bridle to old Paul. "So the Plankenhorst ladies are still in the city, are they?" he asked, as he proceeded with Fritz toward the entrance of the convent. "And you say they are friends of the revolutionists. Do you know these women?"

"It is one of our chief concerns to know them," was the reply. "Their past is not unknown to us, but now they declare themselves unconditionally on our side. Nothing catches fire like a woman's heart at the cry of freedom. But our confidence in them is a guarded one. We, too, have our secret police, and all their movements are carefully watched. Should they attempt to open communication with their former friends, we should learn the fact at once and the two ladies would be summarily dealt with. Oh, I assure you, our forces are well organised."

"I haven't a doubt of it. And is my brother Jenö one of your number?"

"One of the foremost. He holds the rank of second lieutenant."

Richard shook his head incredulously.

The mob was meanwhile gradually making a path for itself through the flames of burning brandy, and as the intrepid Fritz caught sight of one form after another through the blue-green fire, he became more and more aware of the magnitude of the task before him. Distinguished from the rabble about him was one man, no less ragged and dirty than his fellows, but of colossal size and brandishing above his head a six-foot iron bar as if it had been a wooden wand. He was pushing his way forward in a sort of blind frenzy. Seeing the hussars, however, drawn up in formidable array, he paused for his comrades to join him, when he raised aloft his powerful weapon and, pointing to the building before them, shouted, in a hoarse, brutal voice : " Into the fire with the nuns ! " A bloodthirsty howl answered him from behind.

But suddenly the shrill notes of a bugle were heard above the howling of the mob. It was a signal to the horsemen to hold themselves in readiness for action, and it dampened the ardour of the rioters.

" For heaven's sake," exclaimed Fritz, " don't give the order to attack. We must avoid bloodshed. I will try to make these fellows listen to me."

" Speak, then, in God's name ! I will stay at your side," said Richard, as he lighted a cigar and waited for his companion to try the effect of his eloquence on the unruly mob before them.

The convent steps served Fritz as a platform. Addressing his hearers as "brothers," he spoke to them about freedom and the constitution and civic duties, about the schemes of the reactionaries, about their common fatherland and emperor and the glorious days they had just witnessed. Now and then a hoarse outcry from his auditors forced him to pause, and more than once his remarks were punctuated by a flying potato or bit of tile hurled at his head. Richard, too, was hit twice by these missiles.

"Comrade," cried the hussar officer, "I have had quite enough of these potatoes. Wind up your speech as soon as you can and let me try my hand. I shall find a way to make them listen, I promise you!"

"It is a difficult situation," returned Fritz, wiping his brow. "The people have no love for the religious houses; but these nuns are women, and toward women even the revolutionist is chivalrous."

"So I see," rejoined the other dryly, glancing up at the windows of the building, many of which had been shattered by missiles. Fortunately for the inmates, the cells were protected by inner shutters, which were all securely closed.

The rioters now began to pelt the hussars, whose horses were becoming more and more restless. As Fritz opened his mouth to continue his speech, the man with the iron bar began to harangue also, and the people could understand neither of them.

At that moment there appeared from the opposite direction an odd-looking, long-legged student, with three enormous ostrich plumes waving in his hat and a prominent red nose dominating his thin, smooth-shaven face. A tricoloured sash crossed his breast, while a slender parade-sword, girt high up under his arm to prevent his stumbling over it, hung at his side. With a quick step and a light spring, the young man was presently at the side of Richard and Fritz.

"God keep you, comrades!" he cried in greeting. "Calm your fears, for here I am, — Hugo Maus-mann, first lieutenant in the second legion. You are hard pressed just now, I can well believe. Friend Fritz is a famous orator, but only in the tragic vein. Tragedy is his forte. But a public speaker must know his audience. Here a Hans Sachs is called for rather than a Schiller. Only make your hearers laugh, and you have carried your point. Just let me give these folks a few of my rhymes, and you shall see them open their eyes, and then their mouths, and all burst out laughing; after that you can do what you will with them."

"All right, comrade," returned Richard; "go ahead and make them laugh, or I shall have to try my hand at making them cry."

Hugo Mausmann stepped forward and made a comical gesture, indicating his desire to be heard. Deliberately drawing out his snuff-box, he tapped it with his finger, and proceeded to take a pinch, an action which struck the spectators as so novel, under the circumstances, that they became silent to a man and thus permitted the speaker to begin his inexhaustible flow of doggerel. With frequent use of such rhyming catchwords as, "in freedom's cause I beg you pause; " "your country's fame, your own good name;" "our banner bright, our heart's delight;" "we're brothers all, to stand or fall," — he poured out his jingling verse, concluding in a highly dramatic manner by embracing the hussar officer at his side, in sign of the good-fellowship which he described as uniting all classes in the brotherhood of freedom.

"Comrade, you haven't made them laugh yet," said Richard.

Hugo continued his rhymed address, but the people would listen no longer. "Down with the friend of the priests!" sounded from all sides. "Into the fire with the nuns!" And the shower of missiles came thick and fast. An egg hit the speaker on the nose, and filled his mouth and eyes with its contents.

"Give us a rhyme for that, brother!" shouted the successful marksman, and all laughed now in good earnest; but it was the brutal laugh of malice and ridicule at another's discomfiture.

Richard threw his cigar away and sprang down the steps. Fritz intercepted him, and insisted on being heard.

"Brother," he cried, "do nothing rash. Avoid the shedding of blood — not that I fear bloodshed in itself, but the hatred that is sure to grow out of it. We must not hate one another. Your sword must not drink our people's blood. A peaceful issue is still possible."

"What, then, do you advise?"

"Go and speak to the prioress, and persuade her to leave the building with all her nuns ; they have no costly possessions to carry with them, and you can soon clear the house. Then we will admit the leaders of the mob and show them that there is no booty to be had, and no nuns there to burn. We will write on the outer doors: 'This is state property,' — as it really is, — and no further injury will be done to the building. Mausmann and I will keep back the mob while you do your errand. By that time the rest of our party will be here, and we will go among the people and make them listen to reason, and cease from violence."

Richard pressed the other's hand. "You are a brave fellow," he exclaimed, "and I will do as you say. Only keep the 'brothers' amused while I go and talk with the 'sisters.'"

With an added respect for these two young men

who were bravely trying to gain their ends by peaceful means, Richard returned to the entrance of the convent, and knocked at the door. The cautious doorkeeper was at length persuaded to open to him. The captain of hussars felt somewhat ill at ease in playing any other rôle before the helpless nuns than that of their defender at the head of his cavalry; he consoled himself, however, with the thought that a nun was after all not the same as other women, but a sort of sexless creature who was not to be treated according to the conventional rules of society.

He found the passages all deserted, the nuns being assembled in the refectory. Pausing on the threshold of this room, the young officer beheld a scene that could not fail to move him deeply. In the middle of the room lay a dying sister, while about her were grouped her companions, ministering to her wants and seeking to comfort her. In the group one face caught his eye and held him spellbound.

It was Edith. This, then, was where her aunt had placed her to await her marriage. She stretched out her hands to her lover in despairing appeal, as the bloodthirsty howls of the infuriated mob fell on her ears. With wrath in his bosom the young man ran down the stairs, and out of the door. As he sprang into his saddle he thought he saw a shutter of one of the upper windows pushed partly open. Perhaps Edith was looking out, and watching him.

"Well, if she is looking, she shall see that her lover is a man," he said to himself.

"Clear out of here, you dirty rascals!" were his words to the mob. Insolent laughter and mocking shouts were the answer he received.

The officer's sword flashed over his head, the bugle gave the signal to charge, and Richard dashed forward into the very heart of the raging mob, straight toward the giant form of its leader. The latter brandished his iron weapon and made it whistle through the air. At that moment Richard seemed to hear a scream from the window above; then the six-foot iron bar came down toward his head with a hiss as it cleft the air.

All honour to the Al-Bohacen sword that was raised to meet the blow; and all honour to the arm and hand that received the brunt of its force on the sword-hilt. There was a clash and a shower of sparks, but the Damascus blade stood the test and suffered not a nick or a scratch. Before the giant could lift his weapon again he found himself lying under the horse's hoofs. Five minutes later the square was empty.

CHAPTER XIV.

TRUE LOVE.

THROUGH the unlighted streets of Vienna a carriage was slowly making its uncertain way by night. The gas-mains had been wrecked, — that was one of the results of the glorious days of "liberty," — and only the feeble coach-lamps lighted a path for the equipage.

The carriage halted before the Plankenhorst house, and the coachman stepped down and held the door open while two women alighted, after which he drove into the courtyard, leaving his passengers to make the best of their way up the unlighted stairs. The hostess, coming to meet them with a lamp in her hand, kissed one of her callers, who was evidently a nun, and gave her hand to the other. The latter's hood falling back revealed Edith's bright face.

"Heaven must have guided you hither, Sister Remigia!" exclaimed the baroness, in a guarded tone.

"We had need enough of Heaven's guidance in this fearful darkness," was the reply. "Not a street lamp is lighted in the whole city, and the pavement is torn up in many places."

"Heaven watches over its chosen ones," said Antoinette, leading her guests into the dining-room, where the table was spread in readiness for them, while the water was already boiling in the tea-kettle.

First assuring herself that no one was in the next room, the hostess locked the door, bade her daughter serve the tea, and then drew her chair to Sister Remigia's side. "What word does the general send?" she asked.

"To-morrow is fixed upon for a general attack," replied the sister, in an anxious tone.

"Did you know that things were going badly?" asked Antoinette.

"How so?"

"The insurgents are counting on a secret understanding with a part of the investing forces. Goldner told me the whole plan. Of course I pretended to be very much alarmed as to what would become of us who have played so important a part in the uprising, if the city should be taken. But the good young man bade me have no fear: in case of any mishap, a plan of escape was arranged for those whose lives would be endangered by remaining. He said that between the Mariahilf and Lerchenfeld cemeteries the line of investment was held by a squadron of hussars with whom the Aula had for some time been fraternising, and that it was hoped this squadron would not only offer a free escape to fugitives in case of danger, but would also join in their flight and cover their rear, thus securing them a safe retreat into Galicia or Hungary. The only thing in the way of this plan, it appears, is the obstinacy of the squadron's commander, Captain Richard Baradlay."

" The same who drove the rioters away from the convent ? "

" Yes."

" So far as I have learned," said Sister Remigia, "he has not since then associated with the members of the Aula and the popular leaders."

" No," rejoined the baroness, "he has held himself aloof from them and refused to be drawn into their scheme. His men would have yielded, but they stand by their commander : if he bade them fight against their own kith and kin, they would obey him. Lately, however, the rebels have gained a new and unhoped-for ally."

" In whom ? "

" In a woman, and a very dangerous one, too. She does not shrink from the boldest and most perilous undertakings. She is the young Baradlays' mother."

" But how, pray, could she have made her way through the investing lines ? " asked the sister, in astonishment.

" By a daring stroke that seems hardly credible.

Fritz told me all about it. This delicate widow of the late Baron Baradlay procured from an old market-woman in Schwechat, the costume and basket of a vegetable-vender, and then proceeded with this woman, on foot, her basket of onions and potatoes on her back, through the lines of the investing army, selling her wares on the way, until she reached the city. She is now here in Vienna, at number 17 Singer Street, in the shop of her attendant market-woman."

"And what is her object in all this?"

"To take her sons home with her. She wishes to persuade them to return to Hungary and enter the government service there."

"Has she spoken with them yet?" asked the nun.

"Not yet, fortunately. She only arrived this afternoon. Goldner has spoken with her, and she is to have an interview with her son Richard, the cavalry officer, to-morrow morning. She is allowed to go to him unmolested, and as surely as she speaks with him, he will yield to her. The general will then be informed of the affair through his secret agents, and before the hussars can carry out their plan, the whole squadron is to be surrounded. Who is the commanding officer in your section now?"

"The cuirassier major, Otto Palvicz."

"Ah, he is the right man for the business. The hussars will be decimated, and Captain Baradlay shot."

K

To all this Edith was forced to listen, but she suffered no look of hers to betray how keenly it affected
her. On hearing her lover's probable fate, she nearly
choked over a piece of ham, and had to resort to a dose
of vinegar to conquer a sudden faintness.

Alfonsine could not refrain from venting her spite
on her cousin. "Your appetite," said she, "does not
seem to suffer greatly at the prospect of losing your
lover."

Edith helped herself composedly to another slice
of ham. "Better to be executed than buried alive,"
she rejoined. Holding out her glass, she begged her
cousin to pour her some chartreuse. "I must get
used to it if I am to be a nun," she remarked play-
fully.

Alfonsine handed her the bottle and bade her help
herself, and Edith's hand never once trembled as she
filled her cognac glass to the brim with the green
liquor; then she poured out a glassful for Sister
Remigia.

"Drink with me, Sister Remigia," she cried, with
a roguish smile; "we must take something to keep
up our spirits."

The nun made a show of reluctance, but was finally
obliged to yield to the seductions of her favourite
beverage. Meanwhile the hostess proceeded with
her instructions.

"Don't forget the address," said she, — "number

17 Singer Street, the vegetable shop in the basement. The mother will be sure to return for her youngest son, and we must not let her escape us. Give the general full information of these details in the morning, but take care that Captain Baradlay doesn't get wind of the affair. That man must die, and we must leave him no loophole for slipping out of our hands."

An incomprehensible child, that Edith! Even now she asks nonchalantly for a piece of *fromage de Brie,* sips her chartreuse like an epicure, and refills her companion's glass as often as it is emptied. A well-spread table in this world, her soul's salvation in the next, and meanwhile the quiet life of a cloister, seemed to satisfy her every desire. Soon she was nodding as if overcome with sleepiness, and finally she leaned back on the sofa, and her eyes seemed to be closed; but through her long lashes she was watching intently the three women before her. They thought her asleep.

"Is she always like this?" asked the Baroness Plankenhorst.

"She is incorrigibly lazy," replied Sister Remigia. "No work, no books seem to interest her. Eating and sleeping are her sole delight."

"Well, we must make the best of the matter," returned Antoinette. "I hope she will enjoy her convent life. An allowance will be made for her

support as long as she lives; that has been provided
for."

"Are you, then, sure that she has lost her lover?"

"Quite. If he once has an interview with his
mother, he will be persuaded to desert. Her eldest
son she has already drawn into the net: he is now
a recruiting officer in the Hungarian service, and is
busy raising troops. But if Richard fails to meet
his mother, and still refuses to join the insurgents,
a ball will be sent through his head at the critical
moment — so Fritz assures me. Two of his own
men have vowed to shoot him if he opposes their
wishes. So he has but a short shrift in any case.
By to-morrow evening he will be either a dead man,
assassinated by one of his troopers, or, if he attempts
to desert, a prisoner in the hands of Major Palvicz;
and, in the latter case, he will be shot day after to-
morrow. It is all one to me how it turns out. I
don't wish him the ignominy of a public execution,
although he has given me reason enough to hate
him."

When Sister Remigia at length aroused Edith and
led her, apparently half asleep, down to the carriage,
Antoinette accompanied them with a light, explaining
as she went that all the men-servants had been called
away to the barricades. Her real purpose was to see
Edith safely seated in the coach, and sound asleep
by the nun's side. She had only the vaguest suspi-

cions regarding her niece, but it was best to take no chances.

The heavy coach rumbled slowly through the dark streets. Perhaps the driver himself was half asleep. When they were well on their way, Edith opened her eyes and peered cautiously about. Her sole thought was to make her escape, even if a thousand devils stood guard at the carriage door, and the ghosts of all who had fallen in the last few days haunted the unlighted streets of the city. Sister Remigia was already fast asleep ; it was her eyes, not Edith's, that refused to hold themselves open after the evening's ample repast. The chartreuse had done its work.

Assuring herself of her companion's condition, Edith softly opened the door at her side and sprang lightly to the ground, unperceived by the deaf and sleepy coachman. Swiftly, and with wildly beating heart, she ran back toward the heart of the city, leaving the coach to lumber on its way without her. It was only with difficulty that she could find her way in the dark. The tall tower of St. Stephen's loomed up ahead of her, and thither she turned her steps, hoping to find some one in that neighbourhood to direct her farther. With limbs trembling, and heart anxiously throbbing, now that she was safe from observation, the poor girl hastened on as best she could. Twice as she ran she heard the great tower-clock strike the quarter-hour, and she knew she must have gone astray; for half an hour suffices to go from one end of the inner city to the other. Coming to a street corner, she paused and looked about for the tower, and at last made it out on her right. Then she knew where she was, and concluded that Singer Street must be somewhere in the vicinity. As she stood there in uncertainty, the great clock struck again — midnight this time — and, as it struck, a fiery rocket shot upward from the turret's summit, — a signal seen and understood by some one in the distance.

By the bright but momentary glare of this rocket, Edith's eyes sought in all haste the name of the street in which she stood. With a thrill of joy, she read on the wall over her head the word "Singer-strasse." Now she had the Ariadne clue in her hand, and, before the rocket burst and its light suddenly went out, leaving her in apparently deeper darkness than before, she had learned that the house next to her was number 1, and that consequently all the numbers on that side of the street were odd. By simply counting the doors she could soon find number 17.

Feeling her way with her hands like a blind person, lest she should omit a door in her course, Edith moved slowly from house to house, counting the numbers as she went.

"Thirteen, fifteen," she whispered; "now the next will be seventeen. Who is there?" she cried suddenly, starting back in alarm as her hands encountered a human form.

"The blessed Virgin and St. Anne!" exclaimed the unknown, equally frightened. It proved to be an old woman who was crouching in the doorway, and over whom Edith had unwittingly stumbled.

"Oh, I beg your pardon!" panted the girl, recovering from her fright. "You see I was so startled at finding any one here."

"And I was startled, too," rejoined the other. "What do you wish here, miss?"

"I am looking for number 17."

"And what is your errand at number 17?"

"I wish to speak with a woman, a vegetable-vender who arrived here this evening with another market-woman."

"This is the house," said the old woman, "and I have the key in my pocket. Follow me."

She opened the narrow basement door and admitted the girl, following her and locking the door behind them. At the end of the corridor a lamp was flickering on the floor in the draught. The old woman raised the lamp and examined her guest by its light. At sight of the convent dress she started back with an exclamation of surprise. In the young girl's form and face, as she stood there under the feeble rays of

the lamp, was something that suggested to her the
saints and martyrs of old.

Edith was conducted to a low basement room, in
whose corners she saw piles of potatoes and beets,
with strings of onions hanging on the walls.   In the
middle of the room stood two straw chairs, on one of
which was a tallow candle stuck into a hollow potato,
while the other was occupied by a woman dressed
in the costume of a Vienna vegetable-vender.   She
looked up and calmly surveyed the newcomer.   Her
face was not one to betray surprise at any unexpected
occurrence ; indeed, its expression indicated an unusual
degree of self-mastery.   But the girl practised no
such self-control.   Hastening forward and sinking
on her knees before the stranger, she seized her hand
and looked into her face with wide-open eyes.

"Baroness Baradlay," she exclaimed breathlessly,
"they are plotting to murder your son!"

The other started slightly, but stifled the cry that
rose to her lips.   "Richard?" she stammered, forgetting her caution for an instant.

"Yes, yes," cried the other; "Richard, your
Richard! Oh, dear madam, save him, save him!"

The baroness looked into Edith's face with searching scrutiny.   "You are Edith?" she asked.

The girl started in surprise.   "Have you heard
my name already?" she asked.

"I know you from my son's letters," was the

reply. "In your face and your words I read that you can be none other than Richard's betrothed. But how did you learn all this, — that I was here, who I was, and that Richard was in danger?"

"I will tell you all," answered Edith, and she gave a hurried account of what she had overheard at her aunt's that evening. "But they were mistaken in me," she concluded. "They thought my spirit was broken and that they could do what they wished with me. But I ran away from them; I ran all the way here in the dark, and though I never saw you before, I knew you at once. God protected and guided me, and he will lead me still farther."

The speaker's passionate words betrayed so much nobility of soul that the baroness, quite carried away with admiration, put her arm around Edith's neck and let her eyes rest tenderly on the face of the girl who showed such true love for her Richard.

"Calm yourself, my child," said she, "and let us take counsel together. You see I am perfectly composed. This plot is to be carried out to-morrow morning, you say?"

"Yes, I am sure of it."

"Then half the night is still left for defeating it."

The girl clasped her hands with a beseeching gesture. "Oh, take me with you!" she begged.

The other considered a moment. "Very well," she replied, "you may come, too."

Edith clapped her hands with delight, while the baroness opened the door and called the market-woman.

"Frau Babi," said she, "we must set out at once, and this young lady will accompany us."

"Then she must wear another dress," interposed the old woman.

"And have you one for her?" asked the baroness.

"Oh, plenty of them." And with that Frau Babi raised the cover of an old chest and rummaged about for garments suitable for a young peasant girl's wear. She seemed to have an ample stock of old clothes.

"A charming little market-wench!" exclaimed the old woman, when she had wrought the desired metamorphosis. "And now for a basket to carry on her back. You never carried anything like that before, I'll warrant. But don't fear; I'll find you a light one and fill it with dry rolls that won't weigh anything. We two will manage the potatoes and onions."

Edith regarded it all as an excellent joke and hung her basket on her back in great good humour.

The clocks were striking two as the three women at length reached the Kaiserstrasse. At the barricade there was no guard visible. The investing forces here consisted only of a small detachment of cavalry whose main body was encamped at Schwe-chat; and cavalry is never used for storming barricades. Nevertheless, there were sharpshooters posted in the neighbouring houses to guard against a possible assault. Thus the women were able to pass unchallenged.

It was a more difficult task, however, to get through the investing lines. But those who remember the Vienna of those days will recall the unfilled hollow between Hernals and what was then known as the Schmelz, designed to receive the water that flowed from the mountains after heavy rains. Hewn stones and wooden planks lined the sides of this depression. It was not a pleasant spot to visit, but it offered a good hiding-place to any one seeking concealment.

Frau Babi led the way down into this hollow, which was then, luckily, free from water. Climbing out on the farther side, she looked cautiously around and then bade the others follow her, first drawing up their baskets for them.

"Leave them here," said she. "The hussars are over yonder."

At a distance of two hundred paces could be seen a couple of men standing by a watch-fire, while beyond them, within the cemetery, five or six more fires were burning in a group, indicating the encampment of the squadron.

"I was right," added the old woman. "You two go on now; you won't need me any longer."

Taking Edith by the hand, Baroness Baradlay advanced toward the first watch-fire. The sentinels saw their approach, but did not challenge them until they were very near.

"Halt! Who goes there?" cried one of the horsemen.

"Friends," was the answer.

"Give the countersign."

"Saddle horses and right about!"

At this the hussar sprang from his saddle, approached the baroness, and kissed her hand respectfully. "We have been looking for you, madam," said he.

"Do you know who I am, Paul?"

"Yes, madam, and thank heaven you are here safely."

"Where is my son?"

"I will take you to him at once. And that pretty little creature?" he asked, in a low tone, pointing to Edith.

"She comes with me."

"I understand."

The old hussar left his horse in his comrade's care and led the two women toward a small whitewashed house which stood within the cemetery, and had formerly been used as the grave-digger's dwelling, but now served as Richard's quarters. He occupied a little room that looked out upon the city, and this room he had that moment entered after a late night ride.

"There they are again!" he cried, bringing his fist down heavily on the table, upon which the latest newspapers from Pest were spread out, showing a number of articles marked with red. "Into the fire with them!"

But, angry as he seemed to be at finding the papers thrust upon his notice, Captain Baradlay could not persuade himself to burn them unread; and having once begun to read, he could not stop. Resting his elbows on the table and his head in his hands, he read over and over again the marked passages, his brow darkening as he proceeded.

"It is not true, it cannot be true!" he exclaimed, struggling with his feelings. "It is all false, it is utterly preposterous!"

At the sound of approaching footsteps, he crumpled the papers up in his hand. Old Paul entered, and Richard turned upon him in a passion.

"What thieving rascal has been stealing into my room and leaving these infamous newspapers on my table?"

Paul made answer with his accustomed phlegm: "If you told me a thief had carried off something, I could understand it; but that a thief should bring you something is stranger than anything I ever heard of."

"A bundle of newspapers is smuggled through my locked door every day, and laid on my table. Who does it?"

"What do I know of newspapers? I can't read."

"You are trying to fool me, Paul," rejoined his master. "Don't you suppose I know that you have been learning to read these last three months? Who is your teacher?"

"Never mind about him. He was a trumpeter, a student expelled from his university, and he died yesterday. He had been at death's door for a long time. I begged him not to take all his learning with him to the next world, but to leave me some of it."

"And why did you want to learn to read?"

Straightening himself up, the old soldier answered firmly: "Captain, I could easily give you a false reply to that question. If I wished to deceive you, I could say I had learned to read because I wanted to be promoted. But I will tell you the truth: I have learned to read in my old age in order to know what is going on at home."

"So you too read this stuff? How does it get in here?"

"Never mind that now. I have to report that two ladies wish to speak with Captain Baradlay."

The astonished officer thought he must be dreaming when his old servant opened the door and he found himself face to face with his dear and honoured mother, while, peering out from behind her back, was seen the sweet young face of the girl he loved more than life itself. Both forms were clad in coarse peasant garments, bedraggled with rain and mud. What Richard had just been reading with so much incredulity in the newspapers from Pest, he now saw to be true. Women of noble birth were forced to flee from their homes in disguise because of the out-rages committed by bloodthirsty hordes of marauders ; husbands and brothers were slain before their eyes, and their houses were set on fire. The picture of all this passed before him in fancy, as he found himself in the presence of his mother and his be-trothed.

He embraced and kissed the former in a passion of tenderness, but toward the latter he bore himself with shyness and reserve, hardly able to believe it was actually his Edith.

"So it is all true that the papers tell us ?" he asked his mother, pointing to the newspapers on his table.

The baroness glanced at the marked items. "That is but a thousandth part of the truth," she replied.

"I must believe it now," he rejoined, "from the mere fact that you are here before me as a living proof." He struck the table an emphatic blow. "Henceforth no general shall order my movements !

You only shall command me, mother. What would you have me do?"

The baroness drew Edith to her side, and then turned to her son. "This girl has told me what to ask of you. Only an hour ago I myself was at a loss how to proceed."

"Edith!" whispered the young man, caressing the little hand extended toward him. "But how has it all come about?"

"This convent pupil," replied the mother with a tender look at Edith, "overheard a plot that was forming for your destruction. Whatever course you choose, you are a dead man if you tarry here longer. Arrest for desertion on the one hand, and assassination on the other, threaten you. And this dear girl, without a moment's loss of time, without stopping to weep and wring her hands in despair, escaped from her guardians and sought me out in the dead of night, to beg me make all haste and save you while there was yet time."

"Edith!" stammered the young man once more, overcome by his feelings.

"These are times," continued the baroness, "when mothers are calling their sons home; but you have refused to listen to that call."

"I will listen now, mother; only tell me what to do."

"Learn of your own soldiers. The watchword by

which we entered your camp is, 'Saddle horses and right about!' It points your course to you."

"So be it, then," said Richard, and he stepped to the door and issued an order to old Paul.

"The die is cast," said he to his mother as he returned to her side. "But what will become of you?"

"The Father above will watch over us," she returned calmly.

"But you cannot go back into the city," objected Richard; "it will be stormed to-morrow on all sides, and you would be in great danger. I must be off while we still have darkness and rain to cover our flight; and you had best come with me to the next village, where you can get a conveyance and escape into Hungary. Take Edith with you, too, mother."

The women, however, both shook their heads. "I am going back into the city, my son," declared the baroness.

"But the town will surely be taken to-morrow and you will be in danger," protested Richard.

"Nevertheless I am mindful but of one thing: I have another son there, and I am going back for him, no matter how great the peril. I must bring him away at all hazards."

Richard buried his face in his hands. "Oh, mother," he cried, "how small I seem to myself before your greatness of courage and loftiness of

purpose !'' He threw a look at Edith, as if to ask :
" What will become of you, delicate lily uptorn by the
blast ? Whither will you go, where find shelter ? "

Edith understood the questioning look and hastened
to reply. " Don't be anxious about me. Your mother
will accompany me to the convent. Punishment
awaits me there, but it won't kill me ; and I shall be
well taken care of until you come back for me."

The sound of horses' hoofs fell on their ears.

" Time is flying, my son ! " exclaimed the baroness.
" You must not linger another moment."

A slow rain was falling. The hussars were drawn
up in order, and their captain had nothing to do but
mount his horse and place himself at their head.

" Saddle horses and right about ! " sounded the
subdued watchword ; and the squadron wheeled
around. The trumpeter was dead, but the valiant
band needed no bugle blast to spur it forward. In
a moment it had vanished in the mist and darkness.

The two women were escorted by old Paul back
to the watch-fire, where the market-woman awaited
them. Paul himself was to remain behind with one
other sentinel to deceive the patrol and allay suspicions.
Then the two were to hasten after their comrades.

Dawn was breaking when Edith reëntered the convent. A cry of horror was raised in the refectory
over her appearance at such an hour. In the whole

nunnery not an eye had been closed that night, so great was the alarm caused by Sister Remigia's return unaccompanied by her companion. The door of the coach had been found open, Edith was not inside, and the sister, awaking from her slumbers, could not account for her disappearance. And what made matters worse, no one dared take any action that should publish the scandalous occurrence abroad.

Edith found herself besieged with questions on all sides: where in the world had she been, and what had she been doing all night?

"I will give my answer this evening — not before," she declared; and as her unheard-of contumacy yielded to no threats or scolding, chastisement was resorted to.

The pious sisters were horrified when they began to undress their obstinate charge and found her clothes all wet and stained with mud. Who could tell where she had been roaming about in the night? But she would answer not a word to their questions.

The rod and the scourge were applied with no sparing hand, but neither the one nor the other could make her confess. The brave girl only closed her teeth the more tightly when the shameful blows struck her tender body, and after each stroke she whispered to herself: "Dear Richard!" — repeating the words until at last she fainted under the torture. When she recovered consciousness she found herself in bed, her body half covered with plasters. She was in a high fever, but was able to note the approach of nightfall. She had slept nearly all day.

"Now I will tell where I have been," said she to those around her bed. "I went to the camp of the hussars and passed the night in the room of my lover, their captain. Now you may publish it abroad if you choose."

At this fearful revelation the prioress threw up her hands in consternation. Naturally she took every precaution to keep the matter secret; for had it been allowed to leak out, the good name of that nunnery would have been ruined.

CHAPTER XV.

JENÖ had of late made his abode in the Planken-horst house, having formally installed himself there in the room of the footman, who had gone to join the insurgents at the barricades. Thus the young man was able to be in the house day and night. Extraor-dinary events produce extraordinary situations. The young man's cup of happiness held but one drop of bitterness, — anxious uncertainty what the morrow might bring forth. Would the cause of the insur-gents prevail, or would they be defeated? And what would be his fate and that of the Plankenhorsts, in the latter case?

The assault had come to an end on the evening of the third day. The insurgents had in great part laid down their arms, only a few detached companies still maintaining the unequal contest in the outlying dis-tricts. The victorious army was already advancing into the city along its principal streets. In the Plan-kenhorst parlours there were but three persons, the two ladies and Jenö. Those who had of late been such constant frequenters of that drawing-room were now fallen or scattered. As the military band at the head of the conquering forces passed the house, Jenö heard heavy steps ascending the stairs. The victors were coming; they had singled out that particular house, and there was no escape. The young man nerved himself to meet any issue — except the one actually before him.

The old family friends and acquaintances, the pre-revolutionary frequenters of the Plankenhorst parties, came pouring into the room, smiling with triumph, and all meeting with a hearty welcome from the ladies, who seemed to take the whole affair as a matter of course, and to be affected by the sudden change of atmosphere no more than if the past eight months, with their stirring scenes and epoch-making events, had been but a dream.

No one paid any heed to Jenö or seemed in the smallest degree conscious of his presence, until one guest entered who was polite enough to give him a word of greeting. It was Rideghváry. Making his entrance with no little pomp and ostentation, he congratulated the ladies with much effusion and shook a hand of each in both his own. Leaving them upon the entrance of a new guest, he sought out Jenö, who was sitting in one of the windows, a passive spectator of the scene before him.

"Your humble servant, my young friend," was the

elder's condescending salutation. " Glad to find you here, for I have matters of importance to discuss with you which may have great influence on your future. Pray be good enough to go home and await my coming."

Jenö had still spirit enough to resent this summary mode of sending him home. "I am at your Excellency's service," he replied. "You will not need to go out of the house; I am living here at present, — on the third floor, at the right as you go up."

"Ah, I didn't know that," answered the other, in surprise. "Have the goodness, then, to wait for me there." With that his Excellency returned to the ladies, leaving the young man to seek his chamber in no very pleasant frame of mind.

That room, in which visions of rapture had visited the slumbers of the youthful lover, was a paradise to him no longer. The weary humdrum of ordinary life was beginning again. What in the world could that angular gentleman have to say to him, he wondered. He seemed long enough, in all conscience, about coming.

Suddenly the rustling of a woman's dress fell on Jenö's listening ear, and in another moment Alfonsine entered his room. She had run away from the company below and had hurried up alone to her lover. She seemed agitated, and her coming had apparently been a sudden impulse. Falling on Jenö's bosom and embracing him, she burst out with every sign of passionate emotion :

" They want to part us ! "

" Who ? " asked Jenö, no little disturbed by the other's manner.

" They, they ! " cried she, half choked with emotion, and bursting into tears, while she clasped her lover still more closely.

Jenö's agitation increased ; he became thoroughly alarmed. " For heaven's sake, Alfonsine," he begged, " do be cautious ! Rideghváry is likely to come in at any moment, and what if he found you here ? " Poor, kind-hearted youth, more careful of his sweetheart's good name than she herself !

" Oh, he won't come yet," she made haste to assure him. " He and mamma are having a talk, and they have decided that you must return to your lodging at once, — that you are not to stay here a day longer. Oh, I know what that means ; we are to be parted for ever."

Jenö was on the point of fainting ; each word from his sweetheart's lips struck him with dismay. Meanwhile she continued her passionate outburst.

" I will not be separated from you ! " she declared. " I am yours, yours for ever, yours in life and in death, your beloved, your wife, ready to sacrifice all for you, to suffer all ! "

At length she recovered her composure somewhat,

and, lifting her tearful eyes to heaven, breathed a solemn vow : " To you, my friend, my lover, my all, to you or to the grave I dedicate myself. No power on earth shall tear me from you. For your sake I will leave kith and kin, abjure my faith, disown the mother who bore me, if they stand in the way of our happiness. For you I will go into exile and wander over the earth as a homeless beggar. Whatever your destiny, — be it life or be it death, — I will share it."

The exaltation of the moment quite robbed Jenö of his last bit of reason. Was it all a dream, or was it reality, he asked himself.

Neither one nor the other, dear Jenö, but an excellent bit of play-acting. Poor credulous youth ! It is all a part of a well-laid and far-reaching plot, of which you are the innocent victim.

After leaving her lover, Alfonsine did not return to the drawing-room, but hastened to her maid's chamber, where she learned that Sister Remigia was waiting for her in her room. First removing, with Betty's help, the traces of her scene with Jenö, Alfonsine hurried to meet the nun.

" Is Major Palvicz here ? " she demanded.

" No," answered the sister ; " he only returned yesterday from his pursuit of Captain Baradlay, whom he failed to overtake."

" Did he send an answer to my letter ? "

"Yes ; there it is." Sister Remigia handed Alfonsine a note, and then crossed the corridor to Antoinette's room.

Alfonsine remained behind to read her letter. She first locked her door, to guard against surprise, after which she sat down at her table and broke the seal.

"Gracious lady," ran the note, "when you find what you have *mislaid*, you shall recover what you have *lost*."

At these enigmatical words the reader of the message turned pale and the paper trembled in her hand. Her eyes rested on her porcelain lamp-shade, on which was painted the well-known picture of an angel flying heavenward with a sleeping child. The young woman gazed intently at the translucent figures, as if watching to see whither the angel would carry the little child.

Meanwhile Jenö was listening at his door for the departure of the last guest from the drawing-room. Finally they were all gone and he was able to speak with the baroness alone.

"Baroness," said he, "there have been great changes since yesterday. Let me hope that one thing, at any rate, has not altered, — the relation that has hitherto existed between Alfonsine and myself, with the apparent sanction of the young lady's mother. I regard that relation as the very breath of my life, and I beg you, madam, to let me know whether there is any reason why I should fear a discontinuance of your favour."

"My dear Baradlay," returned Antoinette, "you know very well that we are warmly attached to you, and in that attachment you cannot have detected any diminution, nor shall you in the future. My daughter has a sincere fondness for you, and thinks of no one else, while I, for my part, could not but feel myself honoured by a tie that should connect us with the noble house of Baradlay. So far, then, there is nothing to be said against your engagement. The late turn of events, however, has brought with it a change that affects you intimately ; and that change, my dear Baradlay — Do I need to speak further ? "

"Really, I cannot think what you mean, madam," protested Jenö.

"You can't ? H'm ! What, pray, are you now ? "

"What am I ? Nothing at present."

"That is it exactly. Henceforth you are nothing. There are now two hostile parties, and each is striving for the mastery. In this strife it is uncertain as yet which will win, cr whether they may not effect a compromise ; but in any event he is lost who belongs to neither side. Yet do not consider my words as a definite rejection of your suit. We are attached to you, and wish the consummation of that which you so ardently desire. I impose upon you no seven-year probation, like that required by Jacob's father-in-law. So soon as you shall succeed in winning a place in the world, so soon as you cease to be a nobody in our political and national life, I shall be the first to bid you welcome, — whether to-morrow or next month or next year. Meanwhile you have my best wishes."

There was nothing for the young man to do but take his lesson to heart and return to his former quarters. The baroness had told him he was a nobody, and he could not dispute her. He was, moreover, forced to remember that the monthly allowance regularly forwarded to him by his mother had failed to reach him the last month, and, in consequence, he was likely to find himself financially embarrassed within a very few days. There is something decidedly depressing in an empty purse.

Scarcely had he returned to the dreary atmosphere of his old rooms when Rideghváry paid him the honour of a call.

"In the first place," began Rideghváry, "I have a letter to deliver to you. It is from your mother. Put it in your pocket and read it later. For the last two weeks, as you may know, the commanding general has detained all mails and ordered all letters to be opened. It was a necessity of the situation — to prevent treason. On your letter I chanced to recognise your mother's handwriting, and I was fortunately able to rescue it from the common fate and bring it to you. No one has tampered with it, but it probably treats of matters that are no longer of importance in the eyes of the government. Furthermore, the writer will be here in person before many hours have passed."

"Is my mother in the city?" asked Jenö, much surprised.

"Yes, she is here somewhere, and the reason you haven't seen her before is that you kept yourself at the Plankenhorsts', whither she had her grounds for not going. But you may be sure she has sought you here at least a dozen times, and she will come again to-day."

"But what is she doing in Vienna?"

"Nothing good, as we know but too well, alas! She came to persuade your brother Richard to desert with his men and return to Hungary."

"And did she succeed?"

"Yes, and a detachment of cavalry was sent in pursuit of him three days ago. He has fled to the mountains of Galicia, whence he cannot possibly escape on horseback over the border. Your mother, meanwhile, is here in hiding; she is one of those whom the authorities are trying to arrest."

"Merciful heaven!" cried Jenö, starting up from his chair.

"Keep your seat. Until to-morrow morning she will be in no danger. The city is now in the hands

of the army, the civil government being as yet
unorganised.   There is no effective police and detective force; all that takes time, and in the general
confusion now prevailing, any one who wishes can
easily remain in hiding.   But no one can leave the
city undetected, as the lines are closely drawn and
every traveller is stopped and required to show a
passport.   Now, although I have reason enough to
feel embittered against your family yet I cannot
allow your father's widow to come to such an untimely
end as at present threatens her.   So I have provided
a passport with a fictitious name for her use, and you
will hand it to her when she comes.   And now let
us talk about your affairs, my dear Jenö.   You
remained in Vienna after the March uprising, and
have maintained throughout a cool and impartial
attitude which nothing short of genius could have
dictated.   The espousal of a cause before one can
judge of its merits — much less be sure of its ulti-
mate success — indicates weakness of judgment and
a lack of mental stability.   Therefore you were quite
right in holding aloof from either side; yet you must
not continue to hide your light under a bushel.   A
fortunate chance has placed a very important appointment virtually in my hands, since a testimonial from
me is more than likely to decide the choice of an
incumbent.   Your qualifications and ability justify
me in regarding you as the fittest person to fill this

position. It is the secretaryship of our embassy to Russia."

Jenö's heart beat high with gratified self-esteem at the sudden prospect of both realising his proudest ambition and attaining his heart's fondest desire. He had often heard his father refer to this eminent post as the goal for which Ödön was to strive. His head fairly swam at the vision so unexpectedly presented to him. In his wildest dreams he had scarcely dared soar so high.

Meanwhile the other pretended not to note the effect he had produced on the young man. Consulting his watch, he rose hastily. "I have stayed too long," said he. "Another engagement calls me. You will have until to-morrow morning to consider my proposal. Weigh the matter well, for your decision will be of no little importance as regards your whole future career. Look at the question from all sides, and take your mother into your confidence if you wish ; she may have weighty arguments to urge against your acceptance. Consider them all carefully, and then decide for yourself."

So saying, he took his leave, well knowing the impression he had made on his plastic subject, and fully confident that the young man would take good heed not to breathe a word of all this to his mother.

As soon as he had left the room, Jenö broke the

seal of his letter. His monthly allowance was enclosed, and also a few lines in his mother's hand.

"My dear son," she wrote, "I have read your
letter asking me to share in your happiness and to give
my love to the young woman whom you wish to make
your wife. Any happiness that befalls you cannot
fail to rejoice me also. Rank, wealth, birth are
slight matters in my eyes. If you chose a bride
from the working classes, — a virtuous, industrious,
pure-hearted girl, — I should give you my blessing
and rejoice in your happiness ; or if you should select
a spoiled creature of fashion, a coquette and a spendthrift, I should still receive your bride as my daughter, and pray God to bless the union and turn evil
into good ; but if you marry Alfonsine Plankenhorst,
it will be without the blessing of either God or your
mother, and we shall be parted for ever."

That was a cruel thrust. How, he asked himself,
had Alfonsine incurred his mother's displeasure?
What possible offence could she have committed?
He recalled her words, — "For your sake I will leave
kith and kin, abjure my faith, disown the mother who
bore me," — and remembered the passionate kisses
and warm embrace that had accompanied the vow.
And should he be outdone by her in devotion ? Was
his fondness for his mother stronger than his love for
Alfonsine ? Was not the one feeling a weakness and
the other a mark of manly strength ? Surely he was

no longer a child. How scornfully that other mother had told him he was a mere nobody, and bade him make a place for himself in the world if he wished to marry her daughter! What a triumph it would be to appear before that proud woman on the morrow, with a man's full right to claim his own!

He resolved to accept Rideghváry's offer and to listen to no argument or pleading by which his mother might seek to dissuade him. Bidding his servant admit unannounced the lady who had already called a number of times, he sat awaiting her coming. But he waited in vain, and at last threw himself on his bed and fell asleep. His rest was troubled, however, by a succession of bad dreams.

Filled with fears for his mother's safety, Jenö hastened the next morning, as early as propriety would allow, to call upon Rideghváry.

"Do you know anything about my mother?" were his first words after greeting his patron. "She did not come to see me yesterday."

"Yes, I know," replied the other; "she has made her escape. The market-woman, in whose house she hid, was arrested last night and acknowledged having accompanied your mother to the outskirts of the town, where a carriage was waiting for her. She must be in Pressburg by this time."

These words relieved poor Jenö's breast of a heavy

M

load. His mother was out of danger and he was free to act for himself.

"Well, have you considered my proposal?" asked Rideghváry.

"Yes. I have decided to accept the appointment."

Rideghváry pressed the young man's hand. "I was sure you would," said he; "and, to show you my confidence in you, I have your certificate of appointment all made out." He took an official document from his table-drawer and handed it to Jenö. "To-morrow you will take the oath of office, and then you will be free to wind up your affairs here in Vienna."

Luckily the Baroness Plankenhorst was up and dressed betimes that morning, else Jenö would certainly have sought her out in her boudoir. Hastening into the proud lady's presence, he began, without a moment's loss of time, the speech which he had been rehearsing on the way.

"Madam," said he, "you will perhaps recall your parting words to me yesterday, — 'whether to-morrow or next month or next year.' That 'to-morrow' has come, and I am here, — no longer a nobody." To prove his assertion, he produced his certificate of appointment to the secretaryship of the embassy to Russia, and handed it to the baroness.

With a look of the utmost surprise, and a smile of

hearty congratulation, she received the document and read it. "I am indeed delighted," she exclaimed, giving the young appointee her hand. "Do you wish Alfonsine to be informed of this?"

"If you please."

The baroness had to go no farther than the next room to find her daughter. Leading her in by the hand, she presented "the secretary of the Austrian legation at the court of St. Petersburg."

"Oh!" exclaimed Alfonsine, when she had somewhat recovered from her apparent astonishment; and she extended her hand with a gracious smile to the young incumbent of a twelve-thousand-florin position. He eagerly clasped the offered hand in both his own. "It is yours now to keep," she whispered with another smile, and then turned and hid her face in her mother's bosom, overcome, it is to be supposed, by a feeling of maidenly modesty and girlish fear.

Jenö next kissed his prospective mother-in-law's hand, whereupon she impressed a kiss on his forehead. Alfonsine could hardly be induced to raise her modestly downcast eyes again in the presence of the man who was there to claim her as his bride.

"When shall we announce the engagement?" asked the mother, turning to Jenö. "To-morrow, shall we say — at twelve? Very well. And now are you satisfied with me?"

The young man's heart beat high with triumph

and happiness, as he returned to his rooms. He felt that at last he had begun to live; hitherto he had only vegetated, but now he was entering on the full life of a man. Yet there was some alloy in his happiness even then. The thought of his mother, and of her disapproval of his course, refused to be banished from his mind; and though he pretended to rejoice that she had escaped from the city, and had been spared the pain of a meeting and a useless conflict with him, yet his conscience would not be deceived. Too well he knew that he was afraid to meet his mother, and was more relieved at being freed from that necessity than rejoiced at her safe escape.

With the approach of evening poor Jenö's thoughts became such a torment to him that he prepared to go out in quest of distraction. But on stepping before his mirror to adjust his cravat, a sight met his eyes that made him start back in sudden fear. Reflected in the glass he saw his mother enter the room.

"Mother!" he cried, turning toward her.

The woman before him was not the proud, commanding form that he knew so well. It was one of those sorrowing figures which we see painted at the foot of the cross, bowed with grief and spent with watching and weeping, — the very incarnation of bitter anguish. In such guise did the Baroness Baradlay present herself to her youngest son Jenö, and at sight of her, the young man's first thought was one that gave him no cause to blush afterward. Forgetting his dread of meeting her, he thought only of the danger to which she was exposing herself in coming to him, and he put his arms around her, as if to shield her from harm. On his cheek he felt the warm kisses, — so different from those of that other mother!

"How did you manage to come to me, dear mother?" he asked.

"I came by a long way."

"They told me you had left the city, and were in Pressburg."

"So I was. For three days I sought you in vain; then I gave up the hope of finding you, and left the city. But in Pressburg I heard something that made me turn back and seek you once more."

"Oh, why did you do it?" exclaimed the son. "You had but to send for me, and I would have hastened to you. Why did you not command me?"

"Ah, my son, I have forgotten how to command. I have come not to command, but to implore. Do not be afraid of me; do not look at me as if I were a spectre risen between you and your heart's desire. Not thus do I come to you, but only as a suppliant, with one last petition."

"Mother," cried Jenö, much moved, "do not speak to me like that, I beg of you."

"Forgive me. Only a few days ago I could have commanded my sons, but not now. I wrote you a letter — did you receive it? — an arrogant, offensive letter. Destroy it; let it be as if it had never been written. It was an angry woman that wrote it. That proud, angry woman is no more. Grievous afflictions have humbled her, and the end is not yet. She is now but a mourning widow, begging for mercy at the open grave of her sons."

"Dear mother, your sons are still alive," Jenö interposed reassuringly.

"But do you know where they are? One of them is fighting his way over the Carpathians to his native land, pursued, surrounded, and harassed on all sides. At his feet yawns the mountain chasm with the raging torrent at its bottom; over his head the storms vent their fury and the hungry vultures wheel in circles. If he eludes his pursuers, and escapes starvation and freezing, he may, perhaps, be fortunate enough to reach the battle-field, where my eldest son awaits his coming at the head of a volunteer force. Do you know the sort of soldiers who compose that force? Boys that have run away from their homes, and fathers that have left their wives and children. It is as if a feverish madness were driving every one to the field of battle, where certains death awaits its victims."

"But why do they thus rush to their destruction?"

"Because they cannot help themselves, in the bitter woe that oppresses all hearts."

"They may be victorious, mother."

"Oh, yes, they will be. They will win a glorious victory, but it will avail them naught. It will but bring heavier woes upon them. They will show the world wonderful deeds of daring, and compel the admiration of all; their star will shine brightly over all Europe, now wrapped in darkness; but it will be so much the worse for them in the end. Their fate is already sealed by the great world-powers. If they are not prostrated by the first blow, another will be dealt them, and still another, until at last they succumb. I learned this in Pressburg from intercepted letters, and it brought me back here again. How could I resist the longing to come back and see you once more, — the last time in my life?"

"Oh, do not speak so!"

"You are going far away, and it will be a dark day for us that sees your return. The proud and powerful have been putting their heads together, and they have formed a plan for taking vengeance on their mother country for the chastisement she has inflicted on them."

"Who are they?"

"Your friends and patrons. But fear not; I am not here to inveigh against them. They are kinder to you than I am. I would point you the way to ruin ; they show you the road to safety. I offer you a joyless life of trials and afflictions ; they hold out to you happiness and a brilliant career. I cannot compete with them. No, my son, you and they are right, and we are but foolish enthusiasts, sacrificing ourselves for a mere nothing, an idea, a dream. May you never be able to understand us ! Go with those who are now preparing to ally themselves with the Russians against their own fatherland. As Hungarians, you and they are of course pained at the necessity of invoking your old enemy's aid against your own mother and brothers ; but you do it because you are convinced that your mother and brothers must be humbled. The Baradlay escutcheon has received two shameful stains in the conduct of Ödön and Richard. It is reserved for you to wipe out those stains. What a brilliant refutation of all charges it will be in the world's eyes to point to the youngest son, who atoned for the crime of his two elder brothers by joining the party that summoned a mighty power to the pacification of his misguided country ! "

Jenö's face was white and he sat gazing into vacancy. They had not said anything to him about all this ; and yet he might have perceived it clearly enough with a little reflection.

"There can be but one issue," continued the mother : "we are lost, but you will be saved. Two mighty powers are more than we can withstand, be we ever so stanch and brave. Your brothers will fall sooner or later : death is easy to find. You will then be left as the head of the Baradlay family. You will be the envied husband of a beautiful wife, a man of high rank and wide influence, the pride of the new era on which we are entering."

Jenö's head had sunk on his breast ; his heart was no longer filled with pride and exultation. His mother proceeded.

"The unfortunate and the helpless will come and kiss the ground under your feet. You will be in a position to do much good, and I am sure you will make the most of it ; for you have a kind and tender heart. Among the petitions that will be laid before you, do not forget my own. You see I have come to you as the first suppliant."

Alas, how humiliated the young man felt before his mother ! And the more so that she spoke not in irony, but in the gentle tones of pleading earnest.

"Not for myself do I ask anything," she went on ; "our fate will soon overtake us, and if it lingered we should, I assure you, hasten to meet it. Your brother Richard is unmarried and so leaves no family ; but Ödön has a wife and two children, — two dear, pretty children, the younger only a month old. You are sure to be richly rewarded for your great services. Your brothers' property will be confiscated and handed over to you."

Jenö started up in horrified protest.

"And when you are a rich and powerful man," his mother continued, "in possession of all that we now hold in common, and when you are crowned with honours and happiness, then, my son, remember this hour and your mother's petition : let your brother's children never suffer want."

"Mother ! " cried Jenö, beside himself with grief and pain.　Hastening to his desk, he drew forth his certificate of appointment from one of its drawers, tore it into a hundred pieces, and then sank weeping on his mother's breast.　"Mother, I am not going to Russia."

The mother's joy at these words was too great for utterance.　She clasped her youngest, her dearest son in a warm embrace.　"And you will come with me, my boy ? " she asked.

"Yes, I will go with you."

"I shall not let you follow your brothers to the battle-field.　You must stay at home and be our comforter ; your life must be spared.　I wish you to lead a happy life.　May I not hope for many years of happiness for you ? "

Jenö sighed deeply, his thoughts turning to what was now a thing of the past, — his bright dream of happiness.　He kissed his mother, but left her question unanswered.

"Let us hurry away from here at once," said she, rising from the sofa.

Then for the first time Jenö remembered the passport. " This passport," said he, producing it, " was all
in readiness for you had you come yesterday ; and you
can still make use of it."

" Who gave it to you ? " asked the mother.

" An old friend of the family, the same who procured
me my appointment."

" And do you think I will accept any favour from
him ? " Therewith the baroness tore up the passport
and threw the fragments on the floor, among those of
the destroyed certificate.

" Oh, what have you done ? " exclaimed Jenö in
alarm. " How will you make your escape ? Every
outlet is barred."

The other merely raised her head in scorn and
triumph. " As if I could not put all their precautions
to shame ! " she exclaimed. " Get your cloak, my son ;
I will take you by such a way that no man will venture
to follow us."

The next day Rideghváry waited in vain for the
young secretary, in order to escort him to the place
where he was to take the oath of office. In vain, too,
did the bride and her mother, and all the invited guests,
wait for the bridegroom to join them. He failed to
appear. Surely that dreaded mother of his must have
seduced him !

Whither he had vanished, and how he had made

his way through the lines, remained an unsolved riddle. It never occurred to any one that in times like those the Danube offered an excellent road for such as dared trust their lives to a frail boat, in the mist and darkness of the night, with two stout-hearted fishermen at the oars.

CHAPTER XVI.

THROUGH FIRE AND WATER.

AND now whither? That was the anxious query of the deserting squadron of hussars.

On one side was the whole army, from among whose banners they had wrested their own; on the other were two rivers, the Danube and the March, and beyond them a mountain range, the Carpathians.

For an hour and a half they followed a bridle-path through the fields, knowing only that they were riding toward the Danube. Then the sky began to clear, and they were able to determine their position more exactly. On the right lay the river like a dark mirror under the scurrying clouds.

"Now, boys," said Richard, when he had his men all before him, "we have begun a march which will take us either home or to destruction. I have to warn you — what you know well enough already — that we are about to face every sort of peril and hardship. We must ride day and night without a halt, swim rivers, climb mountains, bear hunger, thirst, and want of sleep, and be prepared to fight for our lives at every step. He who faints by the way is lost ; he will be taken prisoner and shot. I ask no man to follow me. I shall go ahead without turning back to see how many of my two hundred and twenty men are behind me. I require no oath of you. It is dark, and whoever chooses to turn back may do so when I start to lead the way ; but when the sun rises, let all who are with me then understand that they are thenceforward under military discipline, and bound to obey my orders without murmur or complaint. Now then, follow me who will ! This is the first test."

The first test was calculated to make the fainthearted, if such there were, shrink with fear. The Danube was to be forded. Richard was familiar with the region from his earlier military manœuvres, and he knew the river's shoals and bars. For him and his old hussars it was mere play to cross the stream without bridge or ferry ; but the less experienced might well fear to breast its waters in the dark, encumbered as they were with their arms.

A young poplar grove received the horsemen on the farther side, and here their leader caused them to be counted by the sergeant-major.

"Two hundred and twenty," reported that officer, after completing the count.

"Impossible !" exclaimed Richard ; "we left two men behind as sentinels."

"Here we are!" sounded a familiar bass, which was at once recognised as old Paul's.

"That you, Paul? Hcw did you overtake us so soon, and what news from the camp?"

"The cuirassiers broke camp and made for the city, as if on purpose to leave us a clear field; and so I said: 'What's the use of standing guard here any longer? Come, brother, let's after the rest!'"

"And was there no sign of an alarm?"

"No, sir; everything was as still as a mouse."

"Good! Now all form a square around me."

The hussars obeyed the order, falling in about their captain in closed ranks. In the east a faint light was beginning to mark the horizon line.

Two hundred and twenty men, gathered together in that quiet grove, swore blind obedience to their commander and fearless execution of his orders until they should see their homes once more. When the sun showed itself like a fiery dome on the horizon, they saw that the standard they were to follow was the familiar tricolour.

"We have half a day's start of our pursuers," said Richard to his men. "The first to discover our flight will be Otto Palvicz, the cuirassier major. When he has followed our trail so far, he will see that we have crossed the river. He can't cross here with his heavy cavalry, but will be obliged to turn back to the floating bridge. By pushing on until late to-night, we shall escape all danger of his over-taking us. So much for our first day's work."

Richard then divided his store of ready money among his followers, and impressed upon them that they were not, under any circumstances, to plunder and rob, but were to pay for all provisions consumed.

Emerging from the poplar grove, the hussars struck into a bridle-path which led them to a castle owned by a Czechic magnate, who was at that time away from home; but his wife gave Richard an audience, with the result that his men received each a drink of brandy, with some bread and smoked meat, while hay and oats were furnished for their horses. Richard also obtained from the good lady a map which showed every road and bridle-path as far as the Moravian and Hungarian borders. This map proved afterward indispensable to the fugitives.

They rested at the Czechic magnate's castle for two hours, when a guide conducted them to the next forest and left them to pursue their way farther. In the depth of the woods the shades of an autumn afternoon closed in on the riders at an early hour. Richard led the way through ravines and over mountains. Reaching an elevated spot of ground that commanded a view of the surrounding country, he had his attention called by old Paul to the beacon-fires visible in the gathering darkness on the distant mountain-tops.

"Those are for our benefit," said Captain Baradlay.

The fires were warning signals of the fugitives' flight, and they soon began to appear not only in the rear, but also on the summits ahead of the riders. Thus the whole country as far as the border was aroused to intercept them. By the light of a newly kindled beacon in their rear Richard could see, through his field-glass, that a body of horsemen was already in hot pursuit.

"They are on our trail much sooner than I expected," said he, "and we have not a moment to waste."

Hoping to elude pursuit, he chose a path leading through a deep ravine which he well remembered from his hunting expeditions. It formed a part of an Austrian noble's estate. A mountain stream flowed through this ravine, its waters being dammed at one place to form a large mill-pond and a fishing basin, and also to supply necessary irrigation at certain seasons. Richard's hastily formed plan was to push on past the mill and open the sluices on his way, thus flooding the narrow valley and cutting off his pursuers, who were seen to be Otto Palvicz's heavy cavalry.

One contingency, however, had not occurred to him, namely, that the trick he intended to play on Otto Palvicz might be played by some one else on himself. At a turn in the ravine not far from the

N

mill, Paul came galloping back with the advance-
guard and reported that the whole valley ahead was
under water. The miller had told him that the dam
had been opened only a short time before by the
forester. It had evidently been done to cut off the
hussars.

Richard spurred forward to the mill. Only a
narrow dike offered a passage across the ravine,
and even this dike had been destroyed for a space
of several yards, leaving only the piles projecting
from the water.

"Never mind," said Richard, nothing dismayed
by the prospect; "go and bring two or three doors
from the mill and lay them on the piles to form a
bridge."

The order was promptly executed, but the horses
refused to cross on this improvised structure.

"They are afraid because it is white," said Paul.

"Cover it with mud," commanded Richard.

"That won't do," objected the old hussar, "because
then we can't burn it behind us."

"Right, Paul; we must set it on fire as soon as
we are over. Perhaps we can find some tar in the
mill."

A whole barrel of tar was discovered after some
search, and a portion of it poured over the bridge.
Now, however, the horses were more recalcitrant than
before; their hoofs slipped on the tarred boards, and

the hollow sound given back by the frail bridge served to increase their fear.

Old Paul swore like a heathen. "Here we are caught in a pretty trap," said he.

"Oh, no," replied Richard, reassuringly. "We two must dismount, and one of us lead the horses by the bridle while the other urges them on from behind. The riders will stay in their saddles."

It was a task, indeed, to get all the rearing, plunging, and thoroughly frightened animals, one after another, over the shaky bridge. The riders cursed, old Paul invoked all the saints in the calendar, and Richard plied his whip with an unsparing hand, until, at last, the passage was accomplished. It had been attended with so much noise, however, that no human ear within miles around could have failed to hear it.

Before long a signal-fire blazed up on the hill from which the fugitives had noted the beacon-lights. Thus far, then, their pursuers had tracked them, and no doubt they would be about their ears in a few minutes. Richard and Paul were bathed in perspiration, and there were still thirty led horses to be driven over the bridge.

"I hear a trumpet behind us," said one of the men; "wouldn't it be best to leave the extra horses and each man look out for himself?"

"No," said Richard; "there must not be a single

horse left behind. Let no one ride on until every horse is over."

His order was obeyed, and not a man stirred from the spot until all the reserve horses were across the bridge. By that time the trumpet notes were very near, and the white mantles of the pursuing horsemen could be discerned in the darkness. Richard gave Paul a whispered order, whereupon the old hussar disappeared with two companions. Then the bridge was heaped with dry brushwood, the rest of the tar poured over it, and the whole set on fire. As the flames shot upward the one band of horsemen could see the other, face to face. Richard swung himself into his saddle, and ordered his men to move forward, carefully, over the narrow dike and down the ravine. He himself remained behind until all had preceded him.

The cuirassiers did not reach the mill in a body, having become greatly scattered in the course of their hot pursuit. Otto Palvicz, however, was in the lead, his full-blooded stallion being best able to stand the strain of the twenty hours' continuous chase. With him were but a score of his men, and there was no telling how long the others might be in joining him; yet he spurred his horse on as if he would have crossed the burning bridge. The animal, however, would not be driven into the fire.

"Captain Richard Baradlay!" shouted Palvicz.

" Here I am, Major Otto Palvicz," came back the answer.

" Surrender yourself my prisoner!"

" Come over and get me!"

"I will, all in good time, you may depend upon it."

" But not to-night."

" Yes, to-night. I sha'n't halt till I have caught you."

" But you can't cross the broken dike."

" It won't delay us more than an hour. By that time we shall be across and at your heels again. You can't escape me."

" We'll see about that."

During this dialogue a rushing of water became audible from the direction of the fish-pond, and Otto Palvicz noticed that an added flood was pouring through the break in the dike and widening the rupture.

"I have had the fish-pond sluices raised," said Richard, "and you will hardly fill in this gap in an hour's time."

Otto Palvicz saw that the other was right. " I see that I cannot cross immediately," he admitted; " but if you are a cavalier, stay where you are and let us fight it out over fire and water. Will you join me in a pistol duel?"

" With all my heart."

"We will fire at each other until one of us falls from his horse."

"Agreed; but first let our men get out of range. Why shoot down our brave lads instead of each other?"

"You are right," assented Otto, and he ordered his men to stand aside.

The two leaders stood facing each other across the burning bridge, whose flames furnished a bright light for a nocturnal duel. Each wore a white cavalry cloak, an excellent target for his opponent's aim.

They exchanged a couple of shots. Palvicz pierced Richard's shako, he himself receiving a shot in the cuirass which left a dent.

"Load again!" cried Otto.

But at that moment the water from the fish-pond, whose sluices had been thrown wide open by old Paul, came rushing over the dike in such a volume as entirely to submerge the burning bridge and leave the duellists in darkness. Indeed, they were forced to seek safety from the rising flood in precipitate flight.

"To-morrow we'll at it again," called out the cuirassier major.

"I'll be with you," answered the captain of hussars.

What had been a fiery Phlegethon before, now became an inky Styx, likely to delay the pursuers for half a day. Meanwhile the fugitives had only to push on as rapidly as possible. The whole region, however, was aroused, and in the first village they reached they could get no provisions for themselves or fodder for their horses.

"You are deserters and bent on mischief," the people said to them, and they were forced to ride on with their hunger unabated.

Coming to a bridge, they were met by a rude company of rustic militia, armed with scythes.

"Shall we do as we did at the St. Bridget Convent?" the hussars asked their captain.

"No, that is out of the question here," was the reply; "we must avoid a fight with the peasantry."

He well knew that a couple of volleys from their pistols would have cleared the bridge; but he chose instead to make a détour that cost them two hours of precious time, being resolved to avoid all bloodshed until he should reach his own country.

And still not a bite to eat. Everything eatable was hidden on their approach. Toward noon, however, they came to a little inn where they obtained a loaf of bread and a little brandy. Richard himself cut up the loaf into as many pieces as there were men, and served it out to his followers as if it had been the Lord's supper. A mouthful of bread and a swallow of brandy, — that was their dinner.

In the afternoon they reached a second mill, and

here the miller was in the act of grinding some buck-
wheat.   Eldorado!   A feast fit for Lucullus! Stirabout for every man, a bellyful!   True, neither dripping nor bacon was to be had; but never mind; it
would taste so good even without.

The hussars unsaddled their horses, and, while
some of the men turned blacksmiths and looked to
the shoeing of their steeds, the rest betook themselves to the kitchen, where, in an immense kettle
hanging over the fire, something was being cooked
with much stirring and pouring in of water, until the
whole was of a uniform and proper consistency.   The
technical name of this dish is "stirabout."

Meanwhile Richard had stationed outposts to guard
against a surprise from the enemy.

When the mush was done, a pole was put through
the handle of the kettle, twelve cavalry cloaks were
spread out on the grass, and on them the steaming
food, which would not have tempted even a wolf's
hunger in its then scalding condition, was served
with a great wooden spoon.   But just as the ban-
queters were about to sit down around the white
cloaks which did duty as table-cloths and plates in
one, the outposts came running in with the cry:
"The cuirassiers are coming!"

To saddle and mount, first folding up the cloaks,
stirabout and all, and throwing them over the pom-
mels. was the work of a moment.   There was not

even time to take one taste of the savoury mess before the men were up and away as fast as their horses could carry them. Without pausing to choose his path, Richard galloped across country, over stock and stubble, taking care only to hold his horse's head toward the east, and spurring on his headlong flight until the sweat ran from the animal's flanks.

"We shall kill all our horses," remarked old Paul, as he pressed hard after his master and glanced back at the ragged line of cavalry behind him. Some of the horses, indeed, broke down under this terrific pace, whereupon the extra mounts were brought into service. It was well they had not been left behind at the mill-dam.

The pursuers were in no better plight. On the highway it had been easy for them to overtake the fugitives, as the latter were forced to make numerous détours; but when they took to the ploughed fields it was a different matter. Richard had been right in his reckoning; in the soft and spongy soil the heavy cuirassiers could proceed only at a walk, while the hussars were able to push forward at a trot.

Richard fell back and remained in the rear to hold all his men together, and when any of them met with an accident he was prompt to lend his aid. Thus he again came within earshot of Otto Palvicz. Glancing back from time to time, he allowed the cuirassier major to come near enough to make conversation possible.

"Stop a moment; I want to speak to you," called Palvicz.

"I can hear you very well as I am," answered Baradlay.

"If you are a brave man, don't run away from me like that."

"I am brave enough to run away so that you'll never catch me."

"That is cowardice. You are showing me your back."

"I shall have a look at yours one of these days."

"Will you stop and fight with me?"

"No; while we fought your men would overtake mine."

"They will do that in any case. Do you see yonder line of willows? Just beyond it lies the March."

"I know that."

"You will be stopped by the river."

"The Danube did not stop us."

This dialogue was carried on very comfortably by the two riders, who were distant from each other only three horse's lengths, an interval which Richard took good care not to let his pursuer diminish.

On reaching the willows that marked the course of the March. the hussars halted.

" See there," cried Palvicz; "your men don't dare take the plunge."

" I'll make them change their minds in a moment," answered the other.

" Are you mad? Both riders and horses will meet their death if you lead them, heated as they are, into the ice-cold water."

"If they meet their death I shall share the same fate."

So saying, Richard put spurs to his horse and galloped forward, Palvicz close at his heels. Presently they came to a stretch of turf where their two noble steeds had a good footing. Palvicz was only two horse's lengths behind when Richard climbed the willow-covered river-bank. The hussar officer had two seconds to spare. He used one of them to survey the danger from which his men were recoiling. The March was swollen by the autumn rains, and its foaming, turbid waters went racing by in an angry tumult. The next moment he called to his men to follow him, and sprang from the high bank into the flood, while his pursuer drew rein with a cry of astonishment. An instant later horse and rider came again to the surface of the water, which had closed foaming over their heads, and Richard called to his enemy with a laugh: " Now follow me if you can!"

At that the whole squadron of hussars plunged with a deafening shout into the boiling current, and followed their leader. Otto Palvicz stood looking at them in amazement as they battled with the waves and perhaps he was even moved with fear lest the gallant band should come to grief. But they all, to a man, gained the farther bank, unharmed by their icy bath; they were rather refreshed and invigorated by it. The cuirassiers, however, did not venture after them. Their leader was forced to desist from further pursuit.

"We shall meet again, Baradlay," he shouted across the river.

"All right; any time you please," returned Richard.

Dripping water at every step, and soaked to the skin, the hussars continued their journey. It was well for them that they did not pause even for a breathing-spell in their wet condition: the cold autumn air would have served them an ill turn had they done so.

A meadow lay before them, in which the horses sank to their fetlocks in the mud. Yet it was a matter of stern necessity to push on. Both the leader and his followers knew that unless men and horses found food and shelter that night, they would all be likely to perish. For two days and nights they had not closed their eyes, and a good night's sleep, with one full meal, seemed indispensable if they were to gain strength for what yet lay before them.

"If the good God would only lead us to a village!"

was the prayer of many a young hussar. But their prayers met with an ill response. They had prayed for some snug little village, and they came to a city instead. Gaining a hilltop, they suddenly beheld in the valley before them a pretty town with six church-spires. Their prayer had been more than answered. The town was girt with a wall, after the old German custom, and it seemed unwise to trust themselves within its embrace. A road led around it, to be sure, but was commanded by a high walled building that looked, to the experienced eye, suspiciously like cavalry barracks. A reconnoissance seemed hazardous where every eye was on the watch for the fugitives; therefore, they were forced to retire to the woods they had just left, and wait for night. Yet they feared to tarry too long, well knowing that Palvicz would send a messenger across the river by boat to notify the garrison commander of their presence in the neighbourhood.

At nightfall the uncertainty of the hussars was dispelled. A bugle sounded its familiar note from the barracks, and the horses pricked up their ears. That well-known "trarara trarara" had always meant to them that their masters were bringing oats for the night and spreading straw for their beds. But no such good luck this time. The fanfare was heard four times, — once at each corner of the wall, — and when the trumpets became silent a roll of drums followed. All this indicated to the listeners that troops were quartered in the town.

To make a détour and avoid both town and barracks was impossible; horses and riders would have perished in the swamp. But go on they must in some way; it was out of the question to bivouac in the open air that cold autumn night. Yet which way were they to turn?

Possibly the reader may wonder that two hundred and twenty Hungarian hussars, those centaurs of modern mythology, should have even stopped to ask such a question, so long as they held their good swords in their hands. But consider, dear reader, that these hussars had not slept for two nights, or eaten anything since the preceding day; that their horses were worn out, their clothes wet through, and their limbs chilled and stiffened by the autumn frost. Military men know only too well how many battles have been lost because of empty stomachs. Many a brave army that has marched out as if to subdue the world has been routed in the end by a despised and inferior enemy, simply because the latter had eaten a good dinner before the battle and the other side had not.

At last help came from an unexpected source, — from that cold and penetrating dampness of which the shivering riders were so bitterly complaining. Such a dense mist arose and spread over the landscape that one could not see twenty steps ahead.

"Now, boys," said Captain Baradlay, turning with satisfaction to his men, "we will play a capital joke on yonder good people. Let every man tear up his saddle-cloth and bind his horse's hoofs with the rags ; then we will start."

The men soon guessed his plan, and in a few minutes were ready for further orders. They left the woods and rode silently along the highway, unable to see ahead, but each man following his nose. Not a soul was abroad at that time of night, all good citizens being long since in bed and asleep.

Suddenly the night watch called the hour, — eleven ; and then a lantern appeared and seemed to be drawing nearer. Advancing until they were within fifty paces of this light, they halted, and then the watchman called again : "Eleven o'clock and all's well ! " If he saw the silent riders, he took them for ghosts wending their noiseless way through the mist. Here and there they passed a window that showed a candle still burning. The dogs bayed at the mysteriously moving forms, and the riders greatly feared the people would be aroused by their barking. The critical moment, however, was yet to come. Where the main street left the town stood a little building for the receipt of customs, and here, too, it was but natural to expect a guard. That one was there soon became evident. When the hussars had approached within a few hundred paces of the spot, they heard the signal for changing the watch, followed by the sound of approaching cavalry.

"It must be a whole troop," muttered Paul, as the steps drew near.

"They are coming straight toward us," whispered Richard. "Draw your swords!"

There seemed no other course left them but to fight their way through. The advancing horsemen, however, were presently heard to turn aside and pass down another street. The danger was averted.

Richard now led his men forward in silence, and the whole squadron rode through the gateway and out of the town under the very nose of the sentry, who doubtless mistook the hussars in the darkness and mist for his own comrades. Their number must have caused him some surprise; but by the time his suspicions were communicated to the sergeant-major, two hours later, and the matter reported to the commandant an hour after that, Richard and his men were far on their way.

"Now, my lads," said Richard, when that danger was safely past, "you may light your pipes and undo the rags from your horses' hoofs."

The success of the ruse had put his men in the best of humours, and even the horses seemed to share their riders' feelings; for they struck out with as much spirit as if they had but just left their stalls. The firm highway was such a relief to the riders, after struggling through bogs and marshes, that they made good progress. At length the road led up into the mountains, and when the sun rose they saw before them, as the mist rolled away, the lofty peaks of the Carpathians, beyond which lay home and friends.

A mountain hamlet received the weary riders with friendly welcome and sympathy. Old and young, men and women, all had a kind word for them, and hastened to throw open their houses and their granaries. The horses were soon standing knee-deep in hay, while the peasants lent their aid in shoeing such as needed to be shod, and in mending broken harness. All that the good people had — and they were not people of much means — was placed before the hungry men for their refreshment.

"Ah, this will be a different kind of dinner from yesterday's," said one hussar to another, as they watched the preparations. But their exultation was premature. Before the baking and boiling were half done, the outposts came galloping in, shouting that the pursuers were in sight.

The soldiers whom the hussars had so cunningly tricked the night before were now bent on getting even with them. Infantry in wagons, and a troop of cavalry riding ahead, were making the best of their way after the fugitives. Nor, indeed, was it any remarkable achievement to overtake the weary hussars on their worn-out horses.

o

Again the order was given to mount and away. The men were disposed to grumble.

"Let us stay where we are and fight it out," they cried. "We'll either beat them back, or fall in our tracks."

Indeed, there seemed at first no choice in the matter. The cavalry was upon them in the rear, while the infantry was making a détour, in order to lie in ambush in a grove just beyond the village, where they would try to check the farther flight of the deserters. In all probability the enemy would reach the grove before the hussars, as the latter had their horses still to saddle.

Meanwhile Richard had made a hasty reconnoissance. To fight their way through the infantry in front would, he felt convinced, result in heavy loss to his men, while the cavalry in their rear would be constantly harassing them until they were entirely destroyed. Not a single hussar would live to see his home. Such a needless sacrifice was to be avoided if possible. One other way was open, — a steep path leading up the mountainside toward its snow-capped summit.

"Is there a path over the mountain, and can we get a guide to show us the way?" asked Richard, of an old shepherd.

"There is a path," he replied, "and if you wish I will show you the way until I can hand you over to another guide. You need fear no pursuit, if you choose that path, but you are likely to perish of hunger."

"We'll try it, nevertheless," returned Richard.

The men were mounted by this time, and drawn up, sword in hand. The order was given to sheath their swords and right wheel.

"Where are we going?" cried the hussars, in a storm of disapproval. "Up the mountainside? We will go to hell first!"

Richard drew his pistols. "Whoever has forgotten his oath had best commit his soul to God," said he sternly. The angry murmurs were hushed. "Those who still have faith in me will follow. I am going ahead."

The swords went rattling into their scabbards. The guide, equipped with alpenstock and climbing irons, led the way, Richard followed him, and the hussars came trailing behind, with old Paul as rear guard.

The enemy, after waiting an hour for the fugitives to make a sally from the village, pulled some very long faces when they caught sight of them, high up on the mountainside, following in single file a steep path along the face of the cliff. Never before had horse's hoof trodden that perilous path; it was so narrow that both steed and rider were in constant danger of being hurled into the mountain stream that ran foaming a hundred fathoms below. One false step or an attack of giddiness would have been fatal.

Amazement was followed by anger on the part of the pursuers. They had no desire to give chase, but, to prevent their intended victims' escape without a scratch, they discharged their rifles at them. Their pieces had a range of a thousand paces, and the target could not have been better, — dark blue uniforms against a white limestone background. The rifle-balls rebounded from the cliff, so that each one went whistling twice by the hussars' ears — as if their position had not been already sufficiently perilous.

Yet in that hour of danger the horsemen sat half asleep in their saddles, with nodding heads and drooping eyelids. Only Richard in the van and old Paul in the rear were still on the alert, and kept calling to their comrades to wake up. A turn in the path presently led the riders out of range, and there was no further cause to fear molestation. A fir grove, as sombre and still as a cathedral, received them in its shelter. Here the starving men unearthed a store of turnips that had been deposited there for feeding sheep. It was not an inviting dish to human palates ; but hunger like theirs is not squeamish, and they were only too glad to feed on the coarse provender. They wished to rest in the grove, but their guide spurred them on once more ; pleasant weather was **too** precious to be wasted in that **region,** where fog and darkness would be sure to afford them all the time they needed for repose.

Forward, then, as long as horse and rider were able to move!

In the afternoon the hussars came to a shepherd's hut, where their guide committed his charge to the care of the occupant of the little shanty, and himself returned to the village. Finding a few trusses of hay, Richard and his men bought them for their horses. But was there nothing, they asked, which might serve to stay a hungry man's stomach? The sheep were feeding below in the valley, and it was too late to go after them. There was, however, a tub of sheep's milk that had been set away to curdle for cheese; it was not an appetising drink, to be sure, but nourishing and strengthening. Each hussar received half a glassful.

As there was some moonlight that night, Richard determined to make the most of it, and the weary hussars were forced to push on. They had but just begun the really arduous part of their journey. The path led upward and was very steep. The fir trees became fewer, and in their stead began to appear juniper trees, of good, sturdy growth at first, but ever becoming smaller, until at last they were no larger than bramble bushes.

When the sun rose over the mountain-tops in front, it hung lustreless and shrouded in mist. The guide began to hint that a snow-storm was in prospect. All vegetation disappeared as they climbed higher; not even a blade of grass showed itself on the bare mountainside; no sign of man or beast or bird greeted the eye; it was all death's kingdom, a landscape of tombstones, the home of the clouds, whither no sound of herdsman's horn, or hunter's rifle, or bell of sheep or goat ever penetrated.

Toward noon, as the hussars were descending into a ravine, a dense mist began to rise from below.

" If it reaches us we shall have a long resting spell," remarked the guide to Richard. " Let us hasten down into the ravine, where there is brushwood and we can at least make a fire if the weather is bad."

The mist rose until it had quite enveloped the band of horsemen. The clouds were returning to their domain, and were asking the intruders by what right they were there. Their challenge had to be heeded, as it became thenceforth impossible to see the way. The guide proposed to go on ahead for a few hundred paces, promising to call back to the others if the path proved to be safe.

A quarter of an hour's anxious waiting followed, while the cold mist powdered every man's beard and hair with hoar frost. Still failing to hear any call from below, Richard descended a few steps and shouted to the guide. No answer. Hungry, thirsty, shivering, the hussars stood waiting.

"Follow me," commanded Richard, and he proceeded to lead his men, as good luck might guide him, down the mountain. All dismounted and led their horses after them. The fog continued to wrap them about as they descended, but at length they reached a thick growth of juniper bushes.

"We must camp here for the night," declared Richard, and bade his men kindle fires.

It was already growing dark. Possibly the sun was still shining up on the heights, but down there in the dense fog it was dark. Brushwood was at hand in plenty, so that the hussars were at least sure not to freeze. They hobbled their horses and left them. Fodder there was none to give them, but the riders themselves were no better off.

The hussars lighted their fires and gathered about them, tired nearly to death and longing for one thing above all else, — sleep. Richard gave orders that one man should remain awake at each fire to tend it ; then he wrapped himself in his cloak and lay down by his fire.

It was too much to expect any one to keep awake. The watchers thought that if they only threw on enough fuel the fires would last.

Scarcely had the sleepers had time to fly home in their dreams and greet the dear ones there, when a sudden uproar wakened them all with a start. It was the whinnying of frightened horses. The thicket had caught fire from the unguarded watch-fires, and was one sheet of flame when the men awoke.

"Up the mountain !" cried Richard, running to his horse and seeking the nearest way of escape from the spreading sea of fire that raged around him.

There was light enough now to show them the way only too clearly, and a perilous, breakneck path it was. The extremity of the danger in their rear, however, gave to men and horses an almost preternatural strength, and they accomplished in a short time an ascent that made them dizzy to look back upon. They stood there a moment, steaming with perspiration in the cold night air, and not daring to linger. They were forced to push on, if only to keep warm. There was no halting for consultation now ; every man made the best of his way forward ; if any should faint by the way they would have to lie where they fell.

Day dawned at last, — the most harrowing day of their long flight. Ice-clad peaks and fields of snow greeted the eye on every side, with nothing to guide a traveller's course but the sun in the heavens. Two days had passed since the men had tasted food. They sought to quench their thirst with lumps of snow, but only made matters worse.

One thing, however, troubled them more than hunger or thirst. Their horses were beginning to fail them, falling exhausted, one after another, in the deep snow ; and whenever one of the animals fell, its rider stood by its side, with tears in his eyes, more than half inclined to lie down too and give up the fight. But old Paul would allow no such nonsense. Alternately swearing and coaxing, and calling upon the saints, he spurred on the stragglers, helped to raise a fallen horse where help was of any avail, brought up the reserve horses to take the places of those left behind, and infused fresh courage into all by the mere force of his example.

"Not a man must be lost ! " he cried. "We shall soon be at home now."

"Yes, at home in heaven," muttered one weary hussar to another.

The men were scattered over a distance of two miles, Richard taking the lead and breaking a path through the deep snow, while Paul brought up the rear. It was almost a miracle that their strength still held out. Their clothes were frozen stiff, and their swords had become a grievous burden to them. The horses' girths flapped loosely against their sides, their shoes had fallen off, and their hoofs were torn and bruised. And no one could tell when or how or where it would all end.

One last trial was in store for the weary fugitives : in the afternoon a dense snow-storm met them in the face. Should Richard lead his men by any mischance into a ravine that offered no outlet, they would all be lost. Occasional avalanches came sliding down the steep cliffs, threatening to bury men and horses. Yet they did not quite lose heart. The terrors of their situation had not yet extinguished the spark of hope.

Evening was again approaching when Richard noted that for some time they had been descending. Before long a well-grown fir grove loomed up ahead and proved a grateful asylum to the wanderers. The wind blew through the tree-tops with the sound of some giant organ, but above its tones Richard heard what was the sweetest of music to his ears, — the sound of a woodman's axe. Human beings and human habitations were near. Taking a few of his men, the hussar captain hastened in the direction of the sound, and soon came upon a wood-chopper cutting the branches from a tree he had just felled. Richard called to him in the Moravian tongue.

"Bless the Lord!" answered the wood-chopper in Hungarian, whereupon the hussars nearly smothered him with kisses and embraces. Then they threw themselves down on their faces in the snow and gave thanks for their deliverance from danger. Yes, blessed be the name of the Lord from everlasting to everlasting!

The wood-chopper told them they were expected in the village yonder, only a short distance down the mountain. Word of their approach had already been brought by the guide, who had left them and hurried on ahead to summon help.

The snow ceased, and as the veil of clouds was drawn aside a view was given of what the hussars had come so far to see, — the fair land of Hungary.

At the base of the mountain lay a little market-town, reached by a winding road up which, with flags and music, a glad procession was now marching to welcome the home-coming hussars. Hearing the band and seeing the banners from afar, Richard and his companions fired their pistols as a signal to their slower comrades, who presently came up with them. All were there, — not a man missing. Dressing their ranks, the horsemen waited to receive the procession. What occurred when it reached them is more than the present generation of readers can be asked to picture to themselves.

A banquet had been spread for the home-coming heroes, and after partaking of it generously, the toil-worn but happy hussars, who had not slept for six nights, danced through the seventh until broad daylight.

All this is no piece of fiction, no picture of the imagination. A young hussar, now a veteran of many wars, wrote it all down in his diary as it occurred, and is to-day ready to take oath that it is every word true as here described.

CHAPTER XVII.

TIMELY AID.

MEANWHILE the Hungarian army had advanced to
meet the enemy; but being ill officered and poorly
drilled, with no experience whatever of actual fighting, it was easily routed. The Austrians had but to
sweep the highway with their twelve-pounders, and
the opposing centre gave way at once. It was a
shameful defeat: all turned tail and ran before the
enemy; and when the Congreve rockets were sent,
ricochetting, hissing, and spitting fire, to explode
among the panic-stricken fugitives, the chaos became
complete.

On such trying occasions, one man with his nerves
under control is invaluable. Ödön Baradlay was no
soldier, no born tactician, but he possessed that first
requisite of success in any calling, self-control. As
soon as he saw that the battle was going against his
countrymen, although his place was in the rear as
commissary-general, he threw himself on his horse
and made an attempt to save the day. To rally the
fugitives, demoralised as they were by the bursting of

shells on every side, was hopeless. Along the highway he saw advancing a troop of the enemy's cavalry, sweeping everything before it.

"Let us give them something to do," said he to himself, scanning the fleeing troops in quest of a few young men who might respond to his call. "Look here, boys," he shouted, "shall we let the enemy capture all our cannon without our striking a blow?"

A little knot of sturdy lads paused in their flight at this call. They were only common soldiers, but they shouted to one another: "Let us die for our country!" and therewith faced about against the cavalry that came charging down upon them.

Suddenly help appeared from an unexpected quarter: out of the acacia hedge that lined the highway such a raking fire was opened upon the cavalry that it was thrown into disorder and forced to beat a hasty retreat, leaving the road strewn with its dead and wounded. With loud huzzas there now sprang out from behind the hedge the Death's-Head Legion, its leader, the long-legged Mausmann, waving his hat and calling to Ödön: "Hurrah, patron! That's what we call barricade tactics."

Ödön welcomed the madcap student who had saluted him as "patron." The German students regarded him as their patron, because he saw to it that they received as good care as the rest of the army, and would not allow his countrymen to put any

slight upon them.   And they deserved all his kindness, the gallant lads ; resolute under fire and always
good-humoured, they were ever ready to fight and
feared neither death nor the devil, — no, nor Congreve rockets, for that matter. They knew their
foe, too, from many a sharp encounter in the past.
A hundred such lads were of untold value at a critical moment like the present.

The students and the other volunteers whom Ödön
had rallied around him amounted to about two hundred in all, — a small but determined band. When
the enemy saw that this handful of young men was
holding the cavalry in check, they caused their
rocket-battery to play upon the little band of patriots.
And the lads took it for play indeed.

"Aha, old friend!" cried Mausmann, as a rocket
came shrieking through the air.   "See, boys, the
first has stuck in the mud; up with a whiz and down
with a thud! The second there bursts in mid-air ;
the third comes nearer, but we don't care.   Here
comes the fourth; its course is straight." (Indeed,
the rocket was so well aimed that it landed in their
very midst, whereupon Mausmann stepped forward,
coolly took it by its stick, although it was spitting
fire in an alarming manner, and hurled it into the
ditch beside the road, where it exploded harmlessly ;
then he finished his rhyme.)   "It bursts at last ; too
late, too late!" The young recruits laughed aloud.

Perceiving that their rockets were effecting nothing, the enemy planned another cavalry charge, this
time sending a troop of cuirassiers to open the road.
The little company of patriots drew up, three deep,
clear across the highway, and awaited the assault.
During this pause Mausmann started the German
student song :

> *" Wer kommt dort von der Höh ?*
> *Wer kommt dort von der Höh ?*
> *Wer kommt dort von der Höh ?*
> *Sa sa, ledernen Höh —*
> *Wer kommt dort von der Höh ? "*

His comrades joined in, and then with a loud
hurrah they gave the oncoming horsemen a volley
from their rifles at twenty paces distance. Aha!
how they broke and turned tail and scampered back,
leaving their dead and wounded behind !

Then the gallant band reloaded, shouldered their
pieces, and marched back to join their comrades.
But presently the sound of approaching cavalry was
again heard on the road behind them. The horsemen
divided to right and left, hoping to surround their
foe. The latter, however, closed in about their
leader, and then faced outward, presenting a bristling
wall of bayonets on every side, like a monstrous
hedgehog ; and again their merry student song rang
out defiantly. Once more the attacking cavalry was

forced to fall back before the lively volleys of this
determined band, which seemed ignorant of the meaning of fear, and proof against all modes of assault.
Its method was to let the enemy advance until a rifle-
volley was sure to do the most execution. The
student song had many stanzas, one for each attack
from the pursuing cavalry; it was sung to the end,
and the enemy repulsed at each onset. The slightly
wounded bound up their wounds, while those who had
fared the worst were laid across their comrades' rifle-
barrels and so carried along, marking their path with
their life-blood, and ever shouting hurrahs for the
cause of liberty.

At last the cartridges ran low.

"Look here, patron," said Mausmann to Ödön,
"we have but one round of ammunition left, and
when that is gone we are lost. But there's a bridge
yonder which we can easily hold, and the cavalry
can't get through the bog to surround us. And now,
boys, swear that you'll save this last shot, and from
now on receive the enemy with your bayonets."

Thereupon the still undaunted students knelt on
the highway, and, with upraised right hands, sang
an oath from some opera chorus — perhaps it was
from "Beatrice" — resolved to play their parts well
till the ringing down of the curtain. Then they
took possession of the bridge, and were preparing to
receive the enemy's cavalry on the points of their

bayonets, when all at once the horsemen slackened their pace and seemed stricken with a sudden panic. Out from the thicket that bordered the road broke a squadron of hussars, and by a flank attack scattered the cuirassiers in all directions.

The fight was over for that day. The enemy sounded the retreat, and the Hungarians were left to go their way unmolested. The hussars turned back to the bridge, led by their captain, a tall and muscular young man with flashing eyes and a smile that played constantly about his mouth. Two of the young men on the bridge recognised that face and form. Those two were Ödön and Mausmann.

"Hurrah! Baradlay! Richard Baradlay!" cried the student, throwing his cap high in the air, and rushing to meet his old acquaintance. In the warmth of his welcome he nearly pulled the other from his horse.

Then Ödön came forward, and the two brothers, who had not met for six years, fell into each other's arms, while hussars and legionaries embraced and kissed one another, each with words of praise on his tongue for the other.

"Heaven must have sent you to us?" exclaimed Ödön. "If you hadn't come when you did, you would have been by this time the head of the family."

"God forbid!" cried Richard. "But what are you doing here? The secretary of war bade me give

P

you a good scolding for exposing your life when you
are commissary-general and your place is with the
transport wagons. You were not sent out to fight,
and you have a young wife and infant children dependent on you. Have you forgotten them, unfeel-
ing man? Just wait till I tell mother what you are
up to!" As he spoke he grew suddenly serious.
"Dear mother!" he exclaimed; "she must have foreseen this when she came to me and bade me hasten
hither to your side."

CHAPTER XVIII.

GREGORY BOKSA.

THE night after the battle Ödön and Richard passed in a neighbouring village, and both were engaged until morning in restoring such order as they could among the defeated troops.

"If we could only offer them something to eat," said Richard. "The smell of a good roast would rally the men quickly enough."

Yes, but a good roast was not to be had. The enemy had passed through that village twice, and had left very poor pickings for those that came after them. Bread was at hand, as the provision train had been saved, but meat was wanting.

"How glad we should be now to see Gregory Boksa, our ox-herd, with his fifty head of cattle!" exclaimed Ödön; and a patrol was sent out to search for the man, who, it was thought, might have found a place of safety for himself and his charge. But the search, which was continued until late in the evening, proved fruitless. At length, however, Boksa made his appearance, but without his oxen, and leading his horse behind him. Evidently he had dismounted to show how grievously lame he was. He groaned and sighed piteously as he came limping into camp, using his pole-axe for a crutch, and appearing utterly exhausted.

"Boksa, what has happened to you?" asked Ödön.

"Ah, sir," moaned the ox-driver, "you may well ask what has happened to me. A good deal has happened to me. I am all done up. I shall never again be the man I was. Oh, oh! my backbone is broken. That cursed cannon-ball! A big forty-pounder hit me."

Mausmann and his comrades burst into a loud laugh at this.

"But where is our herd of oxen?" was the question from every side.

"Ah, if I only knew! Just as the fight was beginning, I took my knife out of my boot-leg and opened my knapsack to get my bread and bacon, and have a quiet little lunch, when all at once the Germans began to blaze away at me, so that I dropped knife, bread, and bacon, and thought for sure my last hour had come. Whiz! a ball grazed by me, and it was a twenty-eight pounder, as sure as I'm alive. It was a chain-shot, too, a couple of twenty-eight pounders joined together."

"You ran away," said Ödön, interrupting the narrative, "we understand that. But where are the oxen?"

"How should I know, with cannon-balls singing about my ears so that I couldn't look around without losing my head?"

"Look here, brother," interposed Richard, addressing Ödön, "that isn't the way to handle this case. Let me try my hand. Now, you cowardly rascal, the long and short of it is, you ran away at the first shot, and left your herd in the enemy's hands. Here, corporal, fetch out the flogging-bench and give him fifty with the strap."

At these words Gregory Boksa changed his limping, broken-backed attitude and suddenly straightened up. Holding his head high and smiting his chest with his clenched fist, he burst out haughtily:

"That is more than I will submit to. My name is Gregory Boksa, nobleman; and, besides, I beg to remind the captain that the Hungarian diet has done away with flogging, even for the common people."

"All right," returned Richard; "when you have received your fifty strokes you may go and appeal to the diet. We are not legislating now."

The order was faithfully executed, poor Gregory bellowing lustily the while, after which he was obliged to return and thank the hussar officer for his lesson.

"Now, then," said Richard, "did the Germans shoot forty-pounders?"

"If you please, sir," replied Boksa humbly, "they didn't even fire a pistol at me."

"Disarm him," was the other's order, "and set him on his horse. Then let him go whither he will. A soldier who is not ashamed to run away deserves to feel the rod on that part of his body which he shows to the enemy."

Stripped of his sword and pistols and pole-axe, and with his whip hung around his neck, poor Boksa was mounted on his piebald nag and ignominiously driven out of camp.

Drawing out his pipe, he looked into the bowl, took off his cap and examined it, and then inspected his tobacco-pouch ; after which he replaced his cap, pocketed his pipe, closed his tobacco-pouch, and rode on. Was he hatching some deep scheme of revenge?

He rode back over the very road by which he had that day taken his flight, — straight toward the enemy's camp. Suddenly he was challenged in the darkness :

"Halt ! Who goes there ?"

"Oh, how you frightened me," exclaimed the ox-herd. "I am a deserter."

The sentinel ordered Boksa to wait there until the patrol came to lead him away. Soon a file-leader appeared with a common soldier and received Gregory's statement that he was a runaway from the Hungarian camp and wished to speak with the commander. He had chanced upon the encampment of a cavalry regiment, whose colonel was at the moment playing cards in his tent with some of his officers. Being told that a deserter was outside, waiting to speak with him, he ordered the man to be admitted.

The officers became interested at once in the newcomer, who appeared at the same time cowardly and haughty, angry and humble; who wore the look of a suppliant and gnashed his teeth with rage, kissed every one's hand, and swore by all the saints while he was doing it.

"Why did you desert?" asked the colonel.

"Because they had me flogged; me, whose family has been noble for seventy-seven generations. And then they took away my arms, which cannot lawfully be taken from a nobleman even for debt, and drove me out of the camp like a dog. All right! There are other people over the mountains, and Gregory Boksa can find a market for his services elsewhere."

"And in what capacity did you serve?" demanded the colonel.

"As ox-herd."

"As a non-combatant, then. Now I understand why you are so fierce."

"Oh, I can handle my man in an honest fight," answered Gregory, "but I'm a bit put out where loud shooting is going on."

The officers laughed at this naïve confession.

"Very well," said the colonel; "it so happens that we need a man now who can manage oxen. We have captured a herd from the enemy, and you shall have the care of it."

At these words Gregory Boksa seized the colonel's hand and kissed it. "Ah, sir," he cried, "may the saints bless you! You shall find me a faithful servant, who will go through fire and water to serve you. I'll soon show you what an artist I am in my calling."

Being introduced to the corporal in charge, Boksa offered, with the zeal of one newly entering upon a responsible position, to take up his quarters for the night among his oxen, with his good horse at his side. Surely, when one is hired to discharge certain duties he must discharge them to the best of his ability. He had a good thick cloak to wrap himself in, and, besides, he could smoke if he chose, out there in the open air, — a solace that would be denied him if he passed the night in the stable.

Accordingly the zealous ox-herd was given permission to lie down with his oxen if he wished. Gregory Boksa first ascertained the direction of the wind, that he might choose his position with the herd to leeward ; and after rehearsing his grievances once more to the adjutant and the corporal and as many others as would listen to him, he wrapped himself in his mantle and bade them all good night. They laughed heartily at the poor man, even while they gave him their assurances of sympathy ; but they

did not forget to keep a watchful eye on his movements through it all.

His actions, however, were not of the sort to
arouse suspicion. First he drew out his pipe and
opened his tobacco-pouch; then he removed his hat.
Perhaps he was wont to pray before going to sleep;
and very likely, too, he found it easier to go to sleep
with his pipe in his mouth. After filling and lighting
that trusty companion of his meditations, he lay down
on his stomach — he had good and sufficient reasons
for not lying on his back — and puffed away in
apparent content. Then, to pass away the time, he
took his knife and began to scrape off the accu-
mulated dirt and grease from the edge of his felt hat,
gathering the scrapings together in the palm of his
hand. The hat was old and dilapidated; it had
weathered many a storm, was full of holes, and was
so stained with sweat and dust and rain that its
original colour had become a matter of pure con-
jecture. Unquestionably it stood in sad need of
the cleaning which its owner now undertook to perform.

When the ox-herd had collected a little heap of
scrapings in the hollow of his hand, he raised the
lid of his pipe and emptied them on the burning
tobacco, whereupon such a penetrating and offensive odour arose as had never before saluted the
nose of man or beast. What the connection may be

between the nervous system of an ox and an odour of this sort, neither Oken nor Cuvier has explained; but all cattle-raisers and ox-herds know that, after inhaling these pungent fumes, an ox ceases to be an ox and becomes a wild animal. It is as if he were reduced to his original untamed condition: he falls into a rage, breaks away, tries to toss on his horns every one who opposes him, runs down and tramples upon all in his path, and, in short, becomes utterly unmanageable.

As soon as the leader of the herd scented the powerful stench which Boksa had raised, he sprang up from his bed on the ground, tossed his head, and sniffed the breeze. A fresh puff of smoke from Gregory's pipe made the now excited animal shake his head till the bell he wore around his neck rang aloud. Then he lashed his sides with his tail and gave a short, hoarse bellow like that of a wild bull. Next he began to leap and plunge and throw his head this way and that, whereupon all the rest of the herd sprang up in great excitement. In a state of evident alarm and panic, the oxen all backed away from the quarter whence came the offensive odour, their horns lowered as if in expectation of attack from some unseen enemy. The consequence of this retreat in a body was that the hedge was broken down — it could not have withstood the strain even had it been of iron — and the whole herd went dashing away over the meadow beyond in the wildest confusion.

At the sound of this outbreak, officers, orderlies, and corporals came running to the scene and called upon Gregory to know what it all meant. It needed no lengthy explanation on his part, however, to show that the herd was running away. It did no good to ply the whip or belabour the animals with the flat of one's sword : they crowded the sentinels to one side, ran over the watch-fires, and broke completely through the lines, with loud bellowing and a deafening thunder of hoofs on the hollow ground. Why they behaved so was a mystery to all. Surely Gregory Boksa had done nothing whatever to them ; he could not have aroused them to such a mad stampede. He had been lying there on his stomach, quietly smoking, all the while.

" What is going on here ? What does this mean ? " cried the colonel, approaching the newly appointed ox-herd.

The latter removed his pipe and put it away in his pocket, as is becoming when a man is addressed by his superiors, and then, with an air of profound wisdom, proceeded to explain matters. " The oxen have seen a vision, sir," said he.

" A vision ? " repeated the colonel, puzzled.

" Yes, sir ; that is no uncommon occurrence. Cattle-dealers and butchers know very well what that means, but the ox-herd understands it best of all. You see, the ox dreams just like a human being, and when he has a vision in his sleep he goes mad and runs till he is so tired he can't run another step. Then comes the gathering of the frightened animals together again and driving them back. But you leave that to me : I understand the business. Once let me get after them on my white-faced horse with my long whip, and I'll have every one of them back again in no time."

"Make haste about it then," said the colonel; "for they might stray away out of your reach. And there is one of the sentinels yonder; he shall mount and go with you."

Painfully and with many groans Gregory Boksa climbed into his saddle; but once seated and with his feet in the stirrups, he seemed to have grown there. "Now, Colonel," he cried, "just watch and see how soon I'll be back again."

The officer failed to note the cunning and ironical tone in which these words were uttered, and which was very different from the ox-herd's earlier manner of speech.

With a loud crack of his whip and a goat-like spring of his piebald steed, Boksa was over the hedge and after the vanishing herd, the dragoon galloping after him. Gregory knew that his long-lashed whip was of more use just then than fifty swords. Three cavalrymen could not, to save their lives, catch an ox that had once gone wild. The task before the ox-herd was like a Spanish bull-fight of gigantic proportions ; but as often as he cracked his whip, marvellous results were sure to follow. With incredible skill he soon had the fifty runaway cattle together. Turning his horse now in this direction, now in that, he gathered the animals, one by one, about their leader. The dragoon meanwhile followed close at his heels, shouting and swearing at the herd as he rode.

When at length the cattle were gathered into one compact body, Boksa suddenly spurred his horse into their very midst and delivered two stinging blows with his wire-tipped whip-lash on the leader's back, which of course made the animal run all the faster. At this the dragoon began to suspect that Gregory was up to mischief, and he called out to know why he did not turn the herd back toward the camp. But he appealed to deaf ears. All at once Boksa refused to understand a word of German, and the dragoon's command of Hungarian did not extend beyond a few oaths.

" *Teremtette !* [1] Don't chase the oxen like that ! " But Gregory was determined not to hear him. " Hold on, *betyár,* [2] or it'll be the worse for you." The ox-herd, however, only lashed his animals the more furiously. " If you can't hear me when I call,"

---

[1] *Teremtette*, zooks !   [2] *Betyár*, stupid bumpkin.

shouted the dragoon, "perhaps you'll listen to this."
And drawing one of his pistols, he discharged it at
the unruly ox-driver.

Gregory looked around as the ball whistled by his
head. "Just see the booby!" he shouted tauntingly; "couldn't hit the side of a barn! Now let's
have the other."

The soldier fired his second pistol, with no better
success.

"Now then, try your sword!" challenged Gregory
Boksa, half turning in his saddle, and bidding the
other defiance. And yet he himself was entirely
defenceless except for his ox-whip.

The dragoon was in deadly earnest. Drawing his
sword, he charged upon the ox-driver at full tilt.
The latter swung his whip and aimed a cut as if at
his pursuer's left cheek. The dragoon parried on the
left with his sword and received a stinging blow on
his right cheek. Then Gregory Boksa aimed his
whip as if at the soldier's right ear, and when the
dragoon parried on that side he got another sharp
cut, this time on his left cheek. A cursed weapon
to deal with, that aimed in one direction and hit in
another! The dragoon swore in German and Hungarian together.

A third time the ox-herd made his whip-lash
whistle through the air, and this time the sharp wire
on the end flew straight at the nostrils of the soldier's

horse. The animal, stung on this very tender spot, reared and pirouetted, and finally, with a leap to one side, threw its rider.

Gregory Boksa, paying no further heed to the dragoon, galloped after his runaway herd, and guided it in the right direction. It was dark, and a thick mist lay over the fields. He was free to go whithersoever he chose.

The two Baradlay brothers, meanwhile, were busy restoring order in their camp, and it was toward morning when Ödön sought his couch. Richard laid his head on the table before him; he could sleep very well so. Suddenly, as the day was beginning to dawn, a trampling of many hoofs and the cracking of a whip awoke the sleepers. Richard ran to the window and beheld Gregory just dismounting from his horse, and surrounded by his herd of oxen. The sweat ran from the animals' panting sides, and their quivering nostrils breathed forth clouds of steam. They saw no more visions; they were tame, submissive, obedient subjects.

Richard and Ödön hastened out. Gregory Boksa drew himself up and gave the military salute.

"Gregory Boksa, you are a man of the right sort!" exclaimed Richard, clapping him on the shoulder. "So the herd is all here, is it?"

"The whole fifty head, sir."

"Aha! Now all respect to you. Paul, hand him

the flask and let him drink to his very good health."

"Pardon me," said Gregory, waving aside the offered flask with a serious air; "first, I have certain matters to attend to." Then, turning to Richard, "Yesterday I swore that the fifty lashes should be paid for, and now I have come to settle the score. There is the payment, — fifty for fifty. Now, Captain, have the goodness to give me a receipt, stating that the fifty strokes with the strap are 'null and void.'"

"What do you want of such a receipt, Boksa?" asked Richard.

"I want it as a proof that the fifty I received yesterday don't count; so that when any one brings them up against me I can contradict him, and show him my evidence in black and white."

"All right, Boksa, you shall have it." And Richard went back to his room, took pen, ink, and paper, and drew up a certificate, stating that the fifty lashes administered to Gregory Boksa were thereby declared to be null, void, and of no validity. The words "null, void, and of no validity" gave Gregory no little comfort, as well as the fact that the document was countersigned by Ödön Baradlay. The ox-herd stuck the certificate into the pocket of his dolman with much satisfaction, and received back his sword, pistols, and pole-axe.

"Now then, where is the flask?" said he.

Old Paul handed him the bottle, and he did not put it down till he had drained the last drop.

"And now tell me," said Richard, "how you managed to get the oxen back.

Gregory Boksa shrugged his shoulders, tightened his belt, drew down one corner of his mouth, wrinkled his nose, raised his eyebrows, and finally thus delivered himself over one shoulder: "Well, you see, I went to the German colonel and asked him kindly to let me have my cattle back again. The German is a good fellow, and, without wasting words over the matter, he gave me the animals all back, and one or two extra, with his compliments and best wishes to Captain Baradlay."

More than this was not to be got from Gregory Boksa. The loud-mouthed braggart, who was never tired of rehearsing deeds which he had not performed, took a fancy, now that he had actually carried through a genuine bit of daring, to keep as still as a mouse about it; and no one ever heard from him the smallest account of how he passed that night.

Q

CHAPTER XIX.

IN THE ROYAL FOREST.

The Royal Forest lies on the left bank of the Rákos, near Isaszeg. Three highroads lead through it, and all three unite at Isaszeg, which thus forms the gateway to Pest.

The Hungarian army was bent on reaching Pest, and it was for this that it was now fighting. The enemy held the forest, and for six hours the Hungarian forces had been fighting their way through, when both sides prepared for a last desperate struggle.

The Austrians planned to strike a decisive blow against their opponents' centre. Sixteen troops of light cavalry, lancers, and dragoons, two cuirassier regiments, eight batteries of cannon, and two mortar batteries crossed the Rákos above Isaszeg and descended like an avalanche on the Hungarian centre. The Hungarians, drawn up in close order, occupied that circular space which even now shows the traces of having once been trampled by many feet. There were three thousand hussars in a body. Against them the enemy levelled their field-batteries, planting

them in the spaces between the different divisions of
their troops and on the wings, and opened a murder-
ous fire. There was but one way to meet this fire,
and that was to make a sudden cavalry charge which
should throw the enemy's ranks into confusion and
make it impossible to distinguish between friend and
foe. Thus the artillerists would be compelled to
desist. This plan was executed. Over the whole
battle-field the trumpets sounded the charge. The
earth trembled under the mighty shock, and the
forest rang with the battle-cry, in which was presently
mingled the clashing of steel, as thousands of swords
met in deadly strife. A cloud of dust veiled the
scene for a space, and when it cleared one might
have witnessed the living enactment of the hero-epics
of old, — six or seven thousand knights indiscrimi-
nately mingled, and every man seeking his foe. Horses
were rearing and snorting, flashing swords rang blade
against blade, red shakos, shining helmets, and four-
cornered caps were densely crowded in one swaying,
surging, struggling mass.

In the stress of the conflict, two leaders who towered
by a head above their fellows suddenly caught sight
of each other. One was Richard Baradlay, the other
Otto Palvicz. It was like the meeting of two lightning flashes from two thunder-clouds. They broke
through the mass of fighting warriors about them and
pushed their way toward each other. The horsemen

opened a lane through their ranks for the two champions, as if recognising that here was the heaven-ordained decision. The swords of these two mighty warriors should decide the issue; let them fight it out.

They fell on each other, neither of them taking thought to parry his opponent's blow, but each striking at one and the same instant with all the strength of his arm and the fury of his passion. Rising in their stirrups and swinging aloft their swords, they aimed each at the other's head. Like two flashes of lightning, both blades descended at once, and both warriors fell in the same moment from their horses. Truly, it was a well-aimed stroke that felled Richard Baradlay, and had he not borne the charmed life of the heroes of the Iliad and the Niebelungenlied, that day had been his last on earth. Otto Palvicz's sword had cleft his opponent's shako, cutting through the metal crown; but, as often happens in such strokes, the blade was so turned in its course that the flat of the sword and not the edge spent its force on the hussar captain's head. Yet the fearful blow was even thus enough to stun Richard, and throw him unconscious to the ground.

His own stroke, however, descending like a thunderbolt from heaven, was more effective. Cleaving the helmet of the cuirassier major, it left a gaping wound on his skull.

No sooner had the two champions fallen than there followed a furious conflict over their bodies, each side striving to rescue its fallen hero. Old Paul, who had spurred his horse after his master, sprang from his saddle and threw himself on Richard's body. The hoofs of trampling steeds soon stamped the life out of the faithful servant, but he had succeeded in saving the one being in this world whom he loved. With unselfish affection, he had shielded his dear master and cheerfully laid down his life for him.

At that moment the sound as of an approaching army fell on the ear. What did it mean? The woods were ringing with the battle-cry, "*Éljen a haza!*"[1] The Hungarian reserve corps had arrived and was pushing to the front. Its batteries opened fire on the enemy, and the militia battalions drove the foe out of the woods. The battle was at last decided. The Austrian trumpeters sounded the retreat, and the battle-field was left deserted, except for the dead and the wounded. When the Hungarians sent out to gather them up, Otto Palvicz was found to be still alive.

[1] Long live our country!

CHAPTER XX.

THE DYING SOLDIER'S BEQUEST.

IT was dark when Richard recovered consciousness. At first the gloom seemed to him like something dense and heavy pressing against his head, and when he raised his hand he was surprised to find its movement unimpeded by this thick, black substance.

"Oho!" he cried, discovering at length that his tongue was movable.

At his call a door opened and Mausmann's face looked in, lighted by a lantern which he held in his hand.

"Well, are you awake at last?" asked the student, still wearing his droll expression.

"Am I really alive?" asked the other.

"Hardly a scratch on you," was the cheerful reply. "You were only a transient guest in the other world."

"But where am I now?"

"In the mill by the Rákos."

"Did we win the fight?" The questioner suddenly recalled the events of the day just passed.

"Did we win, you ask. Isaszeg is ours, and the victory is complete."

At this Richard sprang to his feet.

"That's right!" cried Mausmann; "there's nothing the matter with you, — a lump on your head, and a three-inch *solutio continuitatis* of the skin, that's all."

"And what of Otto Palvicz?"

"Ah, you handled him rather roughly. He is here too in the miller's house, and the staff physician has charge of his case. His wound is thought to be mortal, and he himself is prepared for the worst. His first words to me, when I went to him, were, 'How is Baradlay?' And when I told him you were out of danger, he asked me to take you to him, as he had something important to say to you."

"If he wishes to see me, so much the better," re-joined Richard. "I should have felt bound in any case to visit my wounded opponent. Let us go to him now."

Otto Palvicz lay in a small room in the miller's dwelling. Seeing Richard Baradlay enter, he tried to sit up, and requested that something be put under his head to raise it. Then he extended his hand to his visitor.

"Good evening, comrade," said he. "How goes it? You see I'm done for this time. But don't take it to heart. It wasn't your sword that did the mischief. I have a tough skull of my own, and it has stood many a good whack. The good-for-nothing horses used me up with their hoofs. There must be something wrong inside me, and I shall die of it. You are not to blame; don't be at all concerned. We gave each other one apiece, and we are quits. I have settled my accounts for this life, but one debt remains." He grasped Richard's hand with feverish energy and added, "Comrade, I have a child that to-morrow will be fatherless." A flush overspread the dying man's face. "I will tell you the whole story. My time is short. I must die, and I can leave my secret only to a noble-hearted man who will know how to honour and guard it. I was your enemy, but now I am good friends with everybody. You have got the better of me, and are left to receive your old enemy's bequest; it is your duty to accept it."

"I accept it," said Richard.

"I knew you would, and so I sent for you. I have a son whom I have never seen, and never shall see. His mother is a high-born lady; you will find her name in the papers that are in my pocketbook. She was beautiful, but heartless. I was a young lieutenant when we first met. We were both thought-less and self-willed. My father was alive then, and he would not consent to our marriage, although it would have atoned for the indiscretion of an unguarded hour. Well, it can't be helped now. Yet she needn't

have torn a piece of her heart out, and thrown it into
the gutter. She, my wife before God and by the laws
of nature, went on a journey with her mother and
came back again as a maiden. I learned only that
the hapless being sent into a world where there are
already too many of its kind, was a boy. What
became of him, I did not find out at the time. Later
I won for myself a good station in my military career,
my father died, and I was independent ; and, by heaven,
I would have married the woman if she could only
have told me where my child was. She besieged me
with letters, she begged for an interview, she used every
entreaty ; but to each of her letters I only replied :
'First find my child.' I was cruel to her. She could
have married more than once ; suitors were about her
in plenty. 'I forbid you to marry,' I wrote to her.
'Then marry me yourself,' she answered. 'First find
my child,' I repeated. I tortured her, but she had no
heart to feel the infliction very keenly. She said she
didn't know what had become of the child. She had
not tried to find it ; nay, she had taken the utmost
pains to destroy all traces that could lead to its dis-
covery, either by herself or by another. But, nevertheless, I found the clue. I spent years in the search.
I came upon one little baby footstep after another, —
here a nurse, there a scrap of writing, in another place
a child's hood, and finally the end of the search seemed
at hand. But right there I am stopped ; I must die."

The rough man's breast heaved with a deep sigh. The rude exterior covered a tender heart. Richard listened attentively to every word.

"Comrade," said the dying soldier, "give me your hand, and promise that you will do the errand I can no longer execute."

Richard gave his hand.

"In my pocketbook you will find papers telling where the persons are who will help you to find the boy. He was, at last accounts, in the care of a peddler woman in Pest. I learned this from a Vienna huckster. But I failed to find the woman in Pest, as she had removed to Debreczen. I could not follow her, but I learned that she had sent the child to a peasant woman in the country. Where? She alone can tell. Yet I learned this much from a girl that lived with her, — that the peasant woman into whose care the boy was given, and who made a business of taking such waifs, was often at the peddler woman's house, and complained that she didn't receive enough money to pay for the child's board. The woman lives poorly, I was told, and the boy goes hungry and in rags."

The speaker paused a moment, and his eyes filled with tears.

"But it is a pretty child," he resumed. "The peasant woman brought the little fellow to town with her now and then, to prove that he was alive; he can always be identified by a mole in the shape of a blackberry on his breast. The peddler, out of pity and fondness for the child, used to pay the woman a little money — so I was told — and in that way the poor boy was kept alive. The mother has long ago forgotten him. Comrade, I shall hear the child's cries even after I am under the sod."

"Don't worry about him," said Richard, "he shall not cry."

"You'll find him, won't you? And there is money in my pocketbook to support him until he grows up."

"I will hunt up the boy and take him under my care" promised the other.

"Among my papers," continued the other, "you will find a formal authorisation, entitling the child to bear my name. Yet he is never to know who I was. Tell him his father was a poor soldier, and have him learn an honest trade, Richard."

"You may rely on me, comrade Otto; I promise you to take care of the boy as if he were my own brother's child."

A smile of satisfaction and relief lighted up the dying man's face.

"And comrade," he added, "this secret that I am confiding to you is a woman's secret. Promise me, on your honour, that you will never betray that woman. Not even to my son are you to tell the

mother's name. She is not a good woman, but let
her shame be buried in my grave."

Richard gave his promise in a voice that testified
how deeply he was moved. The pale face before him
grew yet paler, and ere many minutes had passed
the eyes that looked into his became glazed and fixed ;
the wounded soldier had ceased to breathe.

CHAPTER XXI.

SUNLIGHT AND MOONLIGHT.

THE poplar trees on Körös Island are clothing themselves with green, while yellow and blue flowers dot the turf. The whole island is a veritable little paradise. It forms the summer residence of a family of wealth and taste. On the broad veranda, which is shaded from the morning sun by a damask awning, stands a cradle hung with dainty white curtains; and in the cradle sleeps a little baby. In a willow chair at the foot of the cradle sits the mother, in a white, lace-trimmed wrapper, her hair falling in natural curls over her shoulders and bosom. A young man sits before an easel opposite the lady, and paints her miniature, while at the other end of the veranda a three-year-old boy is engaged in coaxing a big New-foundland dog to serve as pony to his little master.

This young mother and these children are Ödön Baradlay's wife and children, and the young man is his brother Jenö. Without Jenö to bear her company, the young wife might lose her reason, thinking of her absent husband, imagining his perils, and waiting weeks for any news from him. Jenö knows how to dispel her fears: for every anxiety he has an antidote, and when all else fails he rides to the next town and brings back cheering tidings — in which, alas, there may be but few words of truth.

The young artist is not satisfied with his picture. He has a decided artistic bent and talks of going to Rome to study; but this likeness that he is now trying to paint baffles him. It seems to lack something; although the features are correctly drawn, the whole has a strange and unnatural look.

"Béla, come here, little nephew."

The boy left the Newfoundland dog and ran to his uncle.

"Look here, look at this picture and tell me who it is."

The little fellow stared a moment at the painting with his great blue eyes. "A pretty lady," he answered.

"Don't you know your mamma, Béla?" asked the artist.

"My mamma doesn't look like that," declared the boy, and ran back to his four-footed playmate.

"The likeness is good," said Aranka encouragingly; "I am sure it is."

"But I am sure it is not," protested Jenö, "and the fault is yours. When you sit to me you are all the time worrying about Ödön, and that produces exactly the expression I wish to avoid. We want to surprise him with the picture, and he mustn't see you looking so anxious and sad."

"But how can I help it ? "

Alas, what tireless efforts the young man had put forth to cheer up his sister-in-law ! How carefully he had hidden his own anxious forebodings and predicted an early triumph for the cause of freedom, when his own heavy heart told him it could not be.

A faint cry from the wee mite of humanity in the cradle diverted the mother's attention, and as she bent over her baby and its cry turned to a laugh, the young artist caught at last on her face the expression he had been waiting for,— the tender, happy look of a fond mother.

In the castle at Nemesdomb the moon was shining brightly through the windows. It fell on the family portraits, one after another, and they seemed to step from their frames like pale ghosts. Brightest and clearest among them all was the likeness of the man with the heart of stone.

Back and forth glided a woman's form clad in white. One might have thought a marble statue from the family vault had left its pedestal to join the weird assembly in the portrait gallery. The stillness of the night was broken from time to time by a sigh or a groan or a stifled cry of pain. What ghostly voices were those that disturbed the quiet of that moonlit scene?

The whole Baradlay castle had been turned into a hospital by its mistress and opened to the warriors wounded in the struggle for freedom; and it was these poor soldiers whose cries of pain now broke the stillness of the night. Two physicians were in attendance; the library was turned into a pharmacy and the great hall into a surgeon's operating-room, while the baroness and her women spent their days picking lint and preparing compresses.

Standing in the moonlight before her dead husband's portrait, the widow spoke with him. "No," said she firmly, "you shall not frighten me away. I will meet you face to face. You say to me: 'All this is your work!' I do not deny it. These groans and sighs allow neither you nor me to sleep. But you know well enough that bloodshed and suffering were inevitable; that this cup of bitterness was, sooner or later, to be drained to the bottom; that whoever would enjoy eternal life must first suffer death. You ask me what I have done with your sons. The exact contrary to what you bade me do. Two of them are fighting for their country; one of the two is wounded, and I may hear of his death any day. But I repent not of what I have done. I await what destiny has in store for us, and if I am to lose all my sons, so be it! It is better to suffer defeat in a righteous cause than to triumph in an unrighteous one."

She left the portrait and sought her own apartment, and the moonlight crept on and left the haughty face on the wall in darkness.

R

CHAPTER XXII.

A WOMAN'S HATRED.

In the Plankenhorst house another of those confidential interviews was being held in which Sister Remigia and her pupil were wont to take part.

Prince Windischgrätz's latest despatches had brought news of a decisive engagement in the Royal Forest near Isaszeg. At seven o'clock in the evening the ban [1] had been on the point of dealing the Hungarians a final crushing blow, and the commander-in-chief had been assured he might go to sleep with no anxiety as to the issue. It was not until seven in the morning that he was awakened by the ban himself with the announcement that he had abandoned the field to the enemy. Despatches to that effect were immediately sent to Vienna.

Baroness Plankenhorst and her daughter, with Sister Remigia and Edith, sat talking over the battle of Isaszeg and the supposed victory of the Austrians. Three of the ladies were in the best of humours. In

[1] The victory of Croatia.

the midst of their lively discussion there came a knock at the door and Rideghváry entered. Both of the Plankenhorst ladies hastened to meet him, greeted him with loud congratulations, and seated him in an armchair. Then for the first time they noticed how pale he looked.

"What news from the front?" asked the baroness eagerly.

"Bad news," he replied; "we have lost the battle of Isaszeg."

"Impossible!" exclaimed Antoinette.

"Yes, it is true," declared the other.

"But why are you so certain of it?" asked Alfonsine. "People are so easily deceived by false rumours."

Rideghváry threw a searching glance at the speaker. "It is more than a rumour, Miss Alfonsine," said he with emphasis. "What I tell you is the truth. The messenger who brought the news was on the spot when Otto Palvicz fell."

The colour suddenly faded from the young lady's cheeks.

"Otto Palvicz?" repeated Sister Remigia. No one else uttered the name.

"Yes," returned Rideghváry, "the courier who was despatched to us was an eye-witness of the encounter between Otto Palvicz and Richard Baradlay. They aimed their swords at each other's heads both at the same time, and both fell at the same instant from their horses."

There were now two pale faces turned anxiously toward the speaker, who continued with cruel deliberation :

"Baradlay still lives ; Otto Palvicz is dead."

Edith sank back with a sigh of relief and folded her hands as one who gives thanks in silence, while Alfonsine, her features convulsed with rage and despair, sprang up from her chair and stood looking down wildly upon the speaker. Her mother turned to her in alarm. Was she about to betray her carefully guarded secret ? But the girl cared little then what she said or who heard her.

"Cursed be he who killed Otto Palvicz !" she exclaimed, with an ungovernable outburst of passion ; and then, overcome by her feelings, she sank down on the sofa, sobbing violently. "Oh, my dear Otto !" she moaned, and then, turning again to Rideghváry : "There is no one in this city or in the whole world that can hate better than you and I. You know all : you have seen me and heard me. Is there any retribution in this world ? "

"Yes," answered Rideghváry.

"Find it for me, even if hell itself has to be searched for it. Do you understand me ? "

"We both understand each other," was the quiet reply.

" And if at any time your hatred slumbers or your zeal slackens, come to me."

" Never fear," returned Rideghváry; we shall see ourselves revenged in good time — though the heavens fall. We will turn all Hungary into such a scene of mourning as will live in the memory of three generations. For the next ten years black shall be the fashionable colour to wear. I hate my country, every blade of grass that grows in its soil, every infant at its mother's breast. And now you know me as I know you. Whenever we have need of each other's aid, we shall not fail to lend it."

So saying, he took his hat and departed without bowing to any one in the room.

Sister Remigia, as in duty bound, sought to administer spiritual consolation and advice to Alfonsine. " Throw yourself in your affliction on Heaven's mercy," said she with unction, "and God will not fail to strengthen and console you."

Alfonsine turned upon her with a wild look. " I ask nothing of Heaven's mercy," she retorted; " I have ceased to pray."

The nun folded her hands piously and sought to soothe the passionate young woman. " Remember," she urged, " that you are still a Christian."

" I am a Christian no longer," returned the other. " I am a woman no longer. Just as there are creatures on earth who cease to be women, call them-

selves nuns, and do nothing but pray, so there are
others that cease to be women and do nothing but
curse — or worse if they can."

Sister Remigia, shocked by these impious words,
which it was sacrilege even to listen to, gathered up
her cloak and hastened to depart, motioning to Edith
to follow. But Alfonsine barred the young girl's
way and held her back.

"You are not to return to the convent," said she ;
"you will stay here with us."

The pious nun did not stop to remonstrate. She
was only too glad to escape from the house.

"Do you know why I have kept you ?" asked
Alfonsine, when the other had gone. "I have kept
you in order that I may whisper in your ear every
night, when you lie down to sleep : 'I will kill him.
The man you love has murdered the man whom I
love, and the murderer must die.' You shall taste
the despair that embitters my heart. You shall not
be happy while I am miserable."

She threw herself into an armchair, weeping pas-
sionately, and Edith sought her old room.

CHAPTER XXIII.

A DUEL BETWEEN BROTHERS.

A WHOLE nation's gaze was turned toward the fortress of Buda. There it stood, weak when it came to self-defence, yet capable of working fearful destruction in case of attack. From the summits of the surrounding mountains one could overlook Buda and examine its interior as if it had been an open book. Old brick walls formed its sole fortifications, with no outworks of any sort.

Wherein, then, lay its mysterious strength? In the fact that Pest lay outstretched at its feet, and for every cannon-ball directed against the fortress it could retaliate with a deadly shower of fire and iron. The enemy on the hill said to his foe across the river: "If you draw your sword against me I will slay your wife and daughters and the infant in its cradle." Nevertheless the sword was drawn.

For the fiery and impetuous, nothing tries the patience more than the forced inactivity of a siege, — the sitting down before a blank wall from behind which the enemy sticks out his tongue and laughs in derision. Before three days had passed, nine-tenths of the besieging army had become fretful with impatience. The men were eager to storm the enemy's stronghold on all sides. Even in the council of war the spirit of impatience was rife and the commanding general was urged to order an assault. Violent scenes were enacted, in which the best friends fell to quarrelling. All were divided between two parties, the hot-headed and the cool-headed. Thus it came about that the two Baradlay brothers, Ödön and Richard, found themselves opposed to each other in the council, and on the fourth day of the siege they went so far as to exchange hot and angry words.

"We must bring the siege to an end," declared the younger brother, vehemently.

"And I say," rejoined the elder, "that we have but just begun it and must wait for our heavier guns before we can think of making an assault. Otherwise we shall provoke a deadly fire on Pest, and all to no purpose."

"What is Pest to us in this crisis?" cried Richard. "Ten years ago the great flood destroyed the city, and we rebuilt it. Let the enemy burn it down; in ten years it will have risen from its ashes, more beautiful than ever."

"Yet even at that fearful sacrifice are we at all sure that we can take the fortress? Can we scale its heights in the face of the enemy's fire?"

"Yes. A subterranean channel, constructed by the Turks, runs from Buda down to the river. Through this a company of infantry could make its way into the fort while a hot attack was maintained from without."

"I have studied the situation, too," returned Ödön, "and I have learned positively that the upper end of the subterranean passage is in ruins; but even if it were not, and a company of our men succeeded in effecting an entrance, would they not, in all probability, be cut down before they could open the gates to us or we could join them?"

"Do you, then, place no confidence whatever in the courage and determination of our soldiers?" asked the other.

"On the contrary," was the reply; "but even courage and determination cannot prevail against such overwhelming odds."

Richard's eyes flashed fire. He was in that tense and irritated condition in which a man feels that he must utter a sharp retort or burst with passion. "You say that," he exclaimed hotly, "because, like all civilians, you are a coward at heart."

No sooner were the words out of his mouth than he regretted them. Ödön turned pale. "No man ever before applied that term to me," said he, in a low but firm tone, regarding his brother steadily, "nor shall you do so with impunity."

This scene was suddenly interrupted by a twelve-pound cannon-ball which burst through the west wall of the room and went out through the opposite side. A second shot struck the roof, and then a bomb landed in the courtyard and exploded.

"There is treason abroad!" cried the members of the council, springing to their feet. "Some one has betrayed our headquarters to the enemy, and we are being fired upon."

"We can't stay here a moment longer, that's certain," said the commanding officer, and he prepared to leave the room.

Richard looked at his brother, who alone kept his seat at the table, a pen in his hand, and gave no sign of leaving his chair, despite the crashing of the enemy's shots. The younger brother was irritated at what seemed to him ostentatious recklessness; and he was, besides, touched with another feeling toward his elder brother.

"Come, old man," said he, "I know well enough you have nerve for anything; but don't stay here now that all the rest of us are leaving."

"I am sitting here," replied the other calmly, "because I am secretary of the council, and I am waiting to record the motion to adjourn, whenever it shall be made."

"He is right," exclaimed the others; "we must adjourn the meeting in due form."

Accordingly all resumed their places around the table, while cannon-balls continued to strike the building, and a formal vote was taken on the motion to adjourn. It was carried unanimously, and all hurried out of the room except Ödön, who lingered behind to complete his minutes. Richard, too, remained at the door until his brother was ready to go.

"Come, hurry up!" he urged; "every one knows you are a man of courage. Coward is the last word to apply to you."

Ödön, however, folded his papers deliberately. "On that point I shall have something to say to you later," said he calmly, freeing his arm from his brother's touch as he walked out.

"Surely you are not going to challenge me to a duel?" exclaimed Richard.

"You will soon see," replied the other, turning proudly away.

The order for a general assault had been given. At midnight of the 21st of May, a sham attack was to be made against the bastions, after which the troops were to retire and remain quiet until three o'clock in the morning. Then, while the enemy were counting confidently on being left undisturbed for another day, a vigorous assault was to be undertaken in earnest, with scaling-ladders and bayonets.

The hardest part would fall to those who should

charge over the crumbling masonry where breaches had been effected, or mount the tall scaling-ladders under a deadly fire from above. For these most dangerous tasks the bravest and most experienced battalions were selected, while volunteers were called for from the whole army to join them. The honour of being among the first to scale the hostile ramparts was eagerly sought by hundreds of brave men.

On the evening preceding the assault, Ödön Barad-lay sought his brother. Since their recent encounter in the council-chamber they had not met, and their relations were felt to be somewhat strained. Richard was delighted to see his brother; he acknowledged in his heart that the other showed great generosity in thus making the first advances, and he gave him a very cordial reception. Ödön's bearing, however, was as calm and undemonstrative as usual. He was dressed in the uniform of the national guard.

"So to-morrow is the decisive day," he remarked as he entered.

"Yes," answered the other; "a sham attack to-night at twelve, and a general assault just before dawn."

"Is your watch right?" asked Ödön.

"Oh, I don't pay much attention to the time," was the answer, in a careless tone; "when the artillery gives the signal I know the dance is about to begin."

" You are not well-informed," rejoined Ödön. " Half an hour before the first cannon-shot, the volunteers from the third army-corps who are to attack the great bastion must be ready to start, and also those from the second army-corps who are to scale the wall of the castle garden. So it will be well for you to set your watch by mine, which agrees with the general's."

"Very well, I'll do it." Richard still maintained a certain condescending superiority in his manner toward his brother, as is customary in the bearing of seasoned soldiers toward civilians, however greatly they may esteem the latter.

" And now please listen to what I have to say," continued Ödön, with his usual calm. " You have allowed yourself to use certain words in addressing me which I cannot repeat even between ourselves."

"What do you mean?" interposed the other. " You surely don't think of calling me out?"

"That is my intention," replied the elder brother composedly. " I challenge you to the most desperate duel ever fought between two men, to the only duel that brothers can engage in who love each other, and yet cannot be reconciled by peaceful means. You have joined the volunteers who are to storm the castle garden at the point of the bayonet; I am enrolled among those whose task it will be to carry the main bastion by scaling-ladders. When the first cannon-shot is fired our duel will begin, and he who first mounts the enemy's fortifications will have obtained satisfaction from the other."

Richard seized his brother's hand with a look of alarm. "Brother," he exclaimed, "you are joking; you are trying to frighten me. That you, who have more sense in your little finger than a great bully like me in his whole head, should rush to almost certain destruction, where some blockhead of an Austrian may easily brain you with the butt end of his rifle; that you should go scrambling up the ladders with the militia, where the first to mount are well-nigh sure to meet their death, and where no one can rush in to save you; that you, the pride of our family, the apple of our eye, our mother's support, our country's hope, should throw yourself against the enemy's bayonets, — oh, that is a cruel punishment you have planned for me! No one demands such a proof of your courage. War is not your profession; that is for us rough men who are good for nothing else. You are the soul of our army; don't try to be its hand or its foot at the same time. We honour superior intelligence, however much we may boast of our physical prowess. Don't think of taking such a revenge on those who love you, just because of a hasty word, long since repented of and retracted. Do what you will with me if you still feel offended; bid me ram my head into the mouth of

one of the enemy's cannon and I will do it. Tell
me you only meant to frighten me — that you are
not in earnest."

"I am in earnest, and shall do as I have said,"
answered the other firmly; "you may do as you
think best." With that he prepared to take his leave.

Richard tried to stop him. "Ödön, brother," he
cried, "I pray you forgive me! Think of our
mother, think of your wife and children!"

Ödön regarded him, unmoved. "I am thinking
of my mother here," said he, stamping with his foot
on the ground, "and I shall defend my wife and
children yonder," pointing toward the fortress.

Richard stood out of his brother's way; further
opposition would have been worse than useless. But
his eyes filled with tears, and he reached out both his
hands toward Ödön. At such a moment the brothers
might well have embraced each other, yet Ödön
never offered his hand. Before a duel the adversaries
are not wont to shake hands.

"When we meet up yonder," said he signifi-
cantly, "don't forget to look at your watch and
note the minute when you first plant your foot on the
fortifications." With that he left the room.

Three o'clock was at hand. The cannoneers stood
at their guns, watches in hand. A deep and peaceful
quiet reigned, broken only by the note of the night-

ingale. At the first stroke of three, fifty-nine cannon burst forth in one thundering volley which was
caught up by the loud huzzas of thousands of voices
on every side. The sun was still far below the
horizon, but the scene was soon illumined by the
destructive fire of hostile artillery. In the glare of
bombs and rockets the volunteers of the thirty-fourth
militia battalion could be seen, like a hill of ants,
swarming up toward the breach in the enemy's wall.
They were driven back, and again they advanced,
fighting with their bayonets in a hand-to-hand struggle. A second time they were repulsed, and their
officers were left, dead and dying, before the breach.

Two other battalions, the nineteenth and thirty-
seventh, with the volunteers who had joined them,
pressed forward with their scaling-ladders. A hot
fire was opened upon them, but in vain ; they planted
their ladders against the wall and ran up the rounds.
To turn them back was impossible ; the only thing
remaining was to shoot them down as fast as they
climbed the ladders.

Leading the way on one of the ladders was Ödön
Baradlay, his drawn sword in his hand. A detachment of the Italian regiment was defending that part
of the wall, and the defence was well maintained. It
was a grim task climbing the ladders in the face of a
deadly fire of sharpshooters, and the air was filled
with the groans of those that fell. Theirs was a

twofold death, shot down as they were by the enemy, and then falling, only to be caught on the bayonets of their own comrades behind them.

Ödön mounted his ladder as coolly as if he had been climbing an Egyptian pyramid on a wager to show himself proof against giddiness. Looking up, he could see a soldier standing at the head of the ladder, half concealed by the breastworks and holding his rifle ready to shoot. That soldier was his opponent in this fearful duel. Reaching the middle of the ladder, he suddenly heard himself hailed from below. The voice was a familiar one.

" Aha, patron, I'm here too! "

Ödön recognised Mausmann's call. The daring gymnast was climbing up the under side of the ladder and making every effort to overtake his leader, eager to gain the top before him. With the agility of a monkey, he passed Ödön and swung himself around on the front of the ladder over the other's head, shouting down to him triumphantly :

" Don't think you are going to get ahead of me, patron. I am captain here, and you are only a private."

Ödön was eager to recover his lead, but the gallant youth only pressed him back with one hand, saying, as he did so :

" Let me go first, patron ; I have no one in the whole world to care if I am killed."

s

With that he sprang upward, two rounds at a time. The soldier above brought his rifle to his shoulder and aimed downward. Mausmann saw him, and shouted tauntingly:

"Take good aim, macaroni, or you might hit me."

The next moment the Italian pulled the trigger. Mausmann's hands relaxed their hold of the ladder.

"Look out!" he called down to Ödön.

"What's the matter?" returned the other.

"Something that never happened to me before; I am killed." Therewith he fell backward over Ödön's head.

Ödön now climbed higher, anxious to reach the top of the ladder before the Italian should have reloaded his piece. But the soldier was too quick for him, and he found himself looking into the very muzzle of his rifle. Still he mounted. He could see the rifleman's finger press the trigger; the piece missed fire, and the next instant Ödön sprang over the breastworks.

Meanwhile the sixty-first battalion had effected an entrance into the castle garden. Three step-like terraces remained to be surmounted, and the men climbed one another's shoulders or stuck their bayonets between the stones of the scarp, and so worked their way upward. The defenders of the garden had retreated to the third terrace. As the

Hungarians were about to scale this also, they were suddenly brought to bay by the arrival of a fresh force of the enemy. It included some of the bravest soldiers of the army, being composed of four platoons of the William regiment.

On the second terrace of the castle garden the two hostile bands met in desperate conflict.

"Surrender!" called the militia major.

"Fire! Charge bayonets!" was the Austrian captain's response, as he gave the commands to his men.

A volley was discharged on each side. The Austrian captain and his lieutenant fell, while the Hungarian major and one of his officers were wounded. Neither party heeded its loss. Richard snatched up the rifle of a wounded soldier and dashed forward to meet the enemy. He was a master of bayonet fighting, and he resolved that, if he had to succumb at last to superior numbers, he would at least sell his life dearly.

An inner voice seemed to whisper to him that he was fighting his last battle. What if he slew ten opponents in succession? The eleventh would surely get the better of him and he must fall. At this thought, and in the thousandth part of a second, he took leave of all that was dear to him, — of the faithful girl awaiting him in Vienna, of the dear mother praying for him at home, of the slain foe to whom he had given a promise that he could not now fulfil. He saw only too well the fearful odds against him, and prepared to die.

His first adversary he sent headlong down the embankment; the second he drove back wounded into his comrades' arms; the third stopped suddenly as he was rushing to the encounter and pointed with his bayonet to the terrace above them. A dense array of flashing bayonets was seen advancing, and it was at once evident that the side which they should join would win the day. To which side, then, did they belong?

The rising sun answered the question. Shooting its beams from behind a cloud at that moment, it lighted up a banner fluttering in the advancing bayonet-hedge. The flag bore the national colours of Hungary.

"*Éljen a haza!*" resounded from the third terrace, and the relief party plunged down the scarp like an avalanche. The Austrians, thus overwhelmed by their opponents, were forced to surrender.

Yonder blue-coated figure which had come with this succour like a rescuing angel, just at the moment when aid was most sorely needed, was Ödön Baradlay. The two brothers fell into each other's arms.

"I am very angry with you," cried Richard, as he folded his brother in a warm embrace.

It was six o'clock in the morning. From every turret and pinnacle in Buda the tricolour waved in the breeze, and all the streets of Pest rang with loud huzzas. Turning his back, however, on these scenes of rejoicing, Richard Baradlay, refreshed by a cold bath and a soldier's breakfast, made his way to a neighbouring village, to fulfil the promise so solemnly pledged to poor Otto Palvicz.

CHAPTER XXIV.

ZEBULON'S BRIGHT IDEA.

THREE thousand six hundred feet above the sea-level, on a height of the Carpathian mountain range, a convivial party, consisting mostly of army officers, was enjoying itself with wine and music. A splendid view lay spread out before the merrymakers, — a wide-reaching landscape lighted by the slanting beams of the western sun as it sank in golden radiance beneath the horizon.

"Look there," Rideghváry was saying, as he named, one after another, the cities and villages that lay before them; "yonder lies the way to Constantinople."

His words were greeted with a shout: "Hurrah! Long live the Czar!" Glasses clinked, and the company struck up the Russian national anthem. Rideghváry joined in, and all uncovered during the singing.

"Don't you sing with us, Zebulon?" asked Rideghváry, turning to his friend, who sat silent and melancholy.

"No more voice than a peacock," was Zebulon's curt reply.

The crags about them gave back the tuneful notes, while far below the long line of Russian cavalry regiments, on their march from the north, caught up the song.

"See there!" cried Rideghváry to Zebulon, pointing to the troops as they wound their way southward toward the heart of Hungary; "now comes our triumph; now we shall tread our foes under our feet. No power on earth can withstand our might." His face beamed with exultation as he spoke.

Zebulon Tallérossy was out of humour. His present part had pleased him so long as he had nothing to do but travel about with his patron, make the acquaintance of foreign celebrities, and receive honours and attentions wherever he went. That, he thought, was the fitting occupation of a great statesman, and he had looked to this same kind of statesmanship to bring everything to a quiet and orderly conclusion. But when he saw that matters were not destined to flow on so harmoniously much longer, he fell out of conceit with his rôle of statesman.

Returning with Rideghváry to the town that lay beneath them in the valley, he gave his friend and patron a hint of his dissatisfaction. "Yes," said he, "she is a mighty power, — Russia; I don't know who could withstand her. But what will be the fate of the conquered ? "

" *Væ victis* — woe to the vanquished ! " returned the other sententiously.

"Well then," continued honest Zebulon, "let us suppose a case : what about such a man as Ödön Baradlay, whom we and all his countrymen esteem and love, and who, if his zeal has led him a little too far, has yet been influenced by none but the loftiest motives, — what will be done to him ?   A good man, fine talents, sure to be a credit to his country — he ought to be spared."

" *Mitgefangen, mitgehangen*," [1] quoted Rideghváry briefly.

For the rest of the drive Zebulon was silent.

In the evening, as Rideghváry was looking over the passport blanks which he kept in one of the pigeon-holes of his desk, he missed the very one to which he attached the greatest value.   It was an English passport with the official signature and stamp of the ambassadors of all the intervening countries, the name and description of the bearer being alone left blank.   Such forms were commonly held in readiness for secret missions.   No one could have taken the missing paper except Zebulon ; and when he had reached this conclusion, Rideghváry smiled.

In his comings and goings, the great man always

[1] Caught with the rest, hung with the rest.

took his friend with him. But how explain the friend-
ship which he manifested for him? Easily enough.
Rideghváry was not a master of the common people's
language, and it was the common people that he
wished to reach. Zebulon was their oracle, their
favourite orator. One needed but to give him a
theme, and he could hold his simple auditors spellbound by the hour. In his expeditions, therefore,
Rideghváry knew that his honest friend would be
indispensable to him when it came to persuading
the good people that the invading hosts which passed
through their villages were not enemies, but friends,
allies, and brothers. That, then, was to be Zebulon's
mission, and he already suspected as much; but he
had no heart for the task before him. Rideghvá-
váry, in his concern lest he should lose his spokesman, hardly let him go out of his sight, and even
shared the same room with him at night; otherwise
he might have found himself some morning without
his mouthpiece.

Zebulon racked his brains for a plan of escape from
his illustrious patron, but all in vain. The patron
was too fond of him. He had even tried to pick a
quarrel with Rideghváry; but the other would not
so much as lose his temper. Since their last talk,
however, Zebulon was more than ever determined to
shake off his affectionate friend.

"If you won't let me run away from you,"

said he to himself, " I will make you run away from me."

He had been pondering a scheme of his own ever since he chanced to see a Cossack eating raw cucumbers on an empty stomach. The Cossack plucked the cucumbers in a garden, and munched them with the greatest apparent relish. The plan was further developed as he watched the preparation of a dainty dish for the epicures of the Russian camp. Turnips and beets were cut up together, mixed with bran, and then boiled in an immense kettle, the finishing touch being added by dipping a pound of tallow candles into the steaming mixture. The candles came out thinner, to be sure, but were still serviceable for illumination, while the stew was rendered perfect.

Zebulon's scheme attained to full development when the cholera broke out so fiercely in the Russian army that even a disastrous battle could hardly have wrought greater havoc. Rideghváry was mortally afraid of the cholera, carried in his bosom a little bag of camphor, wore flannel over his abdomen, shook flowers of sulphur into his boots, always disinfected his room with chloride of lime, drank red wine in the evening and arrack in the morning, and chewed juniper berries during the day.

On this weakness of the illustrious man Zebulon counted largely for the success of his scheme. Entering a druggist's shop one evening, he asked for an ounce of tartar emetic. The apothecary was disinclined to furnish the drug without a physician's order, but Zebulon cut his objection short.

" Doctor's prescription not necessary," said he sharply. " I prescribe for myself — exceptional case. If I say I must have it, that's enough." And he received his *tartarus emeticus*, divided into small doses.

In the night, while Rideghváry was asleep, Zebulon took two doses of his emetic. Honour to whom honour is due! Every man has his own peculiar kind of heroism. In Zebulon it was an heroic deed to bring on himself an artificial attack of cholera at a critical time like that. But his scheme worked admirably. The audible results of the double dose of tartar emetic awakened Rideghváry from his slumbers. With one leap from his bed, he landed in the middle of the room, and ran into the passageway, shouting: " The cholera is here! the cholera is here!" He left his clothes lying in the room, and procured fresh ones to put on. Whatever luggage and papers of his were in the bedchamber, he ordered to be fumigated before he would touch them. Then, calling for his carriage, he drove out of the town in all haste.

Meanwhile, Zebulon, after the drug had done its work, went to sleep again and snored till broad daylight. With this *salto mortale* he disappeared from public life.

CHAPTER XXV.

GOOD OLD FRIENDS.

IT was the evening of the thirteenth of August. The Hungarians had that day laid down their arms. Ödön Baradlay sat at an open window in the fading twilight, writing letters to his mother and his wife, informing them that he should await his fate where he was, even as the Roman senators had calmly awaited theirs, sitting in their curule chairs and scorning to fly before the invader. He viewed the situation with the calmness of a philosopher and showed none of the feverish uneasiness of those who were intent only on their own personal safety. He had not even thought to provide himself with a passport, as so many of his associates had done.

While he thus sat, writing his letters and heedless of his surroundings, a stranger approached him.

"Am I addressing Ödön Baradlay?" he asked.

"That is my name," replied Ödön. "May I ask yours in return?"

"My name is Valentine Schneiderius, evangelical clergyman of Pukkersdorf. I have brought you a letter, but am in haste and must not linger. As long as the Russians are in our rear the way is open ; but presently it will be closed." He delivered his letter and withdrew.

Ödön broke the seal and read :

"DEAR FRIEND, — I shall never forget the ties that unite our families. Your late lamented father was my friend, and nothing could now induce me to look on and see the destruction of a true patriot like yourself. Would to God I could help many more ! I send you an English passport, all signed and sealed, to take you out of the country. Write any name you choose in the blank space. Burn this.

"Your old friend,

"ZEBULON TALLÉROSSY.

"P. S. Go by way of Poland and you won't be known. When safe, think of your country ; perhaps you can yet do something for your poor people.

"Z. T."

Ödön examined the passport and found it complete in every detail, — even to being creased and soiled like a much-handled document. Then he threw it down, ashamed at the thought of using it to save his life when so many of his comrades in arms were in danger of death or captivity. Yet the mere prospect of safety made his pulse beat more rapidly, and involuntarily his thoughts turned to those dear ones at home who looked to him for comfort and support, — his wife and two little children.

He read once more the last words of Zebulon's postscript; they showed no little shrewdness on the writer's part. What if he could really secure aid for his country abroad? The temptation was too great. He took up the passport again and glanced at the signatures on its back. Among them was Ridegh-váry's. No, that man should never enjoy the triumph of hissing in his ear: "This is the last step to that height!"

He burned Zebulon's letter, as well as the two he had just written to his wife and his mother, and, summoning his servant, bade him hasten to Nemes-domb and inform his mother of his flight to a foreign country; she should hear further particulars from him later. Then he completed his preparations for a hasty departure, wrote in the name "Algernon Smith" on the passport, put the paper in his pocket, called a carriage, and set out on his flight.

The enemy's first outpost was successfully passed. The commanding officer examined his passport, found it correct, and affixed his signature. Ödön was free to go on. His second station was Gyapju, whence he wished to continue directly to Várad, and thence by way of Szigeth into Galicia. At Gyapju he was conducted to the commandant's quarters. Entering with an unconcerned air, he inquired to

whom he should show his papers. There were several officers in the room, one of whom asked him to
wait a few minutes until the commandant came in.
Meanwhile an adjutant made the necessary examination of his passport and found it apparently all right ;
the one thing now required was the signature of the
commanding officer.

The entrance of the latter caused Ödön a violent
start. The man before him was — Leonin Ramiroff,
grown to manly proportions and wearing the stern,
soldierly look of one entrusted with military responsi-
bility. The adjutant called his attention to the paper
awaiting his signature, assuring him that it was all in
order. Leonin took up a pen, wrote his name, and
then turned to hand the passport to Ödön. The
latter felt his heart stop beating as he met that
sharp, penetrating gaze.

"You are not Mr. Algernon Smith," exclaimed the
Russian officer in English, drawing himself up to his
full height; "you are Ödön Baradlay."

Ödön's heart sank within him. "And are you
going to betray me?" he asked, likewise in English.

"You are my prisoner."

"This from you, Leonin Ramiroff, my bosom
friend of old, my faithful comrade on a long winter
journey when we were chased by wolves; you, the
man who plunged into the icy river to save me at
the risk of your own life?"

"I was merely a young lieutenant in the guard then," replied Leonin coldly.

"And now will you hand me over to my bitterest foes, to the derisive laughter of the conqueror, to a miserable death on the scaffold?"

"I am now a colonel of lancers," was the other's only reply; and with that he tore the passport in two and threw it under the table. "Take the prisoner away and put him under guard."

The adjutant took Ödön by the arm and led him out. The house was full of officers and their servants, so that no place could be found for the prisoner but a little shanty built of boards, adjoining the stable. Here he was confined, and a Cossack stationed with his carbine outside as guard.

Every three hours the guard was changed. Being acquainted with Russian, Ödön understood the order given to his jailer, — "If he tries to escape, shoot him."

At nine o'clock in the evening a thunder-storm came up. The rain descended in torrents, and in the flashes of lightning the captive could look through the cracks in his prison-wall and see the Cossack standing ankle-deep in mud and water, his carbine ready for instant use. The storm passed over; the tower-clock struck eleven; in the adjoining stable Ödön heard the Russian cavalrymen snoring, while their horses were stamping under an improvised shed near by.

Suddenly he heard his name called, cautiously and in a whisper.

"Who is calling me?" he asked.

"I — the guard."

"What! do you know me, too?"

"Do you remember your sledge-driver on the Mohilev steppe, — the time we were nearly eaten up by the wolves? You stood by me then, and I'm going to stand by you now. At the back of your shanty is a loose board, — the fourth from the bottom. You can push it aside and crawl out. The horse-shed is behind. My horse has his saddle and bridle on; you'll know him by his white tail. He's the fastest runner in the regiment. Mount him and make for the garden in the rear, and then follow the storm. You'll find the horse a good one, and easy on the bit. Don't be afraid of me if I shoot after you; I'm bound to do it, though I'm not to blame for all the loose boards in your prison. And one word more: when you have mounted my horse, and want him to go, press his flanks with your knees, but don't whip him. If you use the whip he'll stand stock-still, and the harder you whip the stiller he'll stand. More than one horse-thief has come to grief for want of knowing that. His name is Ljubicza, and he likes to be called by it. If you whisper in his ear, 'Hurrah, Ljubicza!' he'll dart away like the wind."

Ödön felt renewed life thrill through his veins.

T

He lost no time in following his humble friend's
directions. Finding the loose board, which seemed
to be secured only by a rusty nail, he softly removed
it, and squeezed through the opening. Making his
way to the horse-shed, he soon picked out the white-
tailed horse, swung himself on to its back and turned
it around. Then, pressing his knees inward, he
whispered, "Hurrah, Ljubicza!" The well-trained
animal darted away through the garden.

At the sound of the galloping horse the guard
sprang forward, drew his carbine to his shoulder, and,
whispering, "St. George preserve him!" pulled the
trigger. At the report all the sleepers leaped to their
feet.

"What's up?"

"Prisoner escaped."

"After him!"

A score of Cossacks threw themselves on their
horses and gave chase, discharging their pieces in the
darkness as they rode. An occasional flash of lightning revealed the fugitive ahead of them, and stimu-
lated the pursuers to renewed efforts. But the fleet
stallion soon overtook the storm, and it proved a good
travelling companion, wrapping the fugitive in its
mantle of rain, and drowning with its thunder-claps
the beating of his horse's hoofs. It took the side of
the escaped prisoner, and he was not caught.

CHAPTER XXVI.

AT HOME.

THE dawn found Ödön alone on the wide heath, — a bare and desolate plain before him, where nothing but earth and sky met the view, except that in the distance the faint outline of a well-sweep could be descried. Ödön turned his horse in that direction. The animal seemed thirsty, and quickened his pace as he drew nearer the well. After watering him and turning him loose to seek what forage the barren heath had to offer, the rider sat down on the low well-curb and gazed over the plain. But he was not long left to his meditations; the distant neighing of a horse aroused him, and his faithful Ljubicza, with an answering whinny, came trotting to his side, as if offering himself for farther flight.

Resting one arm on the saddle, Ödön stood awaiting the stranger's approach. It certainly could not be an enemy roaming the plain in that manner; it must be a travelling companion, a fugitive like himself, who had been attracted thither by the well-sweep, that lighthouse of the arid plains. As he drew nearer, the unknown rider looked like some stray member of a guerilla band. A bright red ribbon adorned his round hat. Upon his closer approach Ödön recognised his old acquaintance, Gregory Boksa, the ox-herd; and he was glad even of this humble man's company in the lonely desert.

"Hurrah!" cried Gregory, as he rode up on his white-faced horse; "how glad I am to see you, my dear sir! May Heaven preserve you! It is well you made your escape, for they're having bad times back yonder. I myself only got away with difficulty."

So saying, the driver of cattle dismounted and patted his horse on the neck.

"Yes, sir," he resumed, "if old White-face hadn't held out as well as he did, it would have been all over with me. You see, when I learned that our people had laid down their arms, I said to myself: 'The Russians sha'n't have my hundred head of cattle for nothing.' So I drove the herd to Várad through the Belényes forest, and walked into the Russian camp. 'I've got some cattle to sell,' said I, 'and if you want to buy, now's your chance.' The stupid Russians snapped at the bait, agreed to my price after a little haggling, and gave me a money-order for the lot. I was to go to Rideghváry, said they, and he would pay me the cash."

"Is Rideghváry in Várad?" asked Ödön quickly.

"Yes, indeed, he's there; but I took good care

not to go near him. I was glad enough to be off before dog or cat could see me. The devil take the money! Rideghváry would have paid me in coin that I had no use for."

Ödön felt lighter of heart. If Rideghváry was in Várad, he himself owed his life a second time to Leonin Ramiroff; for had not the latter arrested him, he would have run into the arms of the former. What if Leonin had foreseen this and stopped him on purpose? Perhaps, too, his escape was really all of his friend's planning, and he had thus shown himself a true friend after all. Whether it was so or not, Ödön clung to the belief that Leonin had behaved with noble generosity toward his old friend.

"I am very grateful to you," said he, "for telling me where Rideghváry is at present. In all the world there is no one I am so anxious to avoid."

"But what are your plans?" asked Boksa.

"I shall go to the very first Austrian officer I can find and tell him who I am. He shall do what he chooses with me. I am going to face the music."

This proposal by no means met with the other's approval. "That is not wise on your part," he remonstrated. "No, indeed! I am a simple man, but I can't approve of your course. When the conqueror is in his first frenzy, I say, keep out of his way, for he is sure to show no mercy to his first victims. Why, then, such haste?"

"You don't suppose I care to lie hidden in the woods month after month, or wander about like a tramp and be hunted from one county to another?"

"No, no," returned Gregory, "I don't say you should do that, though for myself I don't expect anything better. But you are a nobleman with an estate of your own; go home and take your ease, as becomes a man of your station, until they choose to send for you."

"And so make my hard fate all the harder to bear, after seeing again those that are dearest to me in the world? No; both for their sakes and for my own I must refuse to follow any such advice."

"When did you last see your family?"

"It is now four months since I left Nemesdomb."

"And when did you last visit Körös Island?"

"I have never been there at all. My father bought that summer residence while I was abroad, and since my return I have had no leisure for summer vacations."

"Very well, sir. I think now I understand you perfectly. With my poor wits I can easily see that a person of your importance would prefer not to surrender himself a prisoner to the first corporal or sergeant that comes along. You wouldn't enjoy being driven through the nearest market-town with your hands tied behind you, — the sport of your enemies. Now supposing you let me lead you, by lonely paths where we sha'n't meet a soul, to the house of an acquaintance, — an out-of-the-way place, — where you can write a letter to the Austrian commander-in-chief, and quietly wait for things to take their course. A thousand things may happen in the meantime. Why should you rush to your destruction ? Wait and let your fate come to you, I say, and meantime keep your pipe lighted. If I were a great lord, that's what I should do."

"I accept your offer, my good Boksa," returned Ödön. "Your head seems better than mine. Conduct me whither you will."

"All right!" responded the other. "Let us mount and be off."

Throughout the night the full moon lighted the two travellers on their way. Many stretches, too, of dry, hard ground were encountered, where more rapid progress was possible than among the bulrushes and tall reeds. The horses, moreover, found occasional forage, stout grass and blackberry bushes being abundant. Toward morning they came to a river, and here Boksa and his charge rested in the hut of a fisherman who was known to the ox-herd, and who served his guests a hotly spiced fish-chowder. After partaking of it Ödön stretched himself on the rush mat, and, wearied as he was with his long wanderings, slept as soundly as a tired child. When he awoke, Boksa was sitting on the door-sill near him.

"What time is it?" he asked.

"Near sunset," was the answer.

"So late as that? Why didn't you wake me?"

"Ah, that would have been a sin. You were at home, talking with your little boy."

The road lay thenceforth along the riverside. It was late in the evening when they came to an island of some size lying in the middle of the stream, and communicating by a bridge with the bank on which Ödön and his guide were standing.

"Here we are," announced Boksa. "This is where my acquaintance lives, — the one I was going to bring you to."

"What is his name?" asked Ödön.

"You'll know him when you see him," replied the other evasively.

"But shall I not be a burden to him?"

"No, indeed."

They rode over the bridge, and an ivy-covered villa came to view through the foliage. Proceeding up the gravel path to the veranda, they alighted and gave their horses to the stable-boy. Through the long windows that opened on the veranda could be seen a lamp and people gathered about it. A young woman sat with a sleeping child in her lap; an older lady, with a face of marble pallor, sat before an open Bible; and a young man held a little boy on his knee and drew pictures for him on a slate. A big

Newfoundland dog suddenly rose from the corner where he was sleeping, and, with a half-suppressed bark of eager expectation, came bounding to the door.

" Where am I ? " stammered Ödön in great agitation.

" At home."

CHAPTER XXVII.

THE MYSTERIOUS LETTER.

ÖDÖN could not persuade himself that Boksa had done him a kindness in bringing him home. It was a time of torturing suspense for all the family. The Austrian general had been duly informed where Ödön Baradlay could be found, and a summons from him was daily expected. Poor Aranka could not hear a door open, or the sound of a strange step, without starting and turning pale. Every day, when the mail came, they all ran to look over the letters and make sure that the dreaded call to Ödön was not among them.

One day a suspicious-looking letter came to view addressed in German to "Herr Eugen von Baradlay."

Eugen — why, that was German for *Jenö*. He opened the letter, read it, and put it in his pocket. All the family were present, and his mother asked him from whom his letter came, and what news it brought. But Jenö only answered, "I must go on a journey."

"Whither and for what purpose?" asked the baroness.

"I can't sit idle here any longer," he replied. "One of my brothers has vanished from our sight, and the other daily expects to be taken prisoner. Such a life is more than I can bear any longer. It is my turn now to try what I can do."

"But what can you do?" asked his mother.

"That is my secret."

"But I have a right to share it. No member of my family shall adopt a course which affects us all, which I have not first approved."

"You will learn all in due time."

"But what if I then refuse to give my sanction?"

"Your refusal will be too late to be of any avail."

"Then I forbid you to go on."

"I cannot obey you. I am no longer a child, but am responsible to myself alone for my actions."

"But," interposed Ödön, "you are still a son and a brother."

"As you shall soon see," answered Jenö, with significant emphasis.

The baroness took her youngest son by the hand. "You have some plan for saving our family," said she. "I can read your soul; you are an open book to me. I have studied you from your infancy. You think now to rescue us by leaving us and resuming your old connections, thus exerting an influence in our favour upon our enemies. I see that you are planning to return to the Plankenhorsts."

Jenö smiled sadly. "Do you read that in my heart?" he asked.

"You wish to marry that girl in order to save your brother through the powerful influence of her family, — that girl whose dower will be my hatred, and on whom her country's curse and God's anger rest."

Aranka threw herself on her mother-in-law's breast. "Mother," she cried, "do not speak of her like that; he loves her!"

Ödön led his wife back to her seat. "Do not interpose, my dear," said he, firmly. "We are here concerned with matters of which your innocent soul can have not the slightest conception. To purchase life and property by swearing fidelity to the woman who was the inspiring demon of all the woe that so lately befell our poor country; who has nursed the hatred of one people against another; who has played the part of traitress, spy, slanderer; who has stirred up men against the throne only for the purpose of delivering them over to the hangman; who harbours such fiendish plots in her bosom that, if she had her way, she would embitter for ever one country against its neighbour, — to bring such a woman as wife into his father's house is what no Baradlay shall do, or if he should do it I know one who would refuse the gift of his life at such a price."

The baroness sank weeping on her eldest son's bosom. He had voiced the cry of her own proud soul. Jenö said nothing; he smiled sadly, and went about his preparations for departure. Aranka regarded him with compassion in her eyes.

"And do you, too, condemn me?" he asked softly.

"Do what your heart bids you," she sighed.

"Yes, with Heaven's help I will!"

His mother would not let him leave the room; she threw herself on her knees before him and blocked the way. "My son," he scried, "I beg you not to go. Let misery, torture, death itself overtake us; we will bear them all without complaint. Have not ten thousand already died for the cause? But our souls we will keep unsullied. Oh, do not close against us the way to heaven!"

"Mother, I implore you, rise."

"No; if you go, my place is here in the dust, — crushed to the earth."

"You do not understand me, mother; nor is it my will that you should."

"What!" cried the mother, joyfully; "you are not planning to do as I suspected?"

"That question I must refuse to answer."

"One word more," interrupted Ödön; "if you

would relieve our anxiety, show us the letter you have received."

Jenö put his hand to his breast, as if fearful lest some one might try to take the letter from him by force. "That letter you shall not see," he declared.

"I am determined to read it," returned the other.

At this Jenö's face flushed hotly. "Ödön Baradlay," he exclaimed, "the letter is addressed to Eugen Baradlay. I am Eugen Baradlay." So saying, he turned proudly away.

"Then our mother was right, after all," said his brother bitterly.

The baroness rose to her feet. Tears coursed down her cheeks. "Go, then," she cried, "whither your obstinate will leads you. Leave us here in despair and in tears. But know that, though two of my sons are likely to die on the scaffold, I shall not mourn those that are taken, but the one that is left."

At these hard words Jenö looked with a gentle smile at the speaker. "Mother," said he, "remember that my last words to you were, 'I love you.' Farewell!" And he was gone.

The contents of his letter were as follows:

"Herr Commissary - General Eugen von Baradlay: — You are hereby summoned before the military tribunal in Pest."

The judge-advocate's signature followed.

By a slight mistake in translation, " Odön " had been rendered in German by " Eugen " instead of " Edmund."   Such mistakes were not uncommon in those days.

CHAPTER XXVIII.

THE SUMMONS ANSWERED.

In two weeks Jenö's case came up for trial. Meanwhile the prosecution had been busy collecting evidence of the rebel commissary-general's guilt.

"Are you Eugen Baradlay?" asked the judge-advocate.

"I am."

"Are you married?"

"I have a wife and two children."

"Were you commissary-general of the rebel forces?"

"I was."

"Are you the same Eugen Baradlay that drove the administrator from his chair as presiding officer in your county assembly?"

"The same."

"Did you appear during the March uprising at the head of the Hungarian deputation that was sent to Vienna, and did you there address the people in language calculated to stir them to rebellion?"

"I cannot deny it."

304

"Do you recognise these words as having been spoken by you at that time?"

The judge-advocate handed him a sheet of paper covered with pencilled writing in a woman's hand. Jenö had good cause to remember the contents of the sheet, and to recognise the writing. Had he not seen Alfonsine taking down the orator's words on that well-remembered night when they both paused to listen to his brother's eloquence? She had rested her portfolio against his shoulder while she wrote down the most striking portions of the address — for her scrap-book.

"Yes," said he, returning the paper, "those were my words."

The judges consulted together. The prompt and positive acknowledgment of the last charge was more than they had expected; the accused need not have committed himself. The examination was resumed.

"A brother of yours, a hussar officer, deserted with his men. Did you use your influence to persuade him to that course?"

So it was not known who had actually persuaded Richard to lead his men into Hungary; or were they intentionally heaping all the blame on his head to make his condemnation the surer? He hastened to reply:

"Yes, it was I who did it." He answered so eagerly as to excite some surprise.

U

"Have you not another brother, — Edmund or Jenö?"

"Yes; 'Jenö' in Hungarian, 'Edmund' in German."

"Aren't you wrong? Is not 'Eugen' the German for 'Jenö,' and 'Edmund' the German for 'Ödön'? I have heard the matter discussed before now."

"No, it is as I say."

"This brother disappeared from Vienna simultaneously with the hussar officer. Do you know the reason?"

"I believe it was because he found himself thrown out of his place in the chancellor's office, and was unwilling to pass his time in idleness."

"What became of him?"

"Ever since then he has been at home, looking after the estate in his brothers' absence. He took no part whatever in the uprising, but occupied his leisure hours with painting and music, and in teaching my little boy. He is still at home."

"Did you not raise and maintain at your own cost a battalion of volunteers?"

"Yes; two hundred cavalry and three hundred infantry. At the battle of Kápolna I led the cavalry in person."

"You are anticipating the prosecution. Were you present at the Debreczen diet?"

" As one cannot be in two places at the same time, I was not."

" At the battle of Forro did you not exert yourself in rallying the routed forces of the rebels ? "

" Yes, I did."

Jenö had committed himself unnecessarily. He seemed not merely unconcerned as to his fate, but even eager to meet it. The judge-advocate sought to test him. Searching among his papers, he finally looked up and said :

" The charge is here made against you that in the expedition among the mountains you seized and appropriated to your own use all the bullion stored in the public mints."

At this charge Jenö's face flushed with anger. " That is false ! " he cried. " That is a shameless slander ! No Baradlay would commit a crime ! "

This outburst sealed his fate by removing any lingering doubt as to his identity. Such a passionate denial could have come only from him whom the charge actually concerned, that is, from Ödön Baradlay.

" What have you to say in your defence ? " he was asked in closing.

" Our defence is in our deeds," was the proud rejoinder. " Posterity will judge us."

The jury was then sworn in the presence of the accused, and the latter was led into a side room to wait until summoned to hear the verdict and receive his sentence. In a quarter of an hour he was led back again. Omitting the charge which he had denied, he was found guilty on all the other counts, and they were amply sufficient to condemn him to death. He bowed as if well satisfied with his sentence. An early hour the next morning was assigned for his execution. He heaved a sigh. His purpose was accomplished. He had but one favour to ask, — the privilege of writing to his wife, his mother, and his brother, before he died. His request was granted, and he thanked the court with a smile so serene and an eye so clear that more than one heart was touched with compassion.

His judges were not to blame that the Eumenides thirsted for blood.

CHAPTER XXIX.

A POSTHUMOUS MESSAGE.

IN the rainy autumn days the Baradlay family removed from Körös Island to Nemesdomb. The latter was no longer a hospital : the patients had been elsewhere provided for, and all traces of war and bloodshed had disappeared.

One evening, when the little family was gathered about the lamp, the door opened and a guest entered unannounced. It was a guest not wont to stand on ceremony, a guest whose right it was to enter any house at any time, whether its inmates were at table, at prayers, or whatever they might be doing. His uniform — that of the imperial police — was his passport. He raised his hand to his cap in military salute.

" Pardon me for disturbing you at so late an hour," said he in German ; " but I bring a despatch from Pest directed to Baron Edmund von Baradlay."

So the fatal summons had come at last !

Ödön took a lamp from the table. " That is my name," said he, calmly. " Will you please come with me to my room ? "

"Excuse me; I have also letters for the two ladies, — the dowager Baroness Casimir von Baradlay and the young Baroness von Baradlay."

The messenger took from his pocketbook the three letters, and delivered them according to the addresses they bore. "I will await your pleasure in the ante-room," said he, as he saluted and withdrew.

All three looked at their letters with pale faces, as one scrutinises a missive he fears to open and read. Each of the letters bore the government seal, and was addressed in the clear, caligraphic hand of an office clerk.

Each contained, in the same caligraphic handwriting, the following:

"It is my duty to forward to you the enclosed communication, which has been officially examined by me, and found to contain no objectionable matter."

Then followed an illegible scrawl as signature. The "enclosed communication" proved in each case to be a letter from Jenö. Ödön's ran as follows:

"DEAR EDMUND: — To-day I bring to its fulfilment that for which I have lived. I die for the cause I have embraced. Be not bowed down with sadness at my fate; I go to meet it with head erect. I leave you my blessing, and take my faith with me. The blood we shed will moisten no thankless soil: from it will spring golden harvests for our fatherland and for humanity. You who survive will rear again the structure that now falls in ruins over our heads. Sooner or later the helm of the ship of state will come into your hands. I die with entire submission to the decrees of destiny. Dry Aranka's tears; kiss for me little Béla and the baby, and when they ask whither I have gone, say I am in your heart. For yourself, never lose courage; live for our family and our country, which may God prosper for ages to come!   Your brother,

"EUGEN."

The parting message to Aranka was thus conceived:

"MY DEAR, MY BELOVED ARANKA:—Your noble words still ring in my ears,—'Do what your heart bids you.' I have done it. Forgive me for causing you pain by my death. I would have you, while you weep for me, still be comforted. Do not sadden your little ones by showing them a sorrowful face. You know how quickly sadness in you affects them, and how you are thus in danger of blighting the joy of their innocent young lives. Be good to my mother and brothers; they will care for you. Veil the little portrait for awhile, that it may not too often bring to mind sad thoughts of the past. I will spare you the pain of reading more. I would leave you in such a way that you may not be bowed down

with grief at my going. I send you a kiss through
the air; it will reach you from the heavens above.
May God keep you for ever. Even in death,

" Your ever loving

" EUGEN."

To his mother the young man sent the following
message:

" MY DEAR, MY ADORED MOTHER : — The words
with which I parted from you I now repeat once
more, — I love you. You no longer fear that
Aranka's little ones will come to want, do you?
Heaven has ordered all things well, — both for him
who dies, and for those that are left behind. You
have a strong nature, an exalted soul, and I need not
leave you any strength of mine. The mother of the
Gracchi received into her arms her murdered sons,
and wept not. For those that die a glorious death
their mothers need shed no tears, — so you have
told us. Therefore, do not mourn. With true Christian submission say, 'Father, thy will be done!'
And bear no one any malice because of my death;
forgive even her who by her accusation has driven
me to an early grave, and do not let her know how
much good she has really done by her criminal act.
She has made death easy for me, and I thank her. I
die at peace with all the world, and I trust that no
one harbours any ill will against me. An hour more,

and I shall have joined my father up yonder. Of us three boys, you both showed me the greatest affection. When I was small and you used to fall out with each other, I was often the means of effecting a reconciliation. Now once more that shall be my mission. They are calling me. May God preserve you, dear mother. Your loving son,

"EUGEN."

Only a subdued sobbing was heard as they read their letters and exchanged them. In the next room was a stranger who must not hear any loud lamentation. But why did he linger? Who was to go and ask him?

The widow was the first to recover her composure. She dried her tears and rose. "Check your grief for a moment," said she to the other two, and then she went to the door and bade the messenger enter. "Have you any further communication for us?" she asked.

"Yes," he replied, drawing a small package from his breast pocket, and delivering it to the baroness.

She opened it. It contained a blue silk waistcoat which Aranka had embroidered with lilies of the valley and pansies. In the midst of the embroidered flowers were three holes, each as large as a rifle ball, singed and blood-stained at the edges. The embroidery and the bullet-holes explained all.

The government emissary uttered no word, but for a moment, while the packet was being opened, he removed his cap. The baroness forced herself to bear up yet a little longer. With a firm step she went to a cupboard; returning, she handed the man a gold coin. He murmured a "thank you" and something about God's blessing; then he saluted and withdrew.

The necessity of restraint being removed, the grief-stricken family were at liberty to moisten the dear memento with their tears and pay their loving tribute to the noble martyr's memory.

CHAPTER XXX.

THE PRISON TELEGRAPH.

BUT had Jenö held no communication with his
brother Richard before his death? Yes; Richard
was a prisoner in the same building, and it was fitted
with a telegraph which communicated with all the
cells and was never idle. It could not be silenced;
the prisoners could not be prevented from making
use of it at all hours of the day and night. It consisted simply of the prison walls.

No wall is so thick that a knocking on one side
cannot be heard on the other. One rap stood for
A, two for B, three for C, and so on through the
alphabet. The rapping went on continually all over
the building, and each new prisoner learned its meaning on the very day of his arrival, and became a telegraph operator himself. A message sent out from one
cell was passed along until it reached its destination,
when an answer was returned by the same route.

On the day which was destined to be Jenö's last
on earth, the following questions and answers passed
from cell to cell.

315

"What news ? "

" Death sentence."

" Who ? "

" Baradlay."

" Which one ? "

" The oldest."

Through Richard's cell, too, passed this crypto-gram, and he asked again :

" First name ? "

But the only reply he could elicit was a repetition of the above : " The oldest."

CHAPTER XXXI.

A HEADACHE AND ITS CONSEQUENCES.

THE governor plenipotentiary was suffering with a splitting headache, which at times made him inclined to believe that all the bullets he had sent through his victims' heads were holding a rendezvous in his own. On such occasions it was dangerous to approach the great man. In the frenzy of his pain he was wont to rage even against those he loved best, and to find fault with all who were under his authority, as if determined to make others feel some small fraction of the discomfort he was forced to endure. To ask a favour of him in such moments, or even to demand simple justice, was worse than useless. Did he find favour with his torturer, he wanted to know, or was there any justice in his undeserved suffering?

This was the sort of man that was set as judge over a vanquished people.

In the midst of one of these attacks the governor sat alone one evening in his room when his servant opened the door. "Some one here to speak with your Excellency," he announced.

"Send him away."

"But it is a lady."

"The devil take all these hysterical women! I don't want any woebegone faces around me now. I can't see the lady."

Many women, most of them in mourning, crossed his threshold in those days.

"It is the Baroness Alfonsine Plankenhorst who asks to see you," the servant ventured to add.

"Can't she stay at home, I'd like to know? Is this time of night my hour for receiving callers?"

"She says she must see your Excellency — it is important."

"A young person of strong character. Well, show her in. Besides," he added to himself, "she isn't a woman; she is a devil." Then resuming his chair, and without removing the bandage that adorned his head, he awaited his caller.

Alfonsine entered in travelling costume, and closed the door carefully behind her.

"My dear Baroness," began the governor, "I must beg you to be as brief as possible, for I have a fearful headache."

"I will do my errand in a very few words," was the reply. "I learned to-day of your removal from the governorship of Hungary."

"Ha! Is that so? And why am I removed?"
The sufferer felt as if a cannon-ball had crashed
through his head.

"Because there is an outcry against the present
severe measures, and the public is to be told that the
government is not reponsible for them, but you per-
sonally in your excess of zeal."

The sick man pressed both hands to his temples,
as if to keep his head from bursting.

"Beginning to-morrow, a new system is to be
inaugurated," resumed Alfonsine, "and imprisonment
is to take the place of the death penalty."

"Ah, I am very grateful to you for this information — very grateful."

"I made all haste to bring you warning, for to-
morrow morning you will receive official notification
of your retirement. But you still have a night before
you for action."

"And I will use it, I assure you!" exclaimed the
governor.

He rang his bell and summoned his adjutant.
The latter soon appeared.

"Go at once to the judge-advocate and tell him
to have all pending suits drawn up and ready to
submit to the court at midnight, when it will hold
an extra session. At three o'clock all the verdicts
must be in my hands; at five let the accused stand
ready to hear their sentences. The garrison mean-

while is to be kept under arms. Now go ; despatch is the word ! "

The governor turned again to his visitor. "Are you satisfied with my promptness ? " he asked.

Alfonsine answered with another question. "Is Richard Baradlay one of those whose cases will come up to-night ? "

" His name is among the first on the list," was the reply.

"Do not forget, your Excellency," urged the other, "that he has done us more harm than any one else."

" I know all about him, Baroness, and his case shall receive our immediate attention. And now I thank you for bringing me this word so promptly ; I thank you heartily."

" Good night."

" Ha ! ha ! and a royal good night it will be for me ! " exclaimed the governor when his guest had gone.

All that night Alfonsine Plankenhorst never closed her eyes. Fiendish joy and nervous excitement frightened sleep from her pillow. She was impatient for morning to come, that she might take the first train for Vienna and revel in her poor cousin's grief and despair. She counted the hours as they dragged slowly by. Twelve o'clock. The court was now in session ; the accused were hearing the charges read out against them; they were being asked if they had any defence to offer; they had none. Then they were led back to their cells. One o'clock. The verdicts were being considered; no one said a word in the prisoners' favour; the vote was taken. Two o'clock. The verdicts were being recorded. Three o'clock. The man with the bandaged head was signing each sentence. Four o'clock. All was in readiness. Whoever had slept in that prison was now, at any rate, on his feet and was being told to feast his eyes for the last time on this beautiful world, on the rosy flush of dawning day, and on the dying of the twinkling stars in the eastern sky.

Unable to lie longer in bed, Alfonsine rose and went down-stairs. A cab stood in the courtyard. She ordered the porter to bring down her hand-bag, and then drove to the judge-advocate's house. She knew him well, — as the sexton knows the undertaker, — and she felt sure of finding him at home and awake. She was shown into his presence without delay. The judge-advocate was a man of few words.

" Have you finished your night's work? " asked Alfonsine.

" Yes."

" What were the sentences? "

" Death."

" In every case? "

x

" Without exception."

"And Richard Baradlay ?"

"Is on the list."

"He is condemned ?"

"To death."

Alfonsine pressed the judge-advocate's hand and hastened away to her train. The city clocks were striking five, — the last hour they would ever strike for Richard Baradlay, said she, as she hurried on, feeding her imagination with the last grim scenes of his earthly career.

On arriving at Vienna she found the family carriage awaiting her, and she lost no time in reaching her home. Hastening from room to room in quest of Edith, she found her sewing on a black dress for herself.

"I have fulfilled my vow," cried Alfonsine, smiling with gratified malice. "He is dead!"

Edith raised her eyes sadly and met her cousin's gaze. Then she bowed her head on her breast, but she did not weep or cry out.

Hearing her daughter enter, Baroness Plankenhorst hastened to join her and hear all about the success of her mission. Nor did the other omit any detail in recounting her experiences of the night and the early morning. She dwelt with pride on the instant and entire success that had crowned her efforts. Thereupon the mother and daughter embraced and kissed each other in their joy, nearly forgetting in their congratulations the presence of a third person. But was the victim determined not to wince?

"Haven't you a single tear to shed for him?" they asked, scornfully. But perhaps she had not yet grasped the meaning of it all. "Don't you hear me?" screamed her cousin; "your Richard Baradlay is dead."

The other only sighed. "God has taken him," said she to herself, "and I shall mourn him as long as I live." But she could not trust herself to say anything aloud. Her anguish was too keen.

"Weep for him, I tell you!" cried the beautiful fury, stamping her foot, while loose locks of her fair hair fluttered about her face.

At that moment the servant opened the door and announced, "Captain Richard Baradlay." There he stood, but no longer in the uniform of a captain of hussars. He wore plain citizen's clothes.

The tormented victim of the headache had employed the last hours of his tenure of office in causing one hundred and twenty of the chief prisoners under his care to be tried and sentenced with the utmost expedition. They were condemned to death, but he exercised his right of pardon, and set them all free, without exception. He thus, as he had vowed in his hour of torment, took ample revenge — not on the accused, but on the minister who was about to remove him from office. He issued a wholesale pardon. "Now let the minister, in his zeal for milder methods, outdo me if he can!" he exclaimed, as he threw down his pen.

Richard had been summoned before the judge-advocate immediately after receiving the unexpected announcement of his pardon.

"You are set free, it is true," said the high official; "yet for a time you are not allowed to live in Hungary, but are ordered to make your home in some city of the empire outside your own country. Let us say Vienna, for example. The governor, who has to-day given you your liberty, wishes you to call on the young Baroness Alfonsine Plankenhorst, upon your arrival at Vienna, and thank her for her good offices in securing your liberation. Without her intervention you would not so soon have left your prison cell. So give her your heartiest thanks."

"I shall not fail to do so," was the reply.

"And one thing more: your brother Eugen, or Ödön, as you call him, has paid the penalty of his treason with his life—"

"Yes, I know it," interrupted the other; "but I am puzzled how the German and the Hungarian names—"

Here he was sharply cut short. "In the first place," said the judge-advocate, sternly, "it was

against all rules and regulations for you to hear anything about it, since you were a prisoner, and communication with a prisoner is treason. In the second
place, I did not ask you for a lecture on philology;
you are here to attend to what I have to say."
Therewith he took a little pasteboard box out of a
drawer. "Your brother left you a lock of his hair,
which I now deliver to you."

Richard opened the box. "But this is not — " he
began, in great surprise, when the other again shut
him off.

"I have nothing more to say to you. Good morning."

With this, the released prisoner was shown to the
door. A little more, and he would have blurted out
his astonishment at finding blond hair in the little
box, whereas Ödön's hair was dark.

Hastening to the railway station, Richard caught
the early train to Vienna, and so made the journey
all but in Alfonsine's company. She, however, took
her seat in a first-class compartment, while he, as a poor
released prisoner, contented himself with a third-class
seat. And while the young lady was revelling in her
supposed revenge, only a few yards away sat the
object of her hatred, puzzling his brain over three
baffling riddles. The first was: "What is the meaning of the blond lock of hair, and why *Eugen* Baradlay instead of *Edmund?*" The second: "How is

it that I am indebted to Alfonsine Plankenhorst for my freedom?" And the third: "Where shall I find Edith, and when I find her what is to be my next step?"

He could solve neither of the three riddles.

CHAPTER XXXII.

THE SUITOR.

RICHARD entered the Plankenhorst house with the ease and freedom of a man visiting old friends. He did not note the expression of amazement and terror — as if at sight of a ghost — with which the mother and daughter stared at him. He had eyes only for Edith, who, beside herself with joy, sprang to embrace him, stammering as she lay on his bosom: "Richard, is it really you?"

The baroness was the first to regain her composure. "Edith," said she severely, turning to her niece, "I cannot understand your immodest behaviour toward this gentleman. What do you wish, sir?" she asked coldly of Richard.

The young man advanced to Alfonsine and addressed her in words of sincere gratitude and friendliness. "First of all," he began, "it was to pay a debt of heartfelt gratitude that I hastened hither this morning. At daybreak I was to have been executed as a condemned criminal, but at the last moment I was pardoned. The governor, in remitting

my sentence and setting me free, enjoined upon me
as my first duty to pay you, my dear young lady,
my sincere thanks for my freedom. Without your
intervention I should have been sentenced to at least
fifteen years' imprisonment. Accept, I beg you, my
warmest thanks for your kind act."

Every one of his words was a crushing blow on
the viper's head. Did he thank her, Alfonsine
Plankenhorst, for his liberation, he whose destruction had been the end and aim of all her strivings
for weeks and months past, and the sweet vision of
her nightly dreams?

Her mother, whose self-control was greater than
her own, was forced to come to her aid.

"My dear sir," said she to Richard, "there must
be some mistake here. The service which you
ascribe to my daughter cannot have been rendered
by any member of my family, for the simple reason
that we have not concerned ourselves with your
affairs in the slightest degree. We live in strict
retirement, meet no one, never meddle in politics,
and our drawing-rooms are closed to society. This
last I beg leave to emphasise for your benefit."

"I understand you perfectly, madam, and I can
assure you that this is the last time I shall intrude
upon you. A few words more and I have done.
You will remember that a year and a half ago I
became engaged to your niece — "

"An engagement which, of course, must now be considered as broken off," interrupted the baroness. "When you asked for my niece's hand you were an officer in the army, a man of property, and a nobleman. Now, however, you are neither."

"But I am still Richard Baradlay," returned the young man, with dignity.

"And free as a bird!" added the other, scornfully. "But it so happens that the other party to the engagement is not equally free. Miss Edith Liedenwall is bound to comply with the wishes of her relatives on whom she is dependent, and they consider it their duty to discountenance her engagement to Mr. Richard Baradlay. She feels, too, that she has a perfect right to break the engagement and choose again more wisely."

"I beg to ask Miss Liedenwall whether that is so?"

Edith shook her head, but did not venture to speak.

Her aunt was bent on settling the matter once for all. "Edith will do as we think best for her," said she. "We are not only entitled, but in duty bound, to make wise provision for her future. You, sir, are now too late with your wooing. We provided for her while you were still in prison and little likely ever to see your freedom. My niece is promised to another."

Edith started from her chair. "Your niece will

give her hand only to the man she loves," she declared, firmly.

"Edith," commanded her aunt, without losing her composure, "let us not have a scene, if you please. You are my foster-daughter and I have a lawful right to demand obedience of you."

"I will not be your foster-daughter any longer," cried the young lady, asserting herself resolutely; "I will go into service, for which I have been trained in your house. As chambermaid or kitchen girl I can give my hand to whom I choose."

"You will not be allowed to execute your threat, my dear," returned the baroness calmly. "You are under very good care here, and things will take their orderly and proper course until you are called upon to kneel at the altar; and should you choose to weep while pledging your vows there, your tears would be merely regarded as a fitting accompaniment to the solemn ceremonial."

"But I should not weep," cried the girl, excitedly; "I should do something very different. If you really found a man who consented to marry me to please you and against my will, I should say to him, before he led me to the altar, that I once ran away from a convent, — ran away in the night and made my way to the camp where my lover was, in whose room I passed half the night. Some of his comrades, as well as the market-woman in Singer Street, saw me there, and all the nuns in the St. Bridget Convent know about it. Sister Remigia knows that I ran away and where I was. The marks of the punishment I received the next day are still visible. And now, madam, do you wish another than the man for whom I bear those scars to see them?"

Passionate scorn and maidenly indignation spoke in the girl's every look and gesture. Richard was struck dumb with admiration. The baroness fairly choked with amazement and impotent wrath. Of what she had just heard she had entertained not the slightest suspicion. She felt her self-control and will-power slipping away from her in the determined girl's presence; yet she made one last attempt to carry her point.

"You wretched girl!" she cried, clasping her hands and turning her eyes heavenward; "alas, that you should have so far forgotten yourself! Do you know that you have fallen a victim to an unprincipled seducer? This man here whom you claim to be your betrothed is already married to another woman, who, of course, has rights that take precedence of yours, and who will drive you from his side with reviling and insult."

"I — married already?" gasped Richard, in amazement.

"Yes, you!" retorted the baroness. "Or do you choose to deny that you have a son in Pest over whom you watch with tender care, whose education you pay for, and whom you sent to the hospital when he was ill? Deny that, sir, if you can!"

"So you drag a poor innocent child into our unfortunate quarrel," said Richard.

"The child is innocent, but not its father," returned the accuser, pointing her finger at Richard.

"Very well, madam, I will tell you the story of this child. It happened not long ago that I mortally wounded a brave opponent in battle. This man summoned me to him in his dying hour and told me he had, somewhere in the world, a son whom he had long sought in vain, but traces of whom he had recently discovered. The mother had abandoned the child. He begged me to promise that I would find the boy, and I did so, assuring him that I would care for the poor waif as tenderly as if he were my own brother's child. Accordingly, I prosecuted the search and was at last successful. I have in my possession certain letters and other papers which establish the child's identity and parentage."

Baroness Plankenhorst and her daughter were trembling in every limb and seemed powerless to utter a word. Meanwhile the speaker went on, standing proudly erect as he proceeded:

"But I promised my dying adversary never to betray the mother's name to any one, and you may rest assured I never shall."

Edith approached her lover and said, with great gentleness: "Whoever the mother may be of the child to which you have promised to be a father, I will be its mother." And she leaned fondly on his breast and rested her head on his shoulder.

Her aunt, vanquished and prostrate, raised her hand as if in malediction and muttered hoarsely:

"Take her then and begone, in the devil's name!"

CHAPTER XXXIII.

ALL'S WELL THAT ENDS WELL.

RICHARD lost no time in sending to his mother from Vienna a full account of his varied experiences. Her reply was supplemented by the arrival of her steward and his wife, who informed him fully of all that had occurred at home during his absence. The good wife had come with her husband to be of such service as she could to Edith in preparing for the young girl's wedding. Edith had been placed by Richard in a hotel until the marriage should take place.

The riddle of the blond hair was now explained, and Richard's grief and love for his martyr-brother made him prize the little lock of hair more than all other earthly possessions. He was also told that his mother had wished to attend his wedding, but on applying for a passport, — which was now necessary even for the shortest journeys, — she had been refused, and had received instructions not to leave Nemesdomb until farther notice. Then the young baroness had planned to come, but was detained by her baby's illness. As for his brother Ödön, he had the best of reasons for not showing himself in Vienna at present. So the steward and his wife had come to represent the family.

Finally, the good man announced that the Baradlay property had been taken possession of by the government, — not permanently, as only the inheritance of two of the brothers, at most, could be confiscated, while the third brother's share must be restored in the end ; but such matters were settled only after long delay. Meanwhile the total income of the property went into the state treasury, and a mere pittance was returned to the widow, in monthly payments, for the support of her family. Therefore Richard's expenses were to be regulated with extreme economy. The young man found all this only what was to have been expected. He had been granted his life and liberty, and was not disposed to grumble at losing his property. What engrossed his thoughts just then was his approaching marriage with Edith, which was to make him the happiest man in all the world.

When in due time he had attained to that longed-for bliss, he found himself confronted by a situation that demanded earnest consultation with the partner of his happiness.

"Do you know, little wife," said he, "that we are very poor ?"

But Edith only laughed at him. "How can we

be poor when we have each other?" she demanded, triumphantly.

"That makes two millions, I know," admitted Richard; "but it yields no interest in cash. We must economise. Do you know what our monthly income actually amounts to? One hundred florins. More than that my mother cannot spare me, as she is much straitened herself."

"But I don't see how we can spend even that amount," declared Edith. "It is a great sum of money."

"I must confess one thing more to you," pursued the young husband; "even this small income is not all mine. I have a number of little debts here in the city, dating back one and two years, or more, — trifling sums that I owe to honest shopkeepers and working people. These debts were mere bagatelles to me then, but they press me heavily now. Yet I can't allow these poor people who have trusted me to suffer loss. I shall pay them every penny, and for that purpose I propose to set aside one-half my monthly allowance."

"Very well," assented the other cheerfully; "we can live royally on fifty florins a month. I will be cook, and we will get along with only two courses for dinner. You shall see what a good cook I am. I will have a little servant girl to wash the dishes, and I am sure we shall manage famously."

Richard kissed his wife's hand and delivered into her keeping fifty florins for household expenses.

He then asked leave to absent himself for a few hours on business, and Edith told him he might stay out until one o'clock, when she should have dinner ready for him.

Richard appeared punctually at the hour set, like a model husband. And how good the little dinner tasted! He ate like a wolf, and declared that not even the emperor himself fared better. Really it was a splendid meal for fifty-five kreutzers.

"Such a dinner was more than I often got when I was a captain of hussars," declared the gratified husband, "especially when old Paul was cook — Heaven bless him!"

The dinner had been well earned, too. Richard had secured a place as workman in a machine-shop, at fifty florins a month, a splendid salary! He had also transacted other business in the course of the morning. He had called on the old shopkeeper in Porcelain Street, and asked him to take charge of his finances and arrange a settlement with his creditors, to whom he owed perhaps two thousand florins. He wished to pay it off in instalments until the last penny of indebtedness was discharged. Old Solomon had promised to call on him between one and two o'clock, when his shop was always closed.

At half-past one the old man's shuffling steps were

Y

heard in the passageway. Edith was still busy with her dish-washing, and the window was open to let fresh air into the single room that served as kitchen, dining-room, and parlour in one.

"Ah, my dear madam," began the visitor, bowing low, "I kiss your fair hand; I am ever glad to kiss the hand that works — rather than the hand that knows only how to hold a fan. You have a very pleasant home here, — a little cramped for room, perhaps, but that brings you so much the nearer each other. Now then, Captain Baradlay, let us proceed to business," said he, turning to Richard. "The lady of the house will not be inconvenienced, I trust, by our transacting a little business in her parlour. It is here a case of two hearts that beat as one, I am sure." The old Jew took a bit of chalk from his pocket. "Have the goodness, please, to give me a list of all your debts."

Richard's memory in such matters was good, and he named the items, one after another, while old Solomon wrote them down on the table.

"Heavens and earth!" cried the aged Hebrew, raising his eyebrows and causing his round cap to move backward and forward on his bald skull; "a large sum, a big pile of money that makes. H'm, h'm!" He took a pinch of snuff from his black snuff-box, and then resumed his reckoning. "It appears, if I mistake not, that Captain Baradlay was still under age when these debts were contracted."

"But my honour was not under age," said Richard.

"Ah, well said! That should be posted up in large letters, — 'My honour was never under age!' Do you see, madam, what sort of a man you have married? A spendthrift who values his honour at more than two thousand florins.

"But look here, Captain, there's a way we have of settling debts like these, by agreeing with the creditors to pay a certain per cent. They are generally glad enough to get even a small fraction of what they supposed was dead loss. It's a very sensible arrangement all around."

"But it doesn't suit me," returned Richard emphatically. "Florin for florin, it shall all be paid as fast as I get the money. I can't cheat the poor people out of their just dues, even if I have to go hungry to pay them."

"Incorrigible!" exclaimed the other. "Remember, you are no longer a bachelor; you must think of your changed circumstances. Well, well, don't heat yourself. We'll say no more about it, but pass on to consider how all these debts are to be paid."

So saying, he marked off two parallel columns on the table, over one of which he wrote, "Debit," and over the other, "Credit."

"In the first place," began Richard, "I receive a

hundred florins monthly from my mother, half of which is to go to my creditors."

"Half of it? and does your wife agree to that?"

"Oh, yes," Edith hastened to reply.

Solomon made an entry in the second column.

"Fifty florins more will come to me monthly as wages for my work in the machine-shop," continued Richard. "Half of it I shall use toward paying my debts, and the other half is for my wife's wardrobe."

"But how can I ever spend so much?" interposed Edith. "Your dear, good mother sent me so many dresses for wedding presents that I never can wear them out. Let it all go to your creditors." She would give the two no peace until Solomon had written down the whole amount.

Then the old man pushed up the sleeves of his caftan, like one who prepares to execute a master-stroke. "To that must next be added," said he, "the three hundred thousand florins that Miss Edith Liedenwall brought to Captain Baradlay as her dowry." Therewith he wrote "300,000 fl." as the next entry.

The two young people looked at him to see what he meant by such a joke; but he merely rose from his chair, took each of them by the hand, and addressed them as follows:

"I wish you all happiness in your married life. You are worthy of each other. What I just said, and what I wrote, were both in earnest ; and now I will explain."

The three resumed their seats, and the old man proceeded to explain to them the mystery of the three hundred thousand florins.

"You had, my dear madam, a great-uncle, Alfred Plankenhorst, who was a rich man and an old bachelor. He had great family pride, as I have reason to know, having been well acquainted with him and acted as his banker and business agent. I thus came to know a good deal about his family affairs. The old gentleman made a will by which he left all his property — his house in Vienna and his invested funds — to his niece, Baroness Plankenhorst, and her daughter. The old uncle was long-lived, — it is a way with some people, especially when they are rich, — and before he died the young lady had a love affair which resulted unfortunately for her good name. Well, there was no help for it ; but the old gentleman had very strong prejudices in such matters, and he made a new will. Hunting up the orphan daughter of a distant relative, — Edith Liedenwall was the young lady's name, — he left her in the care of the Plankenhorst ladies for her education. The substance of the second will I can give you in a few words.

"Should Alfonsine Plankenhorst ever marry and make good her false step by a union with a man of birth equal to her own, she was to receive the bulk of the property as her dowry; but if she failed to retrieve herself before Edith Liedenwall grew up and married, the latter was to receive this dowry, provided her marriage was a suitable and honourable one, and provided she had committed no act such as had led the testator to destroy his first will. Failing this disposition of the property, as dowry either of Alfonsine Plankenhorst or of Edith Liedenwall, it was to go, after a certain number of years, to the St. Bridget Convent, though the house was in any case to remain in the possession of the Plankenhorst ladies. I was made executor of this will, the contents of which were to be kept secret. But the secretary who wrote it communicated its items to the baroness and her daughter, so that they have long known all about it. If you will now review the events of your courtship and engagement, in the light of what I have just told you, you will find everything explained that has been hitherto mysterious to you. Meanwhile, I was watching the course of events and knew all that was going on. Oh, we quiet old people have sharp eyes; we can see into houses, into pockets, and even into hearts.

"The Plankenhorst mansion will remain in the possession of its present occupants. It is a pretty bit of property by itself, but they'll go through it within ten years. Yet these are not times when one thinks about what is to be ten years hence. He who clothes the lilies of the field and the girls in the ballet will also provide for Alfonsine Plankenhorst.

"And now, Captain and Mrs. Baradlay, are you satisfied with what fortune has brought you?"

THE END.